ROSS O'CARROLL-KELLY

'PURE AND UTTER DICKLIT

The infantile ramblings of a privileged south Dublin airhead.
A Golf GTI ride through a world of moral entropy, social
advantage, conspicuous consumption and alcohol-driven
sexual misadventure. This book sets the women's movement
back forty years. It's like Germaine Greer was never born. Its
author – if he can even be described as such – is Holden
Caulfield on ten pints of Heineken with a pure testosterone
chaser, and what he has to say is puerile, misogynistic trash.
If this is what the Celtic Tiger has spawned, then roll on
the next recession.'
Sunday Tribune

Paul Howard is thirty-three and has been married eight times to women from such Eastern European countries as Bulgaria, Moldova and Azerbaijan. He claims that no money ever changed hands, however his best man on all eight occasions was a man who is known to have Russian mafia links. All eight marriages ended in deportation. He lives in Wicklow under constant fear of arrest.

PS, I scored the brides-maids

Ross O'Carroll-Kelly

[As told to Paul Howard]

Illustrated by Alan Clarke

THE O'BRIEN PRESS
DUBLIN

First published 2004 by The O'Brien Press Ltd,
20 Victoria Road, Dublin 6, Ireland.
Tel: +353 1 4923333; Fax: +353 1 4922777
E-mail: books@obrien.ie
Website: www.obrien.ie
Reprinted 2004.

ISBN: 0-86278-890-0

This book is based on the weekly Ross O'Carroll-Kelly columns
published in the *Sunday Tribune*.

British Library Cataloguing-in-Publication Data
Howard, Paul, 1971-
Ross O'Carroll-Kelly, PS, I scored the bridesmaids
1.O'Carroll-Kelly, Ross (Fictitious character) - Fiction
2.Dublin (Ireland) - Social life and customs - Fiction
3.Humorous stories
I.Title 823.9'14.

2 3 4 5 6 7
04 05 06 07 08

Editing, typesetting, layout and design: The O'Brien Press Ltd
Cover and internal illustrations: Alan Clarke
Author photograph, page 2: Emma Byrne
Printing: Cox & Wyman Ltd

Other books by Paul Howard

Ross O'Carroll-Kelly, The Miseducation Years

Ross O'Carroll-Kelly, The Teenage Dirtbag Years

Ross O'Carroll-Kelly, The Orange Mocha-Chip Frappuccino Years

Hostage, Notorious Irish Kidnappings

The Gaffers – Roy Keane, Mick McCarthy and the team they built

The Joy – the shocking true story of life inside

Celtic Warrior

Dedication

This book is dedicated to the Dublin City Council that finally gives
Bob Geldof the freedom of the city.

Acknowledgements

Thanks to Mum, Dad, Mark, Vin and Rich for the memories. Thanks to
Matt Cooper for making Ross a star. Thanks to Paddy Murray and Jim
Farrelly for not letting it go to the boy's head. Thanks to Ger Siggins,
Maureen Gillespie, Deirdre Sheeran and Colm Voyles for being
inspiring. Thanks to Alan Clarke whose pen has breathed new life into
Ross. Thanks to Emma whose design work makes these books sing.
Thanks to Rachel Pierce, an editor who was once again right about
everything and who made this book twice what it might otherwise have
been. And a very special thank-you to Michelle Murphy and Sarah and
Karl Holmes – the wedding planners.

Contents

Contents

Got this, like,

Valey's Day cord from Sorcha, roysh, we're talking six or seven months ago, when I was throwing her a bone for a little while. She basically arrived home from Australia minus Penis Head, Cian or whatever his name was, that tool she went off with on the so-called romantic trip of a lifetime. Realised the spark wasn't there anymore, she said, and they both wanted different things in life – code for Cian storted rattling some other Sheila. So she comes home and after a couple of days, roysh, and not wanting to sound like a total orsehole here, let's just say it's not just her tail she's got between her legs. The girl's got it bad, alroysh. So sue me. It's, like, phone us now for your free consultation. Just dial 1850 STUD MUFFIN. No foal, no fee.

Anyway, we ended up being together maybe, like, three times, roysh, when this cord arrives and in it she's written, 'You are the first thing I think about when I wake up in the morning and the last thing I think about before I go to sleep at night,' which I was sure she robbed off a Westlife record, or 'Dawson's Creek', or some, I don't know, Patricia focking Scanlon book. Or maybe they learn it in school. Yeah, I can hear a lot of birds out there shifting uncomfortably in their seats. And with good reason. Your secret's out. Goys, remember that time in sixth class when the priest took us all out to play, I don't know, tag rugby or some shit, and all the birds had to stay behind for a chat with some woman teacher who was focking morto? Thought it was about the blob, didn't you? The old period costume drama. Wear loose trousers, hold a hot-water bottle to your stomach and try not to stab any men. News flash, goys. That little chat, it had fock-all to do with telling the birds what to do when Munster are playing at home. It was like, 'How To Get A Goy: Step One – tell him he's the first thing you think about when you get up in the morning and the last thing you think about before you go to sleep at night. They're suckers for that shit,' which we basically are. I even find myself repeating it back to Sorcha, like a total sap, going, 'You're the first thing *I* think about in the morning as well. *And* the last thing I think about at night,' and it's total bullshit and the thing is, roysh, we're talking totally here. I could name fifty things I think about in the morning before Sorcha ever crosses my mind. You want to take that bet?

Jessica Alba. Jade Jagger. Christina Ricci. Anna Kournikova. Ali Landry. Heidi Klum. Halle Berry. Gail Porter. Drew Barrymore. Katie Holmes. Denise Richards. Teri Hatcher. Yasmine Bleeth. Tiffani Amber Thiessen. Angelina Jolie. Isla Fischer. Calista Flockhart. Why not? Estella Warren. Heather Graham. Claudia Schiffer. Gillian Anderson. Andrea Corr. Rachel Stevens. Liz Hurley. Jennifer Love Hewitt. Alicia Silverstone. Natalie Imbruglia. Billie Piper. Alyson Hannigan. Rebecca Romjin-Stamos. What am I up to? Thirty? Amanda Holden. Cat Deeley. Sarah Michelle Gellar. Holly Valance. Britney Spears.

Anna Friel. Shania Twain. Jennifer Aniston. Tyra Banks. Liv Tyler. Charisma Carpenter. Neve Campbell. Elisha Cuthbert. Kirsten Dunst. Hannah Spearitt. Penelope Cruz. Mena Suvari. Claire Danes. Ashley Judd. Kate Beckinsale.

There you have it. Fifty cures for the old morning wood. You wake up at ten o'clock and your little love warrior's already been up an hour. This book was going to be called *The Goy Who Went To Sleep In A Bed And Woke Up In A Tent*, but they couldn't fit it on the focking cover. I know there's a lot of birds out there whose blood is, like, boiling at this point. Hey, I'm called an orsehole on average ten or eleven times a week. Twice that if I venture out to Knackery Doo, which isn't often these days. I've overfished the waters. But the last time I was there, roysh, a bird who I'd never clapped eyes on in my focking life — nobody's bargain, to be honest — she goes, 'Your problem is you think with your dick,' which is basically all true, except for the bit about it being a problem. Because it's not. I do think with my dick. Or at least I listen to it, roysh, and that's because it's hordly ever wrong. Okay, I've woken up with a few mingers in my time, but generally I do alroysh.

Listening to your lad. You know another word — well, two words — for that? Animal attraction. So snap the bracelets on me, roysh, and take me to see the judge, but while you're at it, you're going to have to charge the rest of the animal kingdom as well, because they're choosing who to score and who not to score on exactly the same basis as me. It's nature. Birds — as in women — think they're, like, cleverer than nature. Want to know on what basis they decide whether a goy is worth jumping? Come on, you know this. How many times have you heard a girl say that you can tell a lot about a man by looking at his shoes. His focking SHOES!

'Slip-ons, Orlaith, do NOT go there!' 'OH! MY! GOD! They're not even proper Dubes, Eibhin!'

Get this, roysh. JP was seeing this bird who he was basically mad into. The name's not important, but she had great top tens and an alroysh boat. Chatted her up while showing her old pair around a gaff in Monkstown that they were buying as, like, an investment property. So he gets her number, roysh, and they end up going out with each other for, like, six months. It's so serious, roysh, that me and the goys didn't see the focker for basically ages and when he finally resurfaced he was talking about, like, babies and engagement rings and mortgages and shit. So one night, roysh, they're in Annabel's and JP's wearing a pair of Timberland boots. He's actually sitting down, roysh, shooting the breeze with me, when he stands up to get the Britneys in and doesn't realise that the bottom of his chinos are tucked into his boot, just at the back. So he ends up walking around like this for, like, five full minutes, roysh, and his bird cops it, as do all her friends. So what does she do? *OH! MY GOD! SO embarrassing!* She focking dumps the dude. These are the same creatures who sit crying with the curtains drawn wondering why their hearts are low, their hearts are soooo low ... Want to know what JP's ex is up to now? She's with some tosser who played for Belvo when we were at school and he's already boned two of her friends behind her back. Wears nice shoes, though. And birds think *I'm* focked up? You see, the whole goy-girl thing, roysh, is basically simple. It's birds who choose to complicate things. You meet a bird. If you're attracted to her, you bail in. If she's good, you give her your mobile number the next morning. If she's not, you give her the first ten digits that come into your head. And you don't get married, not this side of forty anyway.

So just as I'm thinking this, roysh, I pull up in traffic outside the church in Donnybrook, and everyone's, like, craning their necks out of their windows to see this bird in a long white dress getting out of a wedding cor, and of course I'm thinking, 'What a dope!' She's only, like, my age, we're talking twenty-two or twenty-three, roysh, a ringer for Abie Titmus, and she's about to walk into that building and swear that she's only going to knob one man for the rest of her days. HELLO? So the bridesmaids are fixing the veil on her, roysh, and fussing around her when all of a sudden, for absolutely no reason – and I did *not* imagine this – she looks over her shoulder, towards my cor, and basically our eyes just, like, lock together. And I can tell, roysh, that in her mind she's wondering if she's doing the right thing. She's wondering why she's settling for the muppet at the altar when there's still people like me in the game. She's basically going to herself, 'I'd love to jump in that cor. Escape. Go wherever the Stillorgan dualler takes us. Make a new life with that incredibly handsome goy.' I wink at her and she just, like, smiles at me, but then the goy behind me beeps me because the traffic has storted moving again, so I give the accelerator some and she's left there thinking

Ross O'Carroll-Kelly. The one that got away ...

CHAPTER ONE
To Have and to Hold

'Do you know how difficult it is to get wisteria in this country?' That's what Oisinn says to me, standing there in his long, white coat, surrounded by hundreds of bottles and, like, test tubes filled with, like, funny coloured liquids, which he's heating over a Bunsen burner. He goes, 'Do you know how difficult it is to get wisteria in this country?' and I'm like, 'I don't know what the fock that is and I don't care either. Come on, dude, let's get mullered,' because the rest of the goys have been in the M1 since, like, half-six.

He goes, 'I was going to maybe mix it with vanilla, ginger and sandalwood, but I'm wondering would it be too close to *Blv Absolute*,' and I'm just standing there staring at him, thinking the goy has seriously lost the plot this time. Couple of weeks ago, roysh, he chucked in that handy number he had going out at the airport to try to basically invent a new smell, lash it in a bottle and flog it to Calvin Klein or one of that crowd for a million sheets. So his old pair's shed suddenly looks like the focking science lab in Castlerock. He's like, 'I suppose if I go easy on the musk accords,' and I go, 'Dude, this is your *last* chance. Are you coming for scoops or not?' He sniffs this one bottle, roysh, then looks at me, cops that I'm serious and goes, 'All work and no play.

Suppose you're roysh,' then he whips off the lab coat and twenty minutes later the two of us are stepping into the Merrion Inn, every set of female eyes in the place glued to us.

Christian greets me by going, 'Why you slimy, double-crossing, no-good swindler. You've got a lot of guts coming here after what you pulled,' and we high-five each other and I get the Britneys in, three Kens and one Probably. JP's in flying form. No sign of Fionn, though, the focking geek. JP goes, 'Looking suave and debonair, my man,' and I'm there, 'Likewise, dude,' which he is, I have to say. The property morket's obviously treating him well. He flicks his thumb in Christian's direction and he goes, 'Did George Lucas there tell you his news?' I look at Christian and he goes, 'I'm making a film, Ross,' and I end up nearly spitting beer all over him, roysh. Making a film? I wouldn't trust him to get one developed, best friend and all as he is. He goes, 'It's no joke, padwan. Got a grant through the college and everything,' and I'm there, 'Yeah, roysh,' and he goes, 'Ten Ks,' and I just freeze, my pint glass about two inches away from my lips. I go, 'Ten thousand bills? They're giving you ten thousand bills to make a movie?' and he just, like, nods his head.

I'm there, 'That's it. It's got to be a porno,' and JP and Oisinn just, like, high-five each other, as if to say, you know, the goy's a focking genius. I can actually see it. I'm like, 'It's Christmas. Everyone's having fun at the office porty. Everyone except, I don't know, twenty-one-year-old receptionist Christine, who the boss has asked to work late. So Christine's pretty fit, roysh, but she doesn't, like, make the most of herself, we're talking glasses, hair up in a bun, and here she is, roysh, slaving away while everyone else is off enjoying themselves. Boss pops back to the office and before you know it she's whipping off the specs, shaking down her hair–' and JP goes, 'And he does her from behind while photocopying her baps and faxing them to the office in Tampere. It's been done before, Ross. But respect to the porno idea.' 'Em, actually,' Christian goes, 'it's going to be more of a science fiction film really. I'm planning to present a distant future in which a space pirate, loosely based on you-know-who, gets a fit of conscience, gives up his roguish ways and settles down on Makkerat, a strange planet where no one grows old and no one dies. There he falls in love with a girl called Azanda who, unbeknownst to our hero, is a shape-changer and also a secret agent for the Empire.' And we're all just, like, staring at him.

Eventually, I go, 'I've got someone in mind to play Christine. We're talking Emer,' and Oisinn goes, 'Howth Emer?' and I'm like, 'Sandycove Emer. Used to be in ballet with Sorcha,' and JP goes, 'Ten-four, I'm hearing you loud and clear, dude. The bird would do *anything* to be famous. Puts her name down for everything. We're talking 'Big Brother'. We're talking 'Pop Idol'.' I go, 'And I was thinking, who better to play the boss than my good self?' and Oisinn and JP both high-five me and go, 'Stud muffin,' and I'm there, 'Well, I've been there before. Me and Emer have this, chemistry, you see. On-screen it'll be pure focking magic.'

Christian goes, 'Our hero has bad debts all over the galaxy and Azanda's job is to bring him in. But of course she soon finds herself falling in love with him,' and I go ape-shit listening to him, roysh, I'm like, 'Christian, don't touch that focking money until we've had a proper talk,' and he looks at me like he's about to burst out crying, roysh, and even though I feel pretty bad for hurting the dude's feelings, I've got to be, like, firm with him. I go, 'It's not going to be a focking science fiction film, okay? I'm putting my foot down, Christian. It's going to be a porno and that's that.'

The focker would end up spending the money on, I don't know, light sabres or some shit. The beauty of my idea, roysh, is that it'll cost pretty much fock-all to make. We're talking seven-and-a-half Ks for my services, leaving two-and-a-half for whatever other overheads there are. Emer will do it for free, that much I can guarantee, and we can use JP's old man's office for the filming. The photocopier can be a bit dodgy, but we'll film it at night so we can do plenty of takes. We're talking lights, camera, action, baby.

✳ ✳ ✳

'Have you heard from that tool you went to Australia with?' That's what I say to Sorcha, roysh, but she just, like, shoots me a filthy and goes, 'His name happens to be Cillian. And yes, Ross, we're still friends.' I'm there, 'After he abandoned you in Sydney?' and quick as a flash, roysh, she goes, 'How's Christian?' which is basically a subtle reminder to me that I'm not exactly the nicest goy in the world myself. Then she goes, 'Sorry. That was uncalled for. Why am I always such a total bitch to you?' and I shrug my shoulders, roysh, and she goes, 'I suppose I *have* been listening to a lot of Mary J Blige lately.'

She looks great. Her year away doing fock-all except spending her old pair's money really suited her. She's still got that just-back-from-holidays look even though she's back, like, six months or something, and looking across the table at her, roysh, I realise that I SO want to be with her today. I go, 'There was no one else, Sorcha. While you were away,' and she nearly chokes on a mouthful of water. She must be back on Weight Watchers, the way she's knocking back that stuff. She goes, 'Sorry, Ross, but I simply can't let that one go. What about Melanie?' and of course I'm like, 'Melanie?' playing the innocent. She goes, 'You know very well who I'm talking about. And Siun.' I'm there, 'Siun was a mistake,' and she's like, 'Was Ali a mistake, too?' and I'm there, 'Who's Ali?' and she goes, 'Ali would be Siun's sister, Ross.' I'm there, 'Was that her name?' and I tell her I can't believe they've taken the tuna melt off the menu, just to try to, like, change the subject. She goes, 'Of course, why should I be surprised that you didn't even ask the girl her name before you slept with her? You were with Tamara as well. Anna. Lucy. Elaine. Lia ...' and I'm like, 'Okay, okay. Didn't know you were keeping score.' She pours herself some more water and sort of, like, smiles to herself, all smug, and goes, 'Not keeping score, Ross. Keeping you in your place,' and I think I've got it bad for this girl again.

We order and the food arrives. She picks all the blue cheese and olives out of her blue cheese and olive salad and leaves them on her side plate. Don't ask. As she's doing this, she goes, 'What are you doing at the moment, we're talking careerwise?' Careerwise? I'm like, 'Well, I'm pretty much chilling at the moment, basically,' and she goes, 'You were pretty much chilling at the moment basically when I went to Australia. Your life is passing you by, Ross, and you've done nothing with it,' and she makes it sound like a bad thing. She's back working in her old dear's boutique, which is hordly, like, the end of the focking rainbow.

She asks me with a totally straight face if I've been following what's been happening in Singapore, and I tell her with a totally straight face that I've kind of lost track of it in the past few weeks. She tells me that fifteen members of the Falun Gong spiritual group were – OH! MY! GOD! – arrested for holding, like, a vigil in memory of the group members who, like, died in custody in China? We're talking, HELLO? I'm there, '*No focking way*,' and I'm wondering was that a bit OTT, but she just goes, 'And now Chee Soon Juan – he's, like, the leader of the opposition – he's facing, like, a defamation suit from the Prime Minister for asking questions – we're talking *questions* – about a multi*billion* dollar loan to Suharto. It's like, *Duuuhhh!* I throw my eyes up to heaven and I go, 'If it's not one thing, it's another, eh?' and she sort of, like, stares into the distance and goes, 'I know. The world is SUCH a focked-up place. Bush is going to attack Iraq as well, whether the United Nations gives him the mandate or not. It's like, OH MY GOD!'

Her phone beeps, roysh, and it's, like, a text. She reads it and goes, 'OH! MY! GOD! I nearly forgot – I'm meeting Andrea this afternoon,' and I wonder if it's the same Andrea I ended up knobbing after Annabel's about two weeks ago. Sorcha goes, 'She's doing politics in UCD.' It's her alroysh. She's there, 'She has to present a paper this afternoon. 'Sterilisation – A Solution to Northern Ireland's Troubles.' She thinks that everyone who earns less than £30,000 a year in the North should be neutered, thus wiping out the working classes who actually cause all the problems. It's a bit extreme for my political taste, but I said I'd look over it for her. Actually, you and her would have a lot in common.'

I try to play it Kool and the Gang, roysh, wondering whether Andrea's actually said anything, but Sorcha breaks her shite laughing and goes, 'I believe you two already know each other?' and I can feel my face go red. She goes, 'It's okay, Ross. I'm not jealous. I am SO over you, it's like, *Aaaggghhh*. Watch her, though. She might be one of my best friends, but I wouldn't trust her as far as I'd throw her.'

We finish lunch and she pays using her gold cord, roysh, and as I get up to go she's just there, '*Leanne Rimes' Greatest Hits*,' and of course I'm there, 'Sorry?' and she goes, 'Andrea said it went missing from her aportment the night you stayed over. Don't tell me you and the other goys are still playing that stupid game?' That *stupid* game, roysh, happens to be called Petty Pilfering and not only are we still playing it, roysh, but we've got, like, a thousand bills riding on the current game. Basically, roysh, me and the goys – we're talking me, Christian, JP, Oisinn and Fionn – we all threw, like, two hundred sheets each into the pot, which adds up to basically a grand, roysh, and it goes to whichever one of us reaches the magical fifty number first. And whoever finishes last, roysh – it'll be Fionn, of course – has to do a forfeit. The winner gets to pick a song off one of his fifty CDs which the loser has to, like, perform while standing on the bor in the Club of Love. Petty Pilfering, you can't beat it.

I go, 'I don't know what you're talking about, Sorcha,' which is technically true, roysh, because the CD I stole from Andrea was, like, *Short Sharp Shocked* by Michelle Shocked. Unless I'm very much mistaken it was Oisinn who stole her Leanne Rimes CD, and if she can't keep track of who's robbing what from her, then she's probably putting it about a bit too much. Sorcha goes, 'When are you going to grow up, Ross?' and I look down at my plate trying to look, I don't know, ashamed I suppose. Then as she gets up, roysh, she kisses me on the cheek and goes, 'Still cute, though,' and she says she'll text me. I watch her leave. Still has a great orse.

✳ ✳ ✳

I walk into the kitchen and, of course, Dickhead's in there being his usual dickhead self. He's got the phone up to his ear, roysh, and the second he sees me he puts his hand over the mouthpiece and goes, 'I take it from your less-than-cheerful countenance that you've yet to hear the joyous news?' and I'm there, 'Shut the fock up, you absolute orsehole.' He goes, 'The Bertie Bowl, Ross. It's history. Charlie Bird's been on the news. Mary Harney's put her foot down. Rugby on the northside. The very idea. I'm on to the florists now.'

I'm about to tell him, roysh, that he's the biggest knob I've ever had the misfortune to meet when he takes his hand away from the mouthpiece all of a sudden and he goes, 'Hello? Yes, I've been holding for ten minutes. Used to love 'The Entertainer', now I wouldn't care if I never heard the damned tune again. Want to order a wreath, please. Just a regular funeral wreath. Doesn't matter what flowers. And could you put on the card: RIP Knacker Park. Yes, Knacker Park. Yes, it's going to Mister Bertie Ahern, Taoiseach, Leinster House, Kildare Street, Dublin 2, thank you very much indeed. Oh and put a couple of exclamation marks after RIP Knacker Park. Three. No, four. Is four overdoing it? No, three then.'

What a tool.

* * *

I get a text from JP and it's like, **Scord Nicki Carney 1st nite. Robbd In Your Time, Mark Owen's nvr-populr solo effrt**, and I text him back, **Respect!** and he just goes, **Affluence!**

* * *

I hit Kiely's, roysh, having basically arranged to meet Fionn for a few scoops, but of course Goggle Features is too busy to even notice me, sat up at the bor he is, with his focking groupies, three or four freshers, total airheads, roysh, and coming from me that's saying something. Should see them, roysh, hanging on his every word, because of course he's, like, lecturing in UCD now. Lechering, more like. He's going, 'Well, yes, Emile Durkheim *is* the father of modern sociology *after a fashion*. But don't forget about Max Weber's contribution,' which I'd rip the total piss out of him for if it wasn't for the fact that I'm here looking for a favour from him. Eventually, roysh, the dude decides to actually acknowledge my existence.

He goes, 'The very man. There we were, talking about human-kind's deepest thinkers and suddenly you walk in,' and I can't make out whether he's, like, taking the piss, but the birds all crack up, so he might be. He does the introductions. One of them, her name's, like, Julie-Ann – nice rack, but a brace on her Taylor Keith – she just gives me this filthy, roysh, looks me up and down, and goes, 'So *you're* Ross O'Carroll-Kelly?' and I'm like, 'The one and only,' playing it like Steve Silvermint, of course. She's there, 'You went to my sister Amy's debs,' like I'm supposed to know what she's talking about. Actually, I think I do. Uh-oh. It's like, *There may be trouble aheeeaaad.* I'm there, 'That was, like, two months ago. Tell her to get laid and get over it,' and then I'm like, 'Anyway, I'm TRYING to talk to my friend here,' and I point to her three mates and I'm like, 'Go and take the dogs for a walk,' because in fairness they *are* all mutts. Fionn goes, 'I'll talk to you later, girls', and they all fock off to the jacks together, to top up their *Eau Dynamisante* and talk about how fanciable I'd be if I wasn't such a bastard to women.

Fionn pushes his glasses up on his nose and goes, 'A tad un-necessary, Ross,' and I'm like, 'Fock's sake, Fionn. *First years?*' and he goes, 'Sorry, remind me who it was went to the Loreto on the Green debs recently?' and it's like, you know, *touché.* I'm there,

'I cannot BELIEVE Amy's still going on about that,' and he goes, 'Ross, you slept with her best friend on the night of her debs,' and I'm like, 'Oh and that's suddenly, like, a big deal, is it?' Fionn goes, 'You see, Ross, because of various demographic and socio-economic factors that you're too pissed to understand at this particular juncture, the debs has assumed a far greater significance in the lives of teenage girls and their families than it enjoyed, say, five years ago.' He loves the sound of his own voice, the Specsavers focker. Knows his stuff, though, you have to hand it to him.

He's going, 'Girls could usually expect to be married with children by their mid-twenties. Not anymore. With house prices being what they are, the single-income household is a thing of the past. In any relationship now, there's an imperative on both porties to have a career, which means they're tying the knot a lot later in life, often in their thirties, if at all. So, you see, the debs has become almost a surrogate wedding. The debs is the big day now. And you ruined Amy's.'

I'm just there, 'Okay, spare me the focking guilt trip. Fionn, I need your help. You're, well, the cleverest goy I know, roysh?' and Fionn's there, 'What about all your friends from Mensa?' which is probably a piss-take as well for all I know, but I just, like, ignore it. I go, 'Fionn, I need you to write something for me,' and he's like, 'Write something? You've changed your mind about that French exchange student who had the hots for you, haven't you?' I just give him daggers, roysh, but I need the focker at this moment in time, so I go, 'It's actually the script for a porno film to be precise. Long story, roysh, but that film-making course that Christian's doing isn't the total waste of time I told him it was. The stupid fockers have given him ten thousand squids to make a movie, Fionn. How focked up is that?'

He goes, 'And Christian wants it to be a porno?' I'm there, 'No, Christian wants it to be about focking spacemen. But I am SO not letting him waste this money.' Fionn goes, 'If it's a porno, I take it that you're going to be the lead?' and I'm like, 'You've got to get the best, Fionn, even if it means paying a few squids over the odds.' I should probably state at this point, roysh, that I have no intention of anyone ever *seeing* this film. For me it's the chance to earn seven-and-a-half Ks, big my end away on camera – a new experience for me, believe it or not – and maybe take home a souvenir copy of the video. If the Head of Christian's course wants to see it, well and good, if that's what pumps his nads, but what I'm saying is it's not going to be on in the focking IMC in Dún Laoghaire.

Fionn goes, 'Why are you asking me? I wouldn't know the first thing about how to write a script,' and I'm there, 'Use your imagination. You used it enough when I was sharing a gaff with you. I remember how many boxes of Kleenex you went through in a week,' and it's true, roysh, the dude has the biggest collection of adult movies this side of Hugh Heffner's front focking door.

I'm there, 'There's two grand in it for you,' and he suddenly looks up, roysh, all interested. He's there, 'Two grand?' and I'm there, 'There's enough in the budget for a good scriptwriter,' and he's so focking happy I'm bulling now I didn't say one-and-a-half instead. Only got, like, five hundred bills left now for overheads. He goes, 'Have you a leading lady? Just so I can have her in mind when I'm doing the writing.' He's a total professional is Fionn. You get what you pay for, you see. I'm there, 'It's almost certainly going to be Emer, as in Sandycove Emer,' and Fionn nods his head and pushes his glasses up and goes, 'Good chemistry there.

It'll work,' which, fair play to him, he didn't have to say. I'm there, 'I think so, too. Just a matter of getting her to agree to it now.'

✳ ✳ ✳

Says in the paper, roysh, that Susan Sarandon – who I'd do in the blink of an eye – has welcomed the release of environmental activists Rodolfo Montiel and Teodoro Cabrera, and she's backing Amnesty International's call on the Mexican government to acknowledge their innocence of terrorism charges and to investigate their claims that they were tortured while in custody. I remember Sorcha banging on about these two dudes before, so I cut the article out, roysh, and, bent as it sounds, I put it in an envelope and lash it in the post for her with a little note just saying, I don't know, I thought she might be interested in this, maybe meet soon for a drink, blah blah blah.

✳ ✳ ✳

'You always said you wanted to work in movies,' I say to Emer. She goes, 'I'm doing four nights a week in Advance Vision. So I already am in a way,' and she gives me one of those stupid girly laughs and I forgot, roysh, that the girl is sappier than an entire Irish debating team. I'm there, 'It's not what you dreamt of, though, is it? Come on, Emer, we're talking a *proper* movie here. We're talking silver screen.' She goes, 'I don't know. What *kind* of movie are we talking about?' like she's focking Nicole Kidman or something, in a position to pick and choose. I'm like, 'It's, em, for mature audiences,' and she goes, 'Mature audiences? Oh, like *The English Patient*?' and I go, 'A bit, yeah,' deciding it's probably best if I break her to it very gently. I'm like, 'Can I get you another Cosmopolitan?' thinking she has focking expensive taste in drinks this bird, we're talking a tenner a pop here, and I must remember to keep the receipts – don't want to end up out of pocket. She goes, 'That'd be lovely, thanks. I, em, very nearly didn't come tonight, I hope you know that,' and I'm like, 'Why, pray tell?' She goes, 'Why? Ross, you never rang me. And that number you gave me didn't exist.' I'm like, 'I'd just gone through a pretty painful break-up,' spinning her a total cock-and-bull story. I'm there, 'I guess I could feel myself falling in love with you. I had to get out before I got hurt again.'

That's rocked her back on her heels. She's there, '*In love with me?* But we were only, like, with each other that one night,' and I go, 'Sometimes a minute is all it takes to fall in love,' and all of a sudden she's as happy as a Tallafornian on Mickey Thursday. She goes, 'OH! MY! GOD! I am, like, SO sorry, Ross. I SO didn't know you felt that way,' and I just shrug my shoulders and take a long gulp of Ken. I don't know how I can live with myself sometimes. She goes, 'I'll never forget what you said to me that night, though,' and I'm thinking, it could have been anything, roysh, because I was off my tits. She goes, 'I had just sent off my application to go on, like, 'Pop Idol' and you were like, "If it went on looks alone, they'd declare you the winner straight away".'

I'm there, 'And I meant it,' really softening her up now for the kill. She's like, 'Can I ask you a question? It's, like, personal?' and I'm wondering did I end up, I don't know, giving her something the night we were together, but she just goes, 'Did you borrow my Sheryl Crow CD? As in *Tuesday Night Music Club?*' I'm there, 'Excuse me?' cracking on to be majorly pissed off. She goes, 'I said *borrow*. It's just, I was sure it was there on the locker beside my bed that night. And the next morning ...' And then she thinks better of it and goes, 'OH MY GOD! what am I saying? I am SO sorry, Ross. I feel like SUCH an orsehole for, like, bringing it up,' and I'm there, 'Just leave it,' and she's like, 'No, Ross, genuinely. I am SUCH an ungrateful bitch sometimes. I mean, here you are, trying to help me out with my, like, career and shit, and I'm practically accusing you of, like, stealing a CD from my room. HELLO? Sometimes I'm like, DUUUHHH!' I'm there, 'You're not the first person to misjudge me,' and she goes, 'I know. You get SUCH a hord time from people,' and I'm like, 'It's mostly because I'm good-looking,' and she nods all, like, sympathetically, I suppose you'd call it. Then she goes, 'I am SO looking forward to working with you. When will I get the script?' I knock back another shitload of Ken and I go, 'You want to *see* the script beforehand?' and she's there, '*Duuuhh?* Naturally! To, like, learn my lines,' and under my breath I'm like, 'Don't think that's going to take long.'

I order her another Cosmopolitan, the thirsty bitch. Suddenly she's all, like, excited and she's going, 'Will I get a chance to use my ballet?' I'm there, 'Can you still do that thing where you wrap your legs around your neck?' and she's like, 'Yeah,' and I go, 'We'll see if there's some way we can include it.'

✳ ✳ ✳

In This Skin by Jessica Simpson is definitely the worst CD I've ever robbed. Total crap. Sara Mooney: shit taste in music, shit taste in men. What star sign does that make her?

✳ ✳ ✳

It's, like, midnight, roysh, and I'm in the Margaret – on my own, for once – when all of a sudden my phone rings and my caller ID says it's, like, Sorcha. I'm there, 'Hey, Hon,' and she goes, 'Hey, Ross. What are you doing?' I'm there, 'Just, em, thinking.' I was actually reading *FHM*, but I don't want her to think I was knocking one off the wrist. She goes, 'I'm SO glad you're doing something you're passionate about.' The focking top tens on Hilary Swank! She's there, 'Hey, thanks for that article. Susan Sarandon does SUCH good work. It's like, OH! MY! GOD!' and she goes quiet for a few seconds, roysh, and the next thing that comes out of her mouth is, 'We live in a cynical, cynical world,' and that's when I cop, roysh, that she's been basically crying.

I'm there, 'Sorcha, what's wrong?' and she's like, 'Nothing,' and I go, 'Sounds like *nothing* as in *something*,' and she storts spilling her guts out to me, about how the Japanese have developed a satellite that will allow them to monitor the movement of minke whales and kill them in greater numbers. She goes, 'And this is *supposedly* in the name of scientific research. They're hell-bent on resuming full-blown commercial whaling, Ross. I know it.' I'm like, 'Sorcha, you've got to stop taking the problems of the world onto your shoulders,' which is a bit, I don't know, deep for me, I suppose. The thing is, roysh, I really do care about her, dickhead and all that I am sometimes. I go, 'It's late. Would you not try to get some sleep?' and she goes, 'HELLO? They're already killing four hundred a year, Ross. How can I be expected to *sleep*? I'm going to look up the Greenpeace website. See if there's an online petition or *something*.'

✱ ✱ ✱

Been living the dream these last few days. Friday night I ended up scoring Heidi Hession, as in studying-to-be-an-auctioneer Heidi, and robbed *Folklore* by Nelly Furtado. Saturday night I bagged off with that Emily Patten who's a real, like, girl-next-door type – if you happen to be Cheryl Tweedy's neighbour! Let's just say that *In the Zone* by Britney Spears is not all I got from her. Then Sunday night it was Blathnad McAuley, who I'm basically convinced knocked back the Wonderbra ad because she thought Eva Herzegovina could do with the work. My selection there was *The Diary of Alicia Keyes* by, funnily enough, Alicia Keyes.

My busy weekend put me basically seven CDs ahead of my nearest challenger – we're talking JP – and that left me pretty much on a high when I called out to Christian's gaff on Monday afternoon. That didn't last long, of course, because I had to listen to him still banging on about space pirates and bounty hunters and how he's thinking of loosely basing the plot twist on the time Princess Leia tried to hire Prince Xizor of the Black Sun organisation to rescue Han Solo from Jabba's palace and Xizor tried to seduce her by emitting a powerful pheromone, except it didn't work because the Force was so strong in her. It's like the dude's not listening to me. I'm there, 'For the last focking time, Christian, this is your big chance. Don't blow it on some outer-space shite,' only going easy on the goy because I've still got to get my hands on that budget money.

He goes, 'But Andy – he's my tutor – he said my ideas are germinating nicely,' and I'm there, 'Well, whatever he meant by that, my idea's going to blow his mind. We're not talking dudes with funny beards getting it on with forty-year-old slappers with tattoos. Get this, Christian – we're talking an adult movie *with* a storyline. Never been attempted before.' He just looks at me, roysh, with those big cow eyes and he goes, 'I told Lauren she could play Leia,' and I swear to God, roysh, I don't know how I manage to keep my calm, although I actually do, roysh, because the dude's my best friend and shit. He just changes the subject, roysh, tells me he met Fionn in, like, Hilper's this afternoon and Fionn gave him, like, a package to give to me and I'll kill the many-eyed focker when I see him, roysh, because it's basically the script and I don't want Christian to know how far down the road I am with my plans for *his* movie. I'm sure Fionn wanted Christian to open it, roysh, but the dude's too honest and, like, trusting to do something like that.

I make some lame-ass excuse to leave, roysh, and when I get into the cor – we're talking a black GTI here, alloys, blah blah blah – I just, like, bell Fionn as I'm reading the thing. He goes, 'You like it then?' and I'm like, '*The Love Boat?* It's been done before. We used to watch it on TV3 when we were supposed to be in college,' but he goes, 'Just read it, Ross,' which I do, roysh, while he waits on the line. And I have to say, roysh, it's focking amazing, and we're talking totally here. I go, 'Fionn, you're a genius,' and he goes, 'I thought we'd steer clear of the office porty motif. It's a pornographic cliché at this stage. Thought we'd set it on a yacht. You'd have no qualms about borrowing your old man's boat, I take it?' I'm like, 'Fock *him*. It gets a bit, I don't know, heavy towards the end, doesn't it? There's laws against animal cruelty, isn't there?' He goes, 'That's the beauty of the boat, Ross. If you film it in international waters, you're in the clear.' I'm like, 'Kool and the Gang. Still not one hundred percent convinced about the ending, but I swear to God, Fionn, don't breathe a word of this to Sorcha. You know how she feels about dolphins.'

✳ ✳ ✳

Unbelievable, roysh, but Oisinn's neighbours showed up at the door of his shed the other night. We're not talking one or two, roysh, we're talking a whole focking posse here, like one of those lynch mobs from 'The Simpsons', we're talking pitchforks, flaming torches, the lot, demanding to know *with what strange powers he be meddling*. Oisinn threatened to douse them all in, like, amber accords and they ended up backing off. I'm not sure how reliable this is, roysh, but it's certainly JP's account and he claims he was there. He goes, 'The dude is going to end up very, very wealthy, or very, very dead.' I'm glad he's in such good form, roysh, because I've asked him to meet me for a coffee – we're talking Davy Byrne's? – to discuss security for the movie, I do NOT want my orse splashed all over *VIP* – not unless they're paying for it. Cut a long story short, I, like, broach the subject with him and he's pretty much game, roysh, but he wants five hundred sheets, which means the budget's basically spent now, and I'm just hoping Christian isn't expecting to make a few shekels out of this himself.

I'm there, 'Five hundred sounds a bit steep to me,' and he goes, 'Actually, there's one other issue,' and I'm thinking, I do NOT like the sound of this. He goes, 'My old man, he wants a port in it,' and I'm thinking, I bet he does, the dirty dog. He goes, 'Not a big port. Something small. Maybe the first mate on the boat or something,' and I'm like, 'Look, Fionn's in charge of the script. I'll ask him can he find room for another cast member, if you'll pordon the pun.'

So there I am, roysh, feeling like Hugh focking Heffner, when all of a sudden who steps into Davy Byrne's, only Erika. She just happened to be passing, she says, on her way down to Blue Eriu when she, like, saw us through the window and she says she's just been talking to Sorcha and she mentions that I should just, like, do her again, roysh, so Erika doesn't have to listen to her crap anymore because basically she says she's sick of it, which I don't think is fair, roysh, although I say nothing. She goes, 'I've never known what she sees in you, Ross. But I think exposure to you for any length of time could help her get over it,' and I decide I'm not taking that, roysh, even though she looks focking amazing.

I'm there, 'What *is* your problem with Sorcha? She's supposed to be, like, your friend.' but she just goes, 'My problem is with *you and Sorcha.* I'm sorry, Ross, I just don't buy it, all this fairy tale rubbish she goes on with. You sent her some crap out of the paper about Mexico or some other shithole of a place and all of a sudden I'm listening to, *Oooh, Erika, he's the one.* She's pathetic. And I don't like seeing orseholes like you reduce her to that,' and I'm there, 'Perhaps it's just plain, old-fashioned jealousy,' and I get up to go and drop the kids off at the pool and I pretend I don't hear her go, 'You have a dick like a babycorn – what is there to be jealous of?'

I go into trap one, lock the door behind me and sit there thinking about Sorcha. She hasn't, like, been herself lately. It's like all this stuff about the whales and those two, I don't know, spics I suppose you'd have to call them, is getting her down, not to mention this Iraq thing, which looks like it's all going to kick off. I decide I'm basically going to stort being, like, nicer to her because even though I'm, like, too damn handsome to be tied down by one woman, I do have feelings for the bird, or girl, if you like. I wash my hands, check myself out in the mirror and head back out. Erika's got this, like, evil look on her face, in other words her usual look. She goes, 'JP's just been telling me about your little *project*. Wonder what Sorcha will think when she hears you've moved into pimping,' and of course I try to bluff it out, going, 'Just helping a friend out with his film-making course,' but JP's basically spilled the beans. No point in blaming the dude, though. Erika can be very, let's say, persuasive. Goys tend to just give her what she wants.

She goes, 'Poor Emer. She's slept with pretty much everybody who's anybody in Lillie's, trying to get famous. Then she's lucky enough to meet you. I'm sure Sorcha will see the *artistic merit* in what it is you'll be doing together,' and I know what her game is, roysh, she's trying to make me feel like a pervert basically. I'm there, 'Erika, I'm asking you not to tell Sorcha about this,' but she just, like, laughs in my face and she goes, 'And *you* in the lead role, Ross. I take it the film will be a short then?' which she didn't have to say, roysh, she just did it to be a bitch.

✳ ✳ ✳

Sorcha's already got the old waterworks on full-tap when I answer the phone. She goes, 'Is it true, Ross?' and straight away I'm like, 'Of course it's not, Sorcha,' totally forgetting to ask her, 'Is what true?' which she picks up on straight away. She goes, 'How can you deny it when you don't even know what I was going to say?' and I'm just there, 'Well, I met Erika this afternoon and I just presume she's been putting the poison. Because I happened to mention how I felt about you,' and she stops crying, roysh, and I can hear the little cogs and wheels in her mind turning, trying to work out how to feel about this. She goes, 'What do you mean, how you felt about me?' and I'm there, 'I told her there were still a lot of feelings there and I could tell she was *not* a happy camper.'

Again, roysh, there's, like, silence. Then she goes, 'It's a simple yes or no answer, Ross. I'm tired of meeting liars and phoneys, Ross, and if there's one person in the world I think I can hear the truth from, it's you. Are you and Emer King making a porno-graphic film together?' and what can I say, roysh, except, 'Yes,' and then the floods really come. She tells me I'm a sicko, that Emer's no better than a prostitute and I'm basically a pimp, which was Erika's word. She tells me she always thought I was, like, a nice goy underneath it all, but now she knows, roysh, that

I'm not, I'm basically like everyone else in the world, a cynical focker who looks after number one first and foremost and doesn't give a fock who I hurt as a consequence. She says she used to tell the rest of the girls that I was the kind of goy she'd like to marry, but now she doesn't care, roysh, if she never, like, speaks to me again.

I try to say something, roysh, but she's, like, ranting now and she won't be stopped. She says that her problem has always been that she takes everything *way* too personally and she realises now she can't carry the weight of the world's problems on her shoulders anymore and that you have to be hord to make it in this world, and that in future she's going to look after herself and fock the seals and fock what's going to happen in Iraq and fock the Mothers of the Disappeared, whoever they are.

I'm there, 'Sorcha, this isn't you,' and she goes, 'Oh it SO is, Ross. This is the *new* me. This is SO the new me. I'm not working in the boutique anymore, Ross. I told my mum tonight. I was offered a new job, which I had certain qualms about. But not anymore. I'm taking it. I'm doing what you do, Ross. I'm looking after number one,' and she just, like, hangs up.

✳ ✳ ✳

Sat the old driving test again, roysh, like a fool thinking, I don't know, fourth time lucky and everything. Orse Face was on my case about my insurance – six miserable Ks a year, the tight focker – but he's there giving it, 'It would certainly help to bring the cost down if you got your licence,' but the fact of the matter is that it would make fock-all difference, roysh, because my name is basically dirt with the insurance companies.

It's, like, any little excuse to hammer you. Hands up, roysh, I've had, like, three accidents in the past year. I rear-ended some old biddy who was doing, like, ten focking miles an hour in the fast lane on the Bray bypass, I suppose to give her a gee-up more than anything. I took half the side off a Honda Civic that was porked with its wheels over my line in Riverview. The one where I *was* in the wrong, roysh, was the time I hit that speed bump on Avondale Road and ended up totalling some old tosser's wall. That one I was prepared to take the rap for, roysh, but the insurance companies couldn't give two focks who's in the roysh and who's in the wrong, they basically settle, and, of course, you end up totally up shit creek without a no-claims bonus. Fionn says I should complain to the Ombudsman, and I fully intend to once someone tells me what the fock it is.

I thought the old man getting elected to the council would mean he could, like, scratch a few backs, pull a few strings and he'd be slipping me it under the table in a brown envelope, but no, muggins here has to actually *sit* the test, which I knew was bad news from the moment I heard. I've got a bit of a, shall we say, history with driving instructors, and I think it's fair to say that there's something about me that they don't like. Believe it or not, some of them feel I come over a bit, I don't know, cocky, and from this dude's questions – we're talking what's the difference between a Stop and a Yield sign, we're talking what is the national speed limit, what does a railway track on a road sign denote – I can tell he seriously has it in for me. JP – why the fock I listen to him, I don't know – but he told me, roysh, that the first thing you do when you get in the car is to, like, crack a joke, just to, like, put the instructor at his, like, ease and shit? And, of course, JP has a lot more experience than me, having sat the test eight times, as opposed to my three.

So the first thing I do when we get into the cor is to try to, like, inject a bit of humour into the proceedings, going, 'Hold on to your hat, Gramps,' then doing a serious wheelspin, which – surprise, sur-focking-prise – the dude doesn't find in the least bit funny. Looks like that goy out of 'One Foot in the Grave'. *I don't believe it!* He goes, 'I could fail you immediately for that,' and I'm there, 'Hey, lighten up, dude.'

I pretty much knew at that stage that I was going to have to drive the perfect test to get any kind of a licence from this orsehole. But that's what I ended up doing, roysh. I ace it, we're talking the hillstort, we're talking backing around the corner, we're talking the handbreak, sorry, three-point turn.

Then he tells me to return to the testing centre, roysh, which is when things stort to, like, fall aport basically. I was probably a bit too cocksure, roysh, and I'm driving with basically one hand, the old mince pies not really on the road, when all of a sudden I run over something, and a mile or so down the road I turn around to him and go, 'What I hit back there, it wasn't, like, living, was it?' and he's like, 'Well, I wouldn't think it is anymore,' and I'm there thinking, you know, Fock you, Paleface. Costs nothing to be nice.

I'm probably a bit distracted at this stage, roysh, because I know he's, like, racking his brains, trying to come up with a reason to fail me. I end up hitting this speed bump, roysh, and I have to admit I'm going at a pretty fair pace when I do. Of course he makes a total meal of it, putting his hands over his eyes and going, 'Please tell me when all four wheels are back on the ground,' which is bullshit, roysh, because we landed ages ago.

Of course the next thing I hear is *nee-naw, nee-naw, nee-naw*, and I'm thinking, 'Oh, it's suddenly a matter for the Feds now, is it?' I pull in and this cop – a bogger, obviously – gets out of his cor and strolls up to me. I've already got the window down, ready for him. He storts writing shit down in a little notepad, roysh, going, 'Fifty miles per hour in a thirty zone – that's two penalty points. Driver not wearing a seatbelt – that's another two. And was that a one-way street I saw you emerging from about a mile back? Yes, I think it was. Two plus two plus two makes ... six.' I'm there, 'Whoa, horsey. This dude here's a driving instructor. He told me to drive down that road,' but he goes, 'I'm afraid, *horsey*, that I don't care if Michael Schumacher was directing you. You'll be hearing from us in due course,' and he focks off, with his big bogger head.

Of course, I'm not unaware of the fact that there's been a bit of a shift in, like, the balance of power now, between me and this driving instructor dude, what with him focking up on the directions front. I'm telling him I'm going to basically report him, roysh, for getting me penalty points I basically didn't deserve and suddenly he's being, like, nice as pie to me, telling me he'll lose his job and two of his saucepans are still in, like, school. I make no bones about it, of course. As we're pulling back into the test centre, roysh, I go, 'Give me my licence and we'll say no more about it,' and he looks over both shoulders, roysh, and goes, 'I could lose my job,' but when I stort singing 'In the Ghetto' he comes to his senses, goes into the centre and comes back five minutes later with a piece of paper telling me I'd, like, passed. But the last laugh, as focking always, was on me. There I am, roysh, pegging it home, wondering if I should be in this bus lane or not, when all of a sudden I remember the penalty points I had from before and I'm trying to, like, add them up, roysh, but my mind is suddenly too all over the place to do, like, sums and shit. I ring Fionn, roysh, and I go, 'What's six plus six, dude, and do NOT yank my chain on this one. It's not twelve, is it?' He goes, 'Usually, yeah. Why, have you won something?' and I'm like, 'Yeah, two years on public focking transport.'

✱ ✱ ✱

Sorcha thinks I don't care about her, roysh, but she is, like, SO wrong. She's basically the reason I got Fionn to write the dolphin out of the script. I mean, I don't think it's physically possible to tie one up anyway, roysh, but I was thinking of her when I dropped it. I've decided to go back to the original idea of an office porty, roysh. Filming it at sea is apparently a bit of a logistics mare, as we say in the film industry, and anyway, Knob Features wouldn't give me the yacht, the scabby focker. He was there going, 'Lend you the boat? Two weeks before the Hennessy Coghlan-O'Hara and Associates Autumn Regatta? Not poss, I'm afraid,' like the complete and total tool that he is. So it looks like it's back to photocopying each other's body ports. JP's going to have a chat with the goy who supplies their photocopier toner to see if there's some kind of, like, product-placement deal we could do where we flash up their logo for, like, ten seconds or something and they give us a few sponds into the bargain.

✱ ✱ ✱

There were a lot of people who thought Oreanna was off her cake having anything to do with me again, especially after I killed her cat. But you can't help who you fall in love with, roysh, and seeing her face this one particular Friday night when I threw the lips on her in Annabel's, well, she looked as happy as a northsider with ten wombs A few of the goys were basically against the idea of me getting involved with her as well – bad karma, Fionn said – but the facts are, roysh, that a) she looks like Ivana Hovart, b) she's fantastic in the sack, and c) actually there isn't a c), but with an a) and b) like that I don't need one.

Didn't want anything heavy, of course. No boyfriend-girlfriend vibe. Call a spade a spade here, roysh, I'm after my Nat King, but getting it off Oreanna means having to, like, crack on that you're more serious than you basically are. I end up letting her believe we're, like, an item, but I tell her that if we're going to, like, give this thing a proper crack, we're going to have to be PONPA for the time being, as in Private Only, No Public Appearances, just because of all the pressure that's going to come on us from all sides, bullshit bullshit bullshit. I don't know how I keep a straight face sometimes. And fair focks to her, roysh, she's making me put in the spadework. Four times I've been with her in four weeks and she's still not putting out, roysh, just keeps saying that she got hurt the last time, and I have to stop myself reminding her that it was Simba who got hurt, and he wouldn't have if he'd moved a bit quicker when I swung the old GTI into the driveway.

Anyway, roysh, to cut a long story short, it's the end of the summer, and this particular Saturday night she sends me a text and tells me her old pair are going out and do I fancy coming out to the gaff in Greystones, we're talking video, bottle of wine, blah blah blah, and of course I'm just there going, HE SHOOTS, HE SCORES!

She rings me up, roysh, and she's like, 'Oooh, my parents are going out at eight. Oooh, come out at seven. I'm dying for them to meet you,' but I decide to skip that bit of the evening, roysh, because I hate that whole, 'Hey, I'm rattling your daughter' vibe. Also it makes it horder to, like, dump a bird if you've met the whole family, although maybe I'm just a bit too, like, sensitive.

Whatever. I hop in the cor – still haven't got the letter telling me my licence is gone – but I don't bother my orse leaving my gaff until, like, eight o'clock, roysh, roll up to hers at about half-past, and when she says I've just missed them, I crack on to be all, like, disappointed, going, 'Those *focking* roadworks in Loughlinstown,' and she's going, 'There'll be other times, Ross,' not knowing how wrong she is. She looks amazing, it has to be said, good Peter Pan and not a pick of meat on her and she's wearing this pink top with, like, one sleeve missing, which I presume is, like, the new fashion or whatever.

Should probably tell you at this stage, roysh, that Oreanna had just got a new dog, we're talking a Jack Russell here, called Scooby, which she basically got as a present from her old pair after Simba bought the farm under my alloys, though let's not dig all that up again. I'm not a big dog-lover myself, roysh – careful! – but you know me, I go with the flow. I even pet the little focking thing, just to show Oreanna that I don't kill *every* animal I lay my eyes on and after, like, twenty minutes or so she begins to relax.

The problem with Jack Russells, though, is that they're horny little fockers, and this Scooby thing hasn't been focking desexed yet. So he's taken all the petting as basically a come-on, roysh, and no sooner have I sat down than he's up on my lap, sniffing the crotch of my chinos, with his little doggy lipstick sticking out. We've all been there and there's, like, nothing more embarrassing. Of course I'm there telling all the little white lies you do in that situation, going, 'He can probably smell my own dog off my clothes,' and of course now Oreanna's gone, 'What kind of dog have you got?' and suddenly I've invented this, like, basset hound called Albert, who Oreanna wants me to bring out so we can walk the dogs together on the beach, and all because I'm too chicken to say, 'Your dog can obviously smell piss off my trousers.' *Sniff. Sniff. Sniff. Sniff. Sniff.* 'For fock's sake, Oreanna, do something, will you?' 'Scooby, stop that!' she goes, letting him know that if anyone in this room is going to get it on with me tonight, it's going to be her. Off Scooby troops into the corner, with his little focking doggy fantasies, and Oreanna lashes on the video, we're talking *You've Got Mail*, which is a film I know my way around. To cut a long story short, long before Meg Ryan is forced out of business, me and herself are there on the floor, basically ripping the clothes off each other. I manage to pull her top over her head, roysh, the one with only one sleeve, and – SHIT THE BED! – I can't help it, I end up totally cracking my hole laughing. I can't believe what I'm seeing. Oreanna's roysh orm and her face are, like, totally brown, roysh, and the rest of her body is, like, milk-bottle white. Turns out the Peter Pan's come from a bottle, roysh, and – this is the hilarious bit – she was running low on it, so she thought, seeing as she was wearing that top, she could get away with slapping it on just the bits that were showing. She looks like she's had her orm up a cow's orse, like in that 'Animal Hospital'.

Of course, she hasn't copped it, roysh, she's giving it, 'I'm getting so turned on,' but I'm basically cracking my hole laughing in her face, roysh, and eventually she goes, 'What's so funny?' and Mr Subtlety here goes, 'Did your orm and your face go off to Ibiza without telling the rest of your body?' and she suddenly cops it and she goes, 'OH MY GOD! OH MY GOD! OH MY GOD!' and pegs it off to the bathroom to clean herself up, pretty much in tears. Actually, she was focking bawling now that I think about it, the sap.

Now I'm not exaggerating, roysh, but the second she's gone – the very second – up hops Scooby out of his corner, obviously thinking, Well, if she's not finishing it, I will, and suddenly he's back sniffing the old Dockers, the lipstick out again. I try to push him away, roysh, but he's basically having none of it. I even hit him a couple of sly slaps, but it seems to make him want it even more. I'm thinking there might even be a port for him in this focking movie we're doing and then – and I'm not being disgusting here or anything – all of a sudden he's up on my leg, basically riding me, his eyes closed, his tail in the air and his orse doing ninety to the focking dozen. So I decide to teach the little focker a lesson once and for all. No means no.

I stand up, roysh, and slowly but carefully move away from the sofa, and he's still clinging onto my leg, eyes shut, getting his jollies. I just take, like, four steps backwards and then, like, three to the left – like O'Gara, the master – then I run and kick my leg in the air, sending Scooby flying into the wall on the other side of the room. SMACK!

But the thing is, roysh, he hits the wall, then the ground and he doesn't move, and at first I'm thinking he's probably focking jetlagged from the flight. But then I get worried, roysh, because he didn't make any sound either, except this sort of, like, yelp I suppose you'd call it, as he was flying through the air. But the second he hit the wall, roysh, there was, like, silence and I'm beginning to fear the worst. I walk over to where he's landed, behind her old man's antique rocking chair, and right enough there's no movement there. Scooby's more than stunned. He's focking toast.

So I'm looking around me, roysh, to see if there's, like, a coal shovel or something around, so I can maybe bury the little focker before Oreanna comes back, then convince her that he ran away from home or some shit. But, of course – and you know what's coming next because I'm basically cursed – Oreanna saw the whole focking thing. Turns out she arrived back in the room just as Scooby was taxiing for landing. She saw him hit the wall. She saw me cracking my hole laughing. She saw me sticking his dead Scooby ass in the coal bucket and getting ready to take him out to the garden. She's looking at me like I'm focking Hannibal Lector or something, and I suppose in the pet world I probably am. I try to explain what happened, roysh. I'm there, 'The little focker was trying to ride my leg,' but she's not going to see reason. She opens her mouth and all that comes out is this, like, high-pitched scream, pretty much the same noise she made when I turned Simba into a focking pizza, thin crust. I turn and get the fock out of there, just as she turns on the waterworks. The secret with birds, you see, is knowing when to walk away.

✱ ✱ ✱

'Have a smell,' Oisinn goes, pointing to his neck, roysh, and of course I'm scoping around me to see if anyone's looking. Don't want the birds in here thinking I've gone Stoke – couldn't handle that many suicides on my conscience. But Oisinn just grabs me by the back of the neck and pulls me towards him. 'Get a good noseful,' he goes. 'Made it myself. It's dedicated to man's innate sense of adventure. Now, ginger you'd know, but guess the other main ingredient.' I'm like, 'Oisinn, I'm finding it hord to breathe here.' He goes, 'Tobacco flower, my man. Don't you think its deep, mellow scent contrasts yet at the same time complements the ginger's spicy freshness?' and I manage to tear myself free and get some air back in my lungs, then look around subtly to see if anyone's, like, copped it.

Have to say, roysh, my awareness when it comes to scenario is every bit as good as it was on the rugby pitch and straight away, roysh, without looking directly at her, I'm aware that I'm getting the big-time mince pies from this blonde bird, roysh, who's a ringer for Alyssa Milano. I listen to Oisinn bang on about work for another five minutes then I mosey on over to her, roysh, with the intention of hitting her with a couple of my world-famous one-liners – 'I think I could fall madly in bed with you' and 'When they made the alphabet, they should have put U and I together' – buying her a bottle of Coors Light and then heading back to her gaff before the rest of the competition arrives in from the Leinster match.

That was the plan, roysh, but she's talking to some goon in a suit. She's nodding, roysh, and going, 'An entire department, exactly,' so I order a pint of Ken and wait till the tool she's talking to focks off to the TK Maxx, then I move in. I'm like, 'Where are you from?' and she says Sutton, except she doesn't, roysh, she says it like, 'Sutting,' which is how you can tell the real money people out there from the blow-ins. I'm like, 'My, my, you're a long way from home,' hoping it doesn't sound too sleazy and shit?

She goes, 'It's my leaving party. Or redundancy party. Same thing, I suppose,' and I'm there, 'Are you a parking ticket? Because you've got fine written all over you,' but she just, like, ignores this, roysh, and tells me she had wanted to leave for ages and this was the kick in the orse that she needed. She's hammered. She goes, 'My boss was SUCH a wanker, pardon my French. Actually, I'm beginning to sound like him,' and I'm there, 'Let's not talk about him. Let's talk about us,' but she goes, 'We have to downsize as part of our efforts to realign ourselves in the market place. That's what he said. Meaning he was sacking a load of us to save himself some money. Ten of us. Of course he didn't have the balls to do it himself. He's hired this new human resources ... bitch is the only word I can come up with to describe her. Bitch with a capital b. Jesus, I *am* beginning to sound like him.'

I'm losing her big-time here, so I go, 'Bum-mer. Suppose you wouldn't say no to another Coors Light then?' sounding all, like, sympathetic. Birds love that drink, you see, because there's, like, fock-all points in it and it doesn't give them a fat orse. She doesn't answer, but I order anyway while she's blabbing away. She goes, 'HOW THE HELL ARE WE TODAY? That's the way he talks. The top of his voice. CHARLES O'CARROLL-KELLY HERE. His initials are ...' and I just stop and all the blood in my body just goes cold, roysh, and she must cop this because she asks me if I know him. Of course I'm there, 'Em, no. Never heard of the goy,' and she goes, 'Well, you wouldn't want to meet him. A big, pompous dickhead. But *she's* the one I really hate. To look at her, you'd think butter wouldn't melt in her mouth, but she is *the* bitch from hell. Focking Sorcha.'

And now my head is focking spinning. She goes, 'Two weeks is all she's been working there. And she's spent all that time coming up with spurious reasons to sack people, so that orsehole doesn't have to pay them redundancy. You know the usual petty stuff. You're back from your lunch a minute late and you've got a verbal warning. Twice and there's a written one on your desk. Oh she's a cold bitch.' I'm in too much of a daze to notice that her mate in the suit is back from the shitter. She sort of, like, flicks her thumb at me and goes, 'I was just telling this goy here about the Ice Maiden.'

* * *

I get a text from JP and it's like, **Stole Damita Jo by Janet Jackson frm Kelly Hammond. Dat makes 22, my man** and I just text him back, going, **Legend!**

CHAPTER TWO
To Love and to Cherish

The stupid dickhead is putting his clubs into the boot of
the Lexus, roysh, when I go out to him. I'm just like, 'I want a
focking word,' and he doesn't even look at me, just goes, 'Will it
take long, Kicker? I'm playing golf with Hookie.' I'm there, 'Why
didn't you tell me?' and of course he plays the innocent, looks at
me like he doesn't know what I'm talking about. That focking hat
of his pisses me off big-time. I go, 'You hired Sorcha. Without
telling me,' and he goes, 'I tried to tell you. In the kitchen, a
couple of weeks ago. I barely got a word in. I said, "Hey, Kicker,"
and you said, "Shut the fock up, Knob Features." I think it was
Knob Features. Then you went back to your room.' Fock, I
remember that now. I'm there, 'I don't remember that. You're a
focking liar.' He shuts the boot and pulls out a cigar and goes,
'What's the problem anyway, Ross? Your mother and I love
Sorcha. You know that. She did that course in human resources.
Very clever girl. She's helping us downsize our cost base at the
moment by realigning–' and I'm like, *'My problem*, if you'll shut
your big focking cakehole long enough to listen, is that you're
using her to do *your* dirty work. She's not cut out to be a bitch.
She's just a bit messed up at the moment and *you're* taking
advantage.'

I tell him that the second he dies, roysh, I'm going to flog absolutely everything he's spent the last twenty years building up and blow the sponds on drugs and lap dancers, immigrant ones, and he goes, 'When I die?' and I go, 'Yeah. And that day can't come quick enough as far as I'm concerned,' and I leave him, like, speechless, roysh, hop into the old black Golf GTI – alloys, the lot – and bell Sorcha on her mobile. She's there, 'Sorcha Lalor, Human Resources,' and I'm there, 'Meet me in the M1 in one hour,' and she goes, 'Ross, I am SO snowed under at the moment,' and I lose it, roysh, and I just go, 'Just focking be there, alroysh?' and I hang up. She arrives, like, half-an-hour late, roysh, just to prove a point, and she's straight on the offensive, giving it, 'There'd better be a good reason for this,' and I'm there, 'Just want to know what your game is?' She's wearing this, like, trouser suit and her face is all hord. She orders a cappuccino, then she goes, 'Let's cut to the chase here, Ross. You have a problem with me working for your father?' and I go, 'Well, yeah,' and she's like, 'Precisely. *You* have a problem with it, Ross. *You* need to deal with it. Now, was there something else?' I'm there, 'What about, I don't know, your old dear's shop? You seemed so happy there,' and she goes, 'I didn't study for all those years to wind up selling over-priced clothes to ladies who lunch. The only thing that would make me happy right now would be to sort out this Niall Nolan issue.' I'm there, 'Who the fock is Niall Nolan?' wondering is it some bloke who's, like, playing her for a fool and surprising myself that I actually care so much. She scrapes the froth off the top of her cappuccino with her spoon and eats it. She goes, 'Basically he's a goy who takes €25,000 a year from the company for doing nothing.' I'm there, 'Ah, roysh. And you're trying to come up with a reason to sack him?' She goes, 'He missed a lot of days. Forty-eight this year if my memory serves and it's still only November.' I'm there, 'Sorcha?' but it's like she's in some kind of trance. She goes, 'Might get a private detective to follow him. See how real this emphysema of his is.' I'm there, '*Sorcha*?' and she suddenly snaps out of it and I go, 'This ... this isn't you.' She goes, 'And what is me, Ross? South Dublin princess in a pink shirt with the collar up? Little rugby groupie following you around?' and I'm there, 'Well, yeah. Not this, like, bitch you've turned into.' She won't look me in the eye, a sure sign that she knows what she's doing is wrong. She goes, 'I'm doing something I'm good at.' I turn the screw. I'm like, 'What about Shut Sellafield? And the World Wildlife Fund? That dolphin you were telling me about?' She goes, 'The North Island Hector's Dolphin? Huh! If they're dumb enough to swim into dragnets, then they don't deserve to live. It's called natural selection, Ross. A bit like this Niall Nolan ... it's going to be hard to prove he doesn't have emphysema. Unless we can get pictures of him running a marathon or something.'

I'm like, 'And this is it then, is it? This is the future you always dreamt about? Sacking people from their jobs? Being my old man's lackey?' She goes, 'Ross, it's 2003. I've grown up. It's about time you did too,' and she goes to stand up, roysh, and I go, 'But what about the animals – the seals, the *dolphins*?' and it comes out all, I don't know, girly and basically bent and everyone in the whole place is suddenly looking at me. She just goes, 'Thank you for the coffee,' and she focks off. I think about what JP said. He turns around to me last night and he goes, 'Ross, with the Celtic Tiger came DVD players, 48-inch televisions and Audi A8s. But the boom is over and now the repo men are at the door. And Sorcha's with the repo men.' Although there's no denying that that trouser suit is seriously focking arousing.

*** ***

Oisinn texts me and it's like, **Wht abt this? Reason by Mel C. Frm Louisa Dowd – as in Aoife Byrne's fat frnd. Legend r wht? Dats 27 now. Read em n weep.**

*** ***

With Emer, roysh, I decided that the less she knew about the actual kind of film we were making, the better. I know it's going to involve her basically getting her kit off, but the plan, roysh, was to basically get her to the venue – we're talking Hook, Lyon and Sinker in Donnybrook – and hope the passion just, like, took over. So you can imagine my surprise, roysh, when she rings me up the other night and tells me she bumped into Fionn in Lillie's and the big-mouthed, greenhouse-faced focker basically blabbed about what kind of movie she'd, like, signed herself up for. She goes, 'Ross, why weren't you upfront with me?' and I'm there, 'I won't lie to you, Emer, I thought you might have a problem getting your kit off in front of the camera.'

But – this is the amazing bit, roysh – she turns around and she goes, 'I've no problem with that at all. I don't know why you didn't just tell me the truth,' and I'm there, 'Are you saying you're happy to do it? You know what's in the script?' and she goes, 'I know the gist of it. Hey, you know my motto – don't knock it till you've tried it,' and I'm like, 'And don't try it in case you like it. Happy days. When suits you? For, like, filming?' She goes, 'It *is* just us, isn't it? OH MY GOD, I SO mean it, Ross, you better not have the goys there, all sniggering behind a curtain or something,' and I go, 'What do you take me for, Emer?' thinking I'll have to tell them it's no-go. I'm there, 'We'll set the camera up ourselves. It'll only be us in the room. I'm not yanking your chain here,' and she goes, 'What about Christmas Eve?' and I'm there, 'Hmmm. Difficult. I'm usually in the M1 getting mullered with the goys.' She goes, 'Oh. It's just I, OH MY GOD, SO love Christmas. I don't know, maybe it's just, like, the romance of it and everything, but I'm always, like, SO horny around Christmas,' and of course what can I say, roysh, except, 'Christmas Eve it is then,' and she goes, 'Gives me time to lose a few pounds as well,' which is good, roysh, because it means she's thinking like a professional.

✳ ✳ ✳

Letter arrives in the post. *Wish to inform you* blah blah blah *that your licence is revoked*, which I'm pretty much sure means gone, and I'm like, FOCK!

✳ ✳ ✳

The nosebag takes forever to arrive, roysh, but there's the old dear blabbing away, like I'm not storving to death here? She's going, 'What do you want for Christmas, Ross?' and I'm there, 'Are you focking deaf? I told you two months ago I wanted sponds,' and she goes, 'Oh. It's just that it's only three-and-a-half weeks away now. Just wanted to check,' and then she goes, 'Money,' and mutters something about remembering this year what the true meaning of Christmas is, and I tell her not to stort with all that Jesus-in-a-manger shite again. I'm like, 'He ruins focking everything, that goy,' and I tell her that if she thinks I'm actually going to Mass this year, she'd better go to the doctor and tell him that her HRT dosage isn't strong enough. She says she never thought she'd hear anybody talk about God like that in her kitchen, but the old man tells her that maybe I have a point, because he read an article in the *Telegraph*, roysh, which said that Mary was actually an unmarried mother and that her and Joseph and the kid were basically refugees, and the old dear goes, 'Refugees? Oh, I don't approve of that.'

Finally she focks off to the kitchen, roysh, and she's back a couple of minutes later and she, like, puts my dinner down in front of me, that's if you could call it that. Focking liver. I take one look at it and I go, 'Not eating that,' and the old man's like, 'Very good for you, Ross. Good for the blood,' and I go, 'It's the organ that all the piss and shit passes through. I'm not eating it,' and I grab my mobile out of my pocket, roysh, and phone for a pizza, roysh in front of them and everything. I'm there, 'A twelve-inch, with everything on it. Everything except focking liver. No, it's just a private joke,' and I'm giving the old dear daggers, roysh, and of course she's about to burst into tears, the attention-seeking bitch. Then I go, 'I'll be in the front room when it arrives. One of you orseholes better answer the door. That's if you could be bothered.'

Then I head into the sitting room, roysh, and I'm there listening to the new Coldplay album, waiting for the old nosebag to arrive, so Hank I'd eat a scabby focking dog at this stage. So it's, like, twenty minutes later when the doorbell finally goes, roysh, and the old man answers it and suddenly there's all this, like, chatting in the hallway, blah blah focking blah, and there's me in the sitting room about to die of focking malnutrition, and I'm thinking, What could he possibly have found to talk about with whatever focking asylum-seeker is delivering my dinner tonight?

So of course I have to actually stand up, roysh, and head all the way out into the hall, and it turns out that it's not my pizza at all, it's, like, Sorcha, who's come around to talk to Knob-End about work. I just, like, follow them into the kitchen and the two of them sit down at the table and stort spouting, like, management bullshit.

Sorcha's going, 'I think if we're going to push ahead with these performance appraisals as we discussed, we're going to have to establish feedback loops so that people and teams know how they are doing *vis-à-vis* expectations,' and I'm there, 'I don't get a hello then?' and she looks up, roysh, but she basically looks roysh through me, and we're talking totally here. She looks hot.

The old dear goes, 'Sorcha, would you like some dinner? It's liver,' and Sorcha goes, 'Yum, oh my God, I *love* liver,' and from the way she licks my old dear's orse, roysh, I know that deep down the girl still wants me. Sorcha goes, 'It helps prevent arthritis, you know,' and I just give it, 'Sack anyone this week, Sorcha?' and she gives me a filthy, roysh, sort of, like, narrows her eyes, and goes, 'We're realigning the workforce to make it better suited to a more competitive morket environment, Ross. Rationalisation is necessary to guarantee efficiency,' and quick as a flash I'm there, 'I liked you more when you were nice,' and she looks me up and down and goes, 'No you didn't, Ross. And we both know it.' The old pair are looking at her, roysh, all smiles, like suddenly *she's* their only child and not me. Then she has to stick the dagger in. She goes, 'How's your *movie* coming along?' and there's, like, no answer to that so I end up just focking off out the door, without even waiting for my pizza. The old man can pay for it when it arrives, the scabby focker.

* * *

JP's full of himself tonight and fair focks to the dude. He's making a basic killing on this new housing development in Gorey, wherever the fock that is, a two-and-a-half-hour commute from Dublin City Centre, he said, in a beautiful country setting, only 4,864 left. He's going, 'A great many people are taking the idea of living outside Dublin offline, Ross. And that's win-win from my POV,' which I can already tell from the thickness of the wad he's flashing, and I'm SO tempted to remind him that I kicked his orse when we were selling gaffs together a year ago.

JP gets them in while Oisinn asks me if I've set a date for filming, roysh, and I tell him that it's in two weeks' time – we're talking Christmas Eve – but that the news is bad from his end because I can't deliver him, or in fact any of the goys the ports I promised them. I tell him that Emer basically won't do love scenes in front of an audience, but he says he understands, roysh, which takes a weight off my shoulders because I was a bit worried about the old performance anxiety as well, not that it's ever, like, happened to me before. I promise the goys they'll all get copies and I go, 'Just for your own education,' and Fionn tells me I should get Christian to splice in five or ten minutes of extra footage, just to make it last longer.

All the goys crack up and I pretend to as well. I'll just do what I usually do, which is wait until he's out on the dancefloor, basically giving it loads, then ask the DJ to stick on 'Five Hundred Miles', that one by The Proclaimers, and get all the rest of the goys to, like, surround him in the middle of the floor and stort, like, pointing at him, because he's got glasses, you see, and he basically looks like one of them. He focking hates that. I'm a happy camper. Everything's going Kool and his Merry Men. All I've got to do now, roysh, is get the camera equipment and that ten grand off Christian who, incidentally, still thinks he's making a focking space movie. He rings me, roysh, and he tells me he thinks 'our hero' is going to have to have an Achilles heel and it's going to be Leskarmic crystals, which are found on the planet Anelsuz, and I just humour the dude.

When I've hung up I text Emer and I go, **Hows d diet comin alng?** and she's there, **Lost 3lb dis wk**, which is good, roysh, because I really don't want be storring opposite to some blimp. It's me who's basically full of myself now. I get my round in and Oisinn goes, 'You look like a happy bunny.' And JP's like, 'Yeah, dude, you look like your dick's been named the official snack food of the French women's beach volleyball team for the 2004 Olympics.' I'm like, 'It might just as well have been, JP. It might just as well have been.'

✷ ✷ ✷

Can't understand why this Sorcha business is, like, wrecking my head the way it is, roysh, but I think it's because – and this is going to sound bent, roysh – if Sorcha turns out to be bad, then what hope is there for the world? I'd never tell her this to her face, roysh, but she's just one of those people who make you want to be a better person than you are. Right now, though, she makes Erika look like Princess Diana.

So on Monday night, roysh, I call out to her gaff in Killiney and her old dear opens the door. She's never really been that pleased to see me since, well, since any of the hundreds of different times I made shit of her daughter's life. She tells me to go on up to her room. Sorcha's sitting at her desk, reading some pretty serious-looking book, which turns out to be some business manual or other. She's got her eyes closed and she's going, 'Total Quality Management is built around the idea that individuals can always improve their work by learning new techniques and applying them.' I knock on the door, roysh, and she turns to look at me and then shakes her head. She goes, 'I'd love to know if the people who write these books have any experience of a real-life working environment. Motivating People.

Encouraging Management Potential. Remunerating Effectively. Creating Portnerships. There's nothing about how to get rid of people who are nothing more than leeches,' and I go, 'From what I've heard, you could write that book yourself.' She looks at me and she goes, 'HELLO? I've sacked fifteen people, Ross. It hordly makes me Rupert Murdoch,' and of course I have to crack on that I know who the fock she's talking about.

She stands up and air-kisses me and then gives me a hug, roysh, which seems to go on forever. I know she's not happy. She goes, 'I'm sorry I gave you such a hord time the other day. It was uncalled for.' I just, like, shrug my shoulders and I go, 'I brought you this,' and I hand her three or four pages of stuff that I, like, printed off from the internet, but she doesn't look at them. I'm there, 'You remember Twingo and Itongo?' and straight away she goes, 'Who?' and I'm like, 'You know very well who, Sorcha. The two giraffes that nearly died in that flood in the zoo in ...' and she goes, 'Prague. I remember. What about them?' and I'm like, 'I found this on the internet. Says they've been given a new home at a wildlife pork in England.'

I can see something flash in her eyes, something of the old Sorcha. Then she goes, 'Sorry, but all of this affects me how?' and I go, 'You gave money to the appeal. I was there in the bank with you when you sent off your entire week's wages. I never told you but, shit, Sorcha, I was so proud of you that day,' and she looks at the pages for the first time. She goes, 'They're Rothschild's giraffes,' and I'm there, 'I know.' She's like, 'Very rare. You ... you went on the internet to get this? Specially for me?' and I nod. She's there, 'Ross, that's very sweet,' and I go, 'You look tired, Sorcha,' and we both sit down on her bed. She goes, 'I *am* tired. It's this whole Frank Vance business,' and I look at her as if to say, you know, who the fock is Frank Vance? She goes, 'It should have been so *bloody* easy. I mean, he doesn't *do* anything, Ross. We've too many accounts clerks. He's just taking the money. So I checked his medical records. Found out he has a bladder problem.' I'm there, 'And?' and she rubs her eyes, roysh, and she goes, 'I banned him from taking toilet breaks,' and I shake my head and go, 'You did *what*?' and she's like, 'You try to get a decent day's work out of a man who's in the toilet every fifteen minutes, Ross. You try it and come back to me. And now, now he's suing me for bullying.' I'm there, 'What does my old man think?' and she goes, 'Haven't told him yet. Thought I might try to sort it out myself before I bothered him with it.' I'm like, 'Sorcha, would you not try to get some sleep. Might all look different in the morning,' and she's there, 'No, I'm going to keep ploughing through these books. The answer must be in there somewhere,' and I can tell she wants me to go. I stand up and she goes, 'It was nice to hear about Twingo and Itongo. Cheered me up.' I give her a hug and tell her I'm here for her, no matter what.

✳ ✳ ✳

Get a text from Oisinn and he's going, **Soundtrk frm Beaches. Dnt even no d brd's name. Dats 31 - rite on ur heels!**

✳ ✳ ✳

The doorbell rings and of course there's no one in the house to answer it, so focking muggins here has to tear himself away from the new Cat Deeley Thai Boxing Exercise Workout video and go and, like, answer it. Turns out it's, like, Hennessy. No hello. He just goes, 'Ross, where's your father?' and I'm there, 'Dead, for all I care,' and he's like, 'It's just I can't seem to reach him on his mobile. He must be out on the course.' I'm like, 'Look, without being rude here, what the fock do you want? I'm actually in the middle of something,' and he goes, 'Yes, your zip is open by the way,' and I look down and do it up.

He goes, 'I won't beat around the bush, Ross. I'm in a spot of bother and I need someone to drive me to the airport.' I'm there, 'No can do, dude. I don't think I have a licence anymore. What does revoked mean?' and he's like, 'Cancelled. Annulled. Withdrawn,' and I go, 'Nope. Definitely don't have a licence.' He goes, 'Ross, if you're caught, I'll pay for the best barrister money can by. I mean, it's way beneath Paddy McEntee, but he's a friend of a friend.' I'm there, 'What's the Jackanory anyway?' and he goes, 'They're looking for me, Ross.' I'm like, 'The Feds? You said that before. That time you pegged it to America,' and he goes, 'They've got the goods on me this time, Ross. They arrived just after seven this morning. Ten of them. Jemmied open my filing cabinet. Left with a lot of, shall we say, paperwork. It's *prima facie* evidence. You want to know the irony in all of this? Your father bought me a shredder for my fiftieth and I haven't even taken it out of the box yet.' He keeps looking over his shoulders, roysh, like he's expecting to be lagged any minute. I'm going, 'What's in it for me?' and he whips this package out from inside his coat and he goes, 'There's two Ks in there, Ross,' and I'm like, 'Okay, OJ. I'll go get the keys,' which I do. The stupid tosser, roysh, he actually thinks he's getting in the focking front with me. I'm there, 'Hennessy, you're a fugitive from the law. I don't want people seeing you in my cor. Get in the boot,' and he thinks about this for a few seconds, and then something catches his eye, roysh, this French bird — we're talking the total spit of Tess Daly — who's two-doors-down's new *au pair*. Hennessy's eyes follow her roysh down the road and then he sort of, like, whistles to himself and goes, 'It's a good job you can't be jailed for what you think,' because he's a focking filthbag basically. By the time he looks back at me I've got the boot open and I'm going, 'In,' and he climbs in without any arguments. I stort up the engine and hit the road and I decide, roysh, to have a bit of craic, so I take a short detour on the way to the airport, basically out The Graduate direction, roysh, where there's a fairly big roundabout. So I end up spending, like, ten minutes going around and around the thing and, of course, Hennessy's in the boot, roysh, with his guts doing somersaults. He's going, 'Ross, I think I'm going to be sick,' and I'm shouting back at him, 'Sorry about this, Hennessy. It's just I can hear a siren somewhere and I want to stall for a bit until I know which one of these roads it's down,' which is total bullshit, of course. Then I turn up Avondale Road, roysh, where there's, like, I don't know, twenty speed ramps all in a row and I hit every single one of them at, like, fifty miles an hour and Hennessy's head is getting whacked off the roof of the boot. Then at the end of that road there's another roundabout. So it's, like, eight or nine times around that and then to the airport.

Well, actually to Blackrock. I'm basically storving, roysh, so I pull into the old Frascati Centre, tell Hennessy I'm going to get change for the East Link toll bridge, back in five minutes, and I leave him there in the boot for an hour-and-a-half, roysh, while I grab a club sandwich and a couple of cups of coffee in Café Java and read One F's interview with God in *The Stor*. I SO have to go to the World Cup next year. Then I saunter over to Roches Stores, roysh, to see if Michaela's working, this bird I ended up nipping in Ron Black's last week, to see if she fancied going for a scoop one night. Turns out she's off today, so I head into the sports section and have a look at the Leinster away jersey, which I'm thinking of buying. Then I mosey on back to the cor. Hennessy's having an eppo, of course. He's going, 'Where have you been? I thought something had happened to you. I thought I was going to end up locked in here forever,' and I tell him he will if he talks to me like that again and all of a sudden he storts minding his manners. He goes, 'Why are we taking the East Link, Ross? Would the M50 not be quicker?' and it would, roysh, but there's a shitload of speed bumps this way, on the coast road in Sandymount and then when you go up that road past the Point Depot.

At one stage, roysh, I actually get worried that I might have knocked the tosser unconscious, that's how hord I hit this one particular bump. But he's wide awake when I turn around and go, 'Don't panic, Hennessy, but there's a checkpoint up ahead,' just putting the shits up him basically. He ACTUALLY bursts into tears, roysh, and he's giving it, 'Please, Ross. I don't want Lauren to have to visit her father in Mountjoy.' The tool. I'm actually stopped at traffic lights, roysh, waiting to pull out onto the airport road, but of course his imagination's doing ninety to the dozen and he thinks the Feds have pulled me over. So just as the lights are turning green, roysh, I roll down the window and shout, 'YOU'LL NEVER TAKE US ALIVE!' at no one basically, then I do what I have to say is a pretty amazing wheelspin and take off at, like, seventy miles an hour.

So Hennessy's seriously bricking it now, thinking the Feds are on our tail, but it turns out the joke is actually on me, roysh, because they *are* on our tail and I am not yanking your chain here. I hear the siren first, roysh, then I check the old rear-view and there's two cops on motorbikes behind us and they're going at a fair old pace as well. I think about pulling into the hord shoulder, roysh, but in the end I decide to try to, like, outrun them, not to save Hennessy's orse but to save my own, because speeding is one thing, roysh, but driving while disqualified is pretty heavy shit.

So old Lead Foot here slams on the accelerator, roysh, and my baby hotfoots up to eighty and I put a bit of light between us. Ten seconds later, roysh, the two boys are back in the mirror, doing over eighty themselves, like a couple of lunatics, basically some-one could get killed. I give it a bit more welly, up to focking, well, literally ninety now and by now Hennessy's in the back, going, 'It's no good, Ross. They know where we're headed. They'll have men there waiting,' but it's like a point of principle for me now to get to the airport before they do, to give some other cop the pleasure of arresting us. So there I am, roysh, just taking the slip road off to the airport, when I realise that the cops have stayed on the main road. I look over my shoulder and I see them just going straight on and, like, five seconds later, roysh, there's two or three Mercs and a big black stretch limo and it turns out I was basically fleeing from some EU muppet or other's Gorda convoy. I pull up outside the departures terminal and let Hennessy out of the boot, which I'm just thinking now must have looked pretty strange to the people who were hanging around outside. He hops out, roysh, and he goes, 'Ross, I owe you for this. More than the money that's in that envelope. I'll phone your dad from JFK, tell him what's happened.' I'm like, 'So where are you going to go?' just so I know where he is in case 'Crimeline' sticks a reward up for the focker. He goes, 'Rio eventually. Brazil has no extradition arrangement with Ireland, you see,' and then his eyes follow and practically undress these two black birds who're getting into a Jo. He's there, 'Plenty of that where I'm going,' then he pulls this, like, leery face, puts an unlit cigar in his mouth, gives me a wink and focks off into the airport.

✳ ✳ ✳

Hennessy phones the old man from New York, tells him the whole suss and the old man spends the next two days pretty much in mourning. He's going, 'An innocent man, pushed to breaking point by this blasted tribunal obsession of ours.' Then his face sort of, like, brightens. He goes, 'I think I'll start a campaign. Prove his innocence. I'm going to bally well do it. Fionnuala, get me my Mont Blanc pen, will you? I'm going to make sure he never spends a minute in jail.' I hit the video shop, roysh, and I rent out *The Shawshank Redemption* and *The Green Mile* and make him sit through them. And *The Great Escape*.

✳ ✳ ✳

It's Christmas Eve, roysh, and the whole gang's in Kiely's, knocking back the drink and basically giving it loads. I buy Sorcha a white wine and ask her if all that bullying shit's been sorted out, roysh, and she says no, and she asks me not to say anything to the old man about it, she's still trying to sort it out without actually having to tell him, and I go, 'I wouldn't even tell that focker my name and even if he guessed it, I'd deny it,' and she laughs, the first time I've seen her laugh – as in *properly* laugh – for ages, and then we overhear Erika going, 'I can't BELIEVE Sophie thinks that top fits her,' and we both crack up laughing again. The vibe is good and the gang's all here. Christian comes over to me, roysh, and hands me a Christmas cord, which is written in total gobbledygook and he tells me it's, like, Rodian, and he obviously cops my reaction, roysh, because he goes, 'The language that Greedo speaks?' and I go, 'Never mind that. Did you bring the video camera?' He looks at me, roysh, all offended and he goes, 'It's in the boot of the cor. You still haven't told me why you want to borrow it,' and I don't want to either, prefer to tell him when it's all done and dusted, hand him the tape and get the sponds off him, that way I don't have to hear another word about this focking space movie of his. I'm there, 'I told you already. We're having a traditional family Christmas and I want to, em, capture it on tape.' He looks me up and down like some, I don't know, alien has taken over my body, and he goes, 'But you hate your parents,' and I go, 'Christian, just go and get the focking thing, will you?' and off he goes with a big face on him. Lauren gives me a filthy, roysh, and I don't know if it's because of the way I boss her boyfriend or if she knows I dropped her old man to the airport. I'm there, 'Have you heard from your old man?' and she goes, 'Yeah, like *you're* really concerned,' and I suppose that answers that then.

I'm looking at my watch. Emer's got a bit of, like, family shit to do tonight, go to the nursing home to see her Gran, then Mass with her old pair – three wise men, baby in a stable, blah blah blah – but she's going to meet me outside Hook, Lyon and Sinker at, like, half-past ten. Fionn's given me the new script and I have to hand it to the dude, roysh, it's pretty amazing stuff, and I mean totally. Some classic lines in it. The whole seduction scene is so good, roysh, I can't understand why Fionn doesn't get his Nat King more often, ugly and all as he is. Emer is playing Debbie, roysh, my secretary who has a mountain of paperwork to get through and has had to, like, work through the Christmas porty to get it, like, finished. I walk in – paper hat on, hammered drunk – and I go, 'Can you take something down for me, Debs?' and of course she grabs her notebook and a pen and she's like, 'What is it you want me to take down, Sir?' and I'm giving it, 'You can stort with that skirt.' Might actually cut a bit of classical music into the love scenes. I'll borrow one or two of Sorcha's CDs. She's into all that shite. Christian arrives back with the camera and, fair focks to him, he's brought the tripod, which means we can set it up in the corner and not have to worry about it. JP comes over, high-fives me and goes, 'Felicitations and best wishes for the festive season, dude. The old man says to ditto that one. Wants to know when you're coming back to Hook, Lyon and Sinker,' and I tell him the only way he'll ever see me working there again is if he gets his hands on a video of tonight's perform- ance and he high-fives me, roysh, and hands me the keys to the office and tells me that I'm a legend, which I already knew, but it's nice to be reminded sometimes.

Everything's in place. I check my watch. Emer's going to be another half-an-hour, so I head over to Sorcha, who's involved in what sounds like a pretty heavy conversation with Fionn about work. She's telling him that she doesn't agree with the manage- ment manual's classic model for dealing with poor performance, involving setting clear objectives for improvements, establishing regular review meetings to monitor progress and explaining the consequences of continued below-par performance. She says she believes in helping people out – out the door. She goes, 'I'm not a mentor–' and I butt in by, like, yawning really loudly and they both just look at me and I go, 'Sorry, that sounds SO focking bor- ing.' Fionn goes, 'Is there something you'd prefer to talk about, Ross?' and I'm trying to think of something, like, witty to say, but before I get a chance he goes, 'Your movie, perhaps?' but Sorcha doesn't cop it, luckily for him. I actually think he's trying to get in there, roysh. He told me one night when he was hammered – the full three pints, he had that night – that he thought he and Sorcha had a connection. The unfortunate thing for him is that she's still got it bad for me.

I tell her she looks well tonight and her face sort of, like, softens, and she's no longer the management bitch from hell, then she asks me am I definitely calling out tomorrow, and I tell her of course I am, I do every year, and she says that's great, that seeing me on Christmas morning was the biggest thing she missed when she was in Australia last year and it doesn't feel like Christmas when I'm not a port of it.

I get a text from Emer and she asks me to meet her in Paddy Cullen's. I text her back to tell her I'm on the way and also that I've got the margarine, the feathers, the thermometer and the Zorro mask – a couple of interesting little twists that Fionn worked into the plot. She asks me to pick up some batteries in the Spar on the way down, roysh, and I text her back, basically asking her what for, and when she tells me, roysh, I'm out of that pub like Linford focking Christie, with a similar bulge in my chinos as well. I shout a general 'Merry Christmas' to everyone, grab the video camera and the old bag of tricks, and ten seconds later I'm pegging it down Anglesea Road. The next thing, roysh, my phone rings and naturally I assume it's her and I'm just there, 'Hey, sexy,' and all I hear back is, 'Hey, Kicker, you sound in good spirits.' I'm there, 'What the fock do you want?' and he goes, 'Just here with your mother, having a glass of mulled wine or six, thinking back to last year.' He's focking hammered. He goes, 'This day last year, in fact. Best Christmas present we ever got, Ross, you coming back home to us after that misunderstanding we had,' and I just go, 'Coming home was the biggest mistake of my life. And tell that focking soak beside you to get a life as well,' and I hang up.

I have to say, roysh, Emer looks tremendous. She's wearing a sort of, like, grey suit, white blouse, hair up in a bun, the whole office worker vibe. She says she just needed a drink, roysh, for Dutch courage, and she orders a Bacordi Breezer and I order a bourbon, which I knock straight back and ask for another. She goes, 'OH MY GOD, Ross, I SO love the script. I just wondered if we could make one tiny change to it?' I'm there, 'I've wasted my money on these batteries, haven't I?' and she goes, 'No, Ross, it's not that. It's this bit here,' and she whips out the script and turns to, like, page two. She goes, 'This bit here. There I am, typing away at the computer, when all of a sudden you burst in, wearing your paper crown and singing.' I'm there, 'What about it?' and she goes, 'Well, I'd like it if you burst in *just* wearing a paper crown,' and I have to say, roysh, I'm really beginning to fall for my co-stor. Wouldn't blame Tom Cruise in the slightest.

She knocks back the rest of her drink, roysh, then we head round to Hook, Lyon and Sinker. I open the door, roysh, and she goes on upstairs to the office. She says she'll set up the video camera while I get undressed and she heads into the office and I'm there whipping the threads off, roysh, thinking how much I love birds who are into control. So there I am, roysh, stark bullock naked, and I put the old paper hat on – it's called method acting – and I knock on the door and I go, 'Are you ready in there?' and she goes, 'Hold on, I'm just putting the batteries in,' and the one-eyed love soldier is suddenly standing to attention. About a minute later, roysh, she goes, 'Okay, I'm sitting at the desk. Now, don't forget to come in singing. I love Take That,' and I'm there, 'No better man,' and I burst in through the door, giving it, 'I want you back, and in the sack, and on your back for gooood.' Looking back, I was probably a bit on the slow side, roysh, but I didn't even suspect anything when the lights were off. I just went, 'Debbie, I thought I asked you to work overtime' – improvising, as we call it in the industry. The next thing, roysh, the lights suddenly go on and – FOCK ME SIDEWAYS! – everyone's there, we're talking Oisinn, we're talking JP, we're talking Fionn, we're talking some of Emer's friends, one or two of which I've been with before, we're talking maybe ten people I know to see from Kiely's, we're talking twenty or thirty people I've never set eyes on before in my life, probably people they picked up at a focking bus stop on the way down. *That's* why Emer wanted to go to Cullen's. Give the fockers time to get down here and set the whole thing up.

Everyone just, like, cheers, roysh, and of course I'm in too much shock to notice that Emer's pointing the video camera at me, filming me basically, standing there in my raw with a paper hat on, still sort of, like, half-singing the song, with the realisation of what's happening slowly dawning on my face. Emer goes, 'Look into the camera, Ross,' and like an idiot I end up doing it. She's there, 'You tried to play me for a fool. You thought I still had feelings for you and you could take advantage of that. So who feels like a fool now?' and I look at the goys, my so-called mates, cracking their holes laughing. I look at Oisinn and I go, 'And you – you goys – what was in it for you?' and JP's there, 'Ah, we just thought it'd be a bit of craic,' and everyone in the room storts laughing their orses off.

The next thing, roysh, the door opens and in walks Christian, carrying a space helmet in one hand and a big stack of papers in the other. He looks at me, roysh, doesn't seem to notice anything unusual, and goes, 'Hey, Ross. Thought you'd gone home. I see you've met the cast then,' and he walks around the room, hand-ing out what turn out to be scripts to everyone, going, 'Now try to set aside a little time over Christmas to learn your lines. Film-ing storts on January sixth.'

He doesn't seem to have been in on the set-up, what with him being a *true* friend and a legend. He holds up the helmet and he goes, 'Oh and those of you playing Carjenbea warriors, these are what you'll be wearing. The rest are arriving after Christmas,' and then completely out of nowhere he goes, 'By the way, Ross, why have you got no clothes on?' and everyone cracks up. Then he looks me up and down and goes, 'Oh, that reminds me, I must get that little light sabre for Sioli, the Elf King,' which, of course, everyone thinks is hilarious. I'm just there, 'Yeah and a Merry Christmas to you lot as well. Tools.'

CHAPTER THREE
To Honour and Obey

How Melissa ended up getting my number, I don't know. The only thing I can think of is that I must have been more locked than I thought when I was with her that night and ended up back in her gaff in Sandycove. But she rings me up, roysh, we're talking ten o'clock in the morning on New Year's Day and she says she heard a rumour from some goy she knows from the Institute that whenever I'm with someone, as in a bird, I always take a CD as, like, a trophy and she says that if it's true, then that makes me SO a sad person and if that's what happened to her Toni Braxton CD – 'you KNOW which one, we're talking *Secrets'* – then she wants it back because it was, like, a Valentine's present from Craig, her ex, who she says is a nicer goy than I will ever be, which basically doesn't bother me one bit. I tell her to get a life and I call her a sap. Can't believe how quick word spreads. The Petty Pilfering Championship ended two nights ago, roysh, with yours truly hitting the magical fifty mork when I scored some former Mountie whose name escapes me and pegged it the next morning with her soundtrack from *Jerry Maguire*. Fionn ended up being last, roysh – no surprise there – with a pathetic *four* CDs, and he probably bought them himself, the steamer.

So I spent, like, three hours going through the PP collection to pick a song that he had to do as, like, his forfeit, and because he made such a tit out of me, roysh, over the porno movie, I knew I had to make it a good one. In the end, roysh, I went for, like, 'Can't Fight the Moonlight' by Leanne Rimes, which he had to do just before midnight last night, roysh, dressed up as one of the birds out of *Coyote Ugly* – we're talking miniskirt, we're talking slut wellies, the lot – standing on the bor in Knackery Doo, which he did, fair focks to him. It was focking hilarious, roysh, but of course the word was out then about the competition, and I think we were all expecting a call or two, though I didn't think it would all kick off so quickly.

Melissa IS a sap, roysh, ringing at that hour of the morning, try-ing to stort my year off on a downer, bad enough as it is waking up like a Toblerone, out on my focking own. Orse Head makes it worse with his blabbering. The second he hears I'm up he's straight into the kitchen behind me, going, 'Young Sorcha's com-ing over tonight, Ross. Toast the New Year with us. Says she has a couple of things she wants to talk to me about. Couple more casualties there before Christmas. I expect it's that. That young idler, worked in security. Worked is a fine word for it. Worked, quote-unquote. Or maybe in italics. Yes, I think so. I can see it in italics. Had some strange notions. Couldn't handle being told he was back three minutes late from lunch. Sorcha laid it on the line and the chap quit in a fit of pique, with a capital P. I'm sure it wasn't much of a Christmas in that household this year. No new crutch for Tiny Tim.' I'm there, 'You're making that girl's life a misery. Even *you* must be able to see she's not happy.' He goes, 'On the contrary, Ross. I think she's found her calling in life,' and I'm there, 'Don't kid yourself. That Boss from Hell shit is just an act. With Sorcha, the good always comes rising to the surface.

And when it does, you're going to be advertising for another mug to do your dirty work.' He keeps clicking the top of his pen, which really focking irritates me. He goes, 'Well, I won't deny I had my doubts about her when I hired her first. At the start it was all Appraisal Systems this and Share Schemes that and Fringe Benefits the other. Wondered if she was a mite soft, quote-unquote. Needn't have worried, of course. Within a week she'd drawn up a hitlist of twenty people and now they're all gone. She's going to save me €500,000 this year alone.'

I'm there, 'Yeah and she's focking miserable.' He goes, 'Oh nonsense, Ross. I know what's eating Sorcha. It's this bullying palaver,' and I'm like, 'You ... actually know about that?' and he goes, 'You don't spend twenty years as a captain of industry without knowing what's going on in your own workplace. Yes I know about it. I'm not a man lacking in sensitivity, Ross. I could tell something wasn't right with the girl. Looked in her drawer after she went home one night and found some, shall we say, books.' I'm there, 'Books?' and he goes, 'Yes, books. Books, thank you very much indeed. Ladies and gentlemen, I give you books. *Developing Basic People Skills. The Boss As Mentor. Raising Group Morale.* Need I go on?' and I shrug my shoulders and go, 'Only if you're going to tell me what the fock you're talking about.'

He goes, 'I took it as a sign, Ross. She wasn't the same girl who insisted on locking the ladies' and gents' toilets outside of official breaktimes. Made some enquiries. Found out about these twelve bullying claims.' I'm there, '*Twelve?*' and he goes, 'Court is nothing to be scared of, Ross. I mean, she loved debating in school. That's all court is. Hennessy says even if they get as far as the Four Courts, the judge will laugh them back down the quays. Did I tell you he phoned this morning? All the way from Rio de

Janeiro. Line as clear as a bell.' I went, 'Oh, and did you tell Hennessy that court is nothing to be scared of?' which, of course, he has no answer to, so I just fock off back to my room. I'm pretty knackered, roysh, after a long, drunken and fruitless search for my bit last night, and I fall asleep.

I actually don't know how long I've been out for when I hear the old man downstairs, going, 'Oh, some of Ross's pals have turned up. Hello, there. Em, yes. Go on upstairs to him. A bit down in the dumps today. Cheer him right up to see you. Wow, there's quite a few of you, isn't there,' and at the beginning, roysh, I actually don't know whether I'm, like, dreaming this or not, but Melissa's suddenly at the end of my bed, roysh, looking like focking Kathy Bates out of *Misery*.

She's not the only one there either. They all stort streaming into the room. Phillipa, who's, like, second-year commerce in UCD. Susanna, Fionn's cousin, who plays the clarinet. Amy, as in Loreto Foxrock. Melanie with the blonde hair. Tina with the armpit hair. We're basically talking every bird I've been with in Annabel's, Reynords and Knackerydoo over the last, like, three months, roysh, and it's obvious what's happened. Melissa's told them all about the Petty Pilfering game and they've all, like, banded together, roysh, real focking *First Wives' Club* vibe, and they've come here for revenge, basically because they all want me, but they can't have me, and that's a fact they can't basically get their heads around.

Melissa's like, 'Where is it?' and I'm there, 'This *is* a nice surprise,' lying there in basically my T-shirt and boxer shorts with my hands behind my head, playing Jack the Lad. She's a big-time – what do you call it? – feminist is Melissa, though not in *that* way, more's the pity. Women are equal and all that shite. She goes,

'Where's my Toni Braxton CD?' and I'm there, 'Take a chill pill, babes. It's over there. Top shelf,' and she storts, like, rooting through the CDs. She's like, 'Your N-Sync one is here as well, Elaine. And the Simon and Garfunkel CD he took from your sister.' Elaine's sister: what a night that was. There must be, like, thirty birds here. They can't all get into the room at the same time. Both the Kelly twins are here, out on the landing. I actually thought I scored the same one twice, but no, I must have done the two. Sheryl Crow and Mark Owen were the albums I took from them, if my memory serves. Of course it's wrecking Melissa's head that I'm not letting her get to me. She's there, like, organising everyone, going, 'Sandra. The Lighthouse Family, wasn't it? There it is, *Ocean Drive*. Carol. I saw your Danni Minogue one there a second ago. And that one your friend said he took. There it is. Whose was *Ennio Morricone's Greatest Hits* again?'

And as they take their CDs and storm out, roysh, all the birds are just, like, staring at me, giving me total filthies, but, like, wanting me at the same time. And I'm just there sniggering away to myself and finally, roysh, when the shelf is almost cleared, Melissa finally cops something and she turns around to me with, like, her mouth open, and she goes, 'Do you mean to tell me that every single CD on that shelf represented ...' and I just wink at her and go, 'Notches on the bedpost.'

She tells me I've no respect for girls and I tell her she's pretty much roysh there. Then she tells me I mustn't have any respect for myself either and I tell her she couldn't be more wrong. I go, 'That shelf will be full again by the end of the summer. You mork my words,' and she turns around, roysh, with a big spiteful face on her, and she goes, 'Do you think you satisfied me that night you were with me?' and I go, 'I satisfied *me*, Melissa. That's all I care about. You want to fake it, you're only fooling yourself. Now take what's yours and spare me the *me heart is looow* act.'

Then I see Alice, roysh, this bird I know from Goatstown, fit as fock, a ringer for Nicole Appleton, and she's got her head sort of, like, cocked to the side, looking through what CDs are left. She goes, 'I can't see my Mary Chapin Carpenter album,' and I'm like, 'It might be on the shelf below. I had to stort a second one a couple of weeks back.'

OH MY GOD, you should have seen Melissa's face.

✳ ✳ ✳

Oisinn sends me a text and it's like, **Smal explsion in wrkshp lst nite. No injuries but Hugo Boss is goin 2 hav to wait 4 the 1st botl of Eau d'Affluence** and even though I crack my hole laughing, roysh, I don't answer him back, because he's just trying to worm his way back in with me, but after the stunt the goys pulled on Christmas Eve, it's going to take a hell of a lot of worming.

✳ ✳ ✳

I'm sitting in, roysh, knocking back a can of beer in the middle of the afternoon while watching 'Judge Judy' and thinking that if this is what the rest of my life is going to be like then I'm going to die grinning from ear to ear. That's when my phone rings, roysh, and I can see from my caller ID that it's, like, JP and for a minute, roysh, I think about just cutting him off, but then I decide that this shit's gone on long enough, the goys only did it as a joke and it's time I storted acting a bit more, I don't know, mature. Besides, I think he's probably calling to talk about this particular case that Judy's deliberating at the moment between these two rednecks who used to be giving each other one and now are arguing over who bought the toaster. Then I remember that he's probably back at work, what with it being the end of January and everything. Turns out there is a reason he's calling.

He goes, 'Ross, I know you're probably still having an eppo over what happened at Christmas, but there's something you should know,' and I'm there, 'Hey, dude. I'm over it. What's this thing I should know?' He goes, 'Kate – as in almost-made-the-Leinster-hockey-panel Kate – well, I met her getting on the Dorsh this morning. She was pretty down. Anyway, she heard from Samantha – as in former deputy head girl in Holy Child – that Sorcha's in some kind of trouble. We're talking, like, work shit?' I go, 'I know. There's, like, twelve people taking a case for bullying against her,' and he's there, 'Fourteen.' I'm there, 'WHAT?' he goes, 'Give her a ring, dude. If anyone can help her sort her shit out it's you.'

So I go back into the kitchen, roysh, shoot the old man a filthy, then tell him I need thirty bills for my taxi fare out to Killiney. He goes, 'Why?' and I just totally lose the rag with him, roysh, and go, 'Because you cost me my focking licence. Making me sit that stupid test,' and he pays up with a big face on him. I call a Jo and arrive up at Sorcha's door. Her old dear answers it, roysh, air-kisses me on both cheeks and tells me she's really glad I'm here.

She goes, 'She's just not herself, Ross. Not since she quit the boutique. I told her, it's all very well being a high-flying business-woman if you're happy. But she's not.' She shouts up the stairs to her – three or four times – and eventually Sorcha goes, 'HELLO? I'm ACTUALLY on the phone up here?' and her old dear goes, 'See what I mean? She was never aggressive like that before. The only time she used to get upset was once a month when her

Amnesty newsletter arrived. Now it's every day. Go on up and talk to her, Ross.' I head upstairs and she's lying on her bed, roysh, on the phone to, I think, Aoife, and she's going, 'Cop ON, girl. You had a slice of, like, Pavlova. HELLO? It's *hordly* the end of the world. Meringue is, like, egg white? Which is, like, no points.' Must be Aoife. Obviously the annual competition to see who can squeeze into the tightest titty-top this summer is already well underway and it's not even, like, February. Sorcha's going, 'The cream is *hordly* going to kill you. Look, I can't talk to you when you're this hysterical. And Ross is here now. I'll text you after 'Sex and the City'.'

She hangs up, roysh, and then gives me a hug, a really big one, like she's really happy to see me. I tell her she's lost weight and she says thanks, even though I didn't mean it as a compliment. I tell her she looks like she's been crying and she suddenly storts getting all, like, defensive, tells me to get a life and I'm just there, 'Hey, I *have* a life. *You're* the one who's not happy.' She gets in a total strop with me then, going, 'You *actually* think I'm not happy? Costs are down eighteen percent. Productivity is up, like, fourteen percent. Your dad gave me an amazing bonus this week. That's my cor insurance paid for the year. HELLO?' 'EastEnders' is on. Ricky's getting bet into that kipper who's married to Barry. I sit down at her desk and I go, 'I hear it's fourteen bullying cases now,' and she totally loses the plot then, focking the television remote at the wall and going, 'HOW MANY SMOKING BREAKS DO THEY NEED? THEY'RE IN THAT LITTLE ROOM ONE WHOLE HOUR OF EVERY WORKING DAY! SINCE WHEN DOES AN ADDICTION GIVE YOU THOSE KINDS OF ENTITLEMENTS?'

I have to, like, grab her, roysh, before she does any more

damage and I'm there giving her a hug, going, 'Come on, babes, relax the kacks,' and even then it takes me a good, like, ten minutes to properly calm her down, and when she does I ask her whatever happened to the girl I used to know, the one who was into saving the trees and the animals and blokes in other countries who were getting their heads lopped off.

She's, like, bawling her eyes out. She goes, 'You know what Sophie said to me the other night?' and I go, 'You don't have to listen to Sophie, she was never a proper friend,' and she goes, 'She said I've changed as a person. She said that a year ago I would have cared about what's going to happen in Iraq. I'd have been on that anti-war morch in town. I probably would have been one of the speakers.' I won't deny it, roysh, I was actually looking out for her on the News. She goes, 'And Chloe told Aoife that since I came back from Australia, all I care about it money. That's what she said, Ross. I was like, HELLO? I pay five euro a week by direct debit to Concern? Is THAT the action of someone who only cares about money?'

I pick up the pieces of the remote control and I ask her what she's doing on Valentine's night. I can tell she's thinking of making something up, roysh, but in the end she just goes, 'No plans,' and I ask her if she'd like to have dinner, just as friends, like old times, no mucking her around, and she smiles and says she'd love that.

✳ ✳ ✳

JP sends me this text, roysh, and it's like, **What have refugees and sperm got in common?** and the answer, roysh, is **They both come in their thousands and only one of the fockers works**, which is a classic.

✳ ✳ ✳

The old man comes into my room – no focking knock or anything – and he sees the humungous stack of Valeys on my bed and he goes, 'Whoah! Mister Popularity!' basically the old best-mates act. I go, 'Why do you have to be such a dick?' and he totally ignores this, roysh, and goes, 'Big weekend ahead, Kicker. Ireland and Scotland on Sunday. Time to see what you're made of Mister Eddie O'Sullivan of Cork Town, thank you very much indeed.' I'm there, 'Look, I'm busy here, catching up with my correspondence and shit?' and suddenly he gets all, like, awkward, roysh, and he goes, 'Yes, yes, of course. Em, I just wanted to, em ... well, been meaning to do it for a long time. Look, I wanted to give you this,' and he opens up his hand, roysh, and there's this, like, pocket watch in it. I look at him as if to say, so focking what. He goes, 'It was my father's. He got it from *his* father. Over a century old, Ross. Passed down from one generation to the next. There's not a day goes by when I don't feel proud of you, son. I think it's time for you to have this.' I just grab it out of his hand, roysh, and I go, 'Great. Now fock off and leave me alone,' and when he's gone, roysh, I fock the thing in the bin and go back to my cords.

There's one where I recognise the handwriting straight away. There's half a bottle of *Issey Miyake* on it. I lash open the envelope and I read the message and it's like, 'To Ross, the dearest person in the world to me, thinking about you on Valentine's Day. Love always. Sorcha xxx,' and she's, like, underlined the word always twice, and the next thing I know I'm, like, picking up the phone and checking if she's still on for tonight.

She goes, 'Thanks for the cord. It was very sweet,' and I'm like, 'Did you get many?' and she's like, 'Just yours. Well, one from Cillian as well, but he doesn't count.' Too focking right he doesn't. She goes, 'Ross, I've come to a decision,' and I'm there, 'Meaning?' and she takes a deep breath and goes, 'I'm quitting my job. You were right, Ross. It just wasn't me, doing all those awful things. Those poor people. I made their lives miserable. And why? Just because I was on some power trip, thinking the world was such a cruel place that that was the only way to survive.' I'm there, 'So what made you decide to, like, chuck it in?' and she goes, 'Portly some of the stuff you said to me the other night. And then portly Erika. She's been ringing me SO much lately. She's never liked me so much as long as we've known each other. I thought, well, if I'm the kind of person Erika likes, then I couldn't be very nice, could I?' I go, 'You haven't told Orse Head yet, have you?' and she goes, 'Your poor dad, Ross. He's going to be SO upset. I thought I'd wait another few weeks to tell him. Don't worry, my mind is made up and I'm not going to change it. I just need a bit of time to decide what I'm going to do with the rest of my life. And anyway, I didn't want to ruin his weekend away in Scotland. He's already like a lost soul without Hennessy.' I'm there, 'Take your time. You know you're doing the roysh thing.'

She goes, 'I'm thinking of going away for a little while, Ross,' and I go, 'Away?' Trying to hide the disappointment in my voice and failing miserably. I'm like, 'Where?' and she goes, 'I haven't decided yet. Somewhere I can find myself again. The person I used to be. George Bush is SO going to bomb Iraq it's not true. And I can't help but think it's portly my fault.' I'm there, 'Why? It's not like you sold the dude the weapons?' and she goes, 'It's not what I did, Ross, it's what I *didn't* do. I should have been out there. Campaigning against this. It was the biggest outpouring of anti-war sentiment since Vietnam, and I was dreaming up ways of making people's working lives so miserable that they'd quit without us having to pay them redundancy money. I feel like I've let the Iraqi people down.' I go, 'I'm sure they'd understand,' and she's there, 'Anyway, wherever I go, it'll be to do something worthwhile, to make a difference to people's lives. The reason I told you now, Ross, is that I didn't want work talk to overshadow dinner. I want tonight to be a celebration. Of everything. Especially our friendship.' I'm there, 'I was thinking Roly's,' and she goes, 'Great, but OH MY GOD, do NOT let me have, like, a storter.'

I hang up and get ready, leaving the other ten or twenty cords unopened, lash on clean threads and a splash of *Bvlgari*, before I realise that I've got a problem. I've basically got no sponds on me, and about ten minutes earlier, roysh, I heard the old pair go out, some romantic bullshit dinner they were going to out in Portmornock. This could be, like, majorly embarrassing, having to ask Sorcha to pay, basically the same stunt I pulled on her birthday. So what do I do, roysh, only forage around in the bin and pull out that piece of focking junk the old man gave me earlier, and I check the time on it and it's only, like, five o'clock. That antique shop that the old pair always go to in Sandycove is open until six and this piece of shit's got to be worth at least a hundred bills. If Sorcha's not having a storter, that should be more than enough.

✳ ✳ ✳

Oisinn rings me in the middle of the afternoon and tells me to turn on Sky News. I switch it on and I'm like, 'What the fock is this?' He goes, 'They're bombing the fock out of Baghdad,' and the two of us watch it for ages without, like, saying anything. Then he goes, 'Cool, isn't it?' and I'm there, 'Focking amazing!'

✷ ✷ ✷

I turn around to the old man, roysh, and I ask him did he get the Wilsons. It's Ireland against England on Sunday and, of course, that's his cue to try to get all palsy with me. He's going, 'The Grand Slam decider, eh? Got the tickets right here. A mite unusual, I must say, you asking for one that's out of sequence with mine and your mother's. Means you're not going to be sitting with us,' and I'm there, 'That's the focking idea.' He goes, 'You know, your mother's wonderful company and everything, Ross – you know that as much as I do – but I'm really going to miss Hennessy on Sunday. Having a bit of trouble accepting the fact that he's not around anymore. Still, I'm sure they'll be televising the game in Rio.' Then he goes, 'Probably not a bad thing that we're not sitting together actually. You know us two when we get stuck into the great out-half debate,' and I'm like, 'I cannot BELIEVE we're actually genetically linked.'

The next thing, roysh, his mobile rings and he answers it and he goes, 'Hello there, young Sorcha. I'm just here talking rugby with Ross. You know what he's like when he gets going.' Then he's just, like, silent, and all of a sudden his face just, like, drops. He goes, 'For heaven's sake, why?' Then there's silence again. I'm thinking, go on Sorcha, stick it to him. He goes, 'You're telling me you're prepared to give up a highly paid career that you happen to be very good at to go off to the Far East on some crusade to save some animal or other?' I presume she says yes. I hope she tells him to go fock himself. He goes, 'Sorcha, if these animals mean that much to you, I could make some kind of donation. On behalf of the company, of course. Tax deductible, you see. Oh, that's very disappointing, Sorcha ... I know you're sorry. I just hate to lose you.' He hangs up, roysh, and I've got this big shit-eating grin on my face. He goes, 'Ross, do you think you could persuade her?' and I go, 'I was the one who told her to tell you to stick your job up your orse.'

✱ ✱ ✱

I asked for a heterosexual coffee, not a frappa frappalappo or whatever the fock this is, roysh, but this could be the last time I ever see Sorcha so I don't bother, like, mentioning it. She eats her last forkful of carrot cake, but leaves the icing on the side of the plate. I'm like, 'What's the name of the place you're going again?' and she goes, 'Indonesia,' and I go, 'Oh yeah, roysh, the tigers,' and she's there, 'Sumatran tigers,' and the words, 'Same difference,' nearly spill out of my mouth, but I catch them just in time. She goes, 'There are less than four hundred of these animals left. And the numbers will continue to fall as their natural habitat gets further eroded away by intensive logging. There could be none by 2010.' She takes off her scrunchy, shakes her hair loose, smoothes it back, puts it back in the scrunchy and then pulls four or five strands loose again, and it suddenly hits me how much I'm going to miss her when she's gone and I have to say, roysh, it hits me hord. I'm thinking, what if she focks off to India or wherever she said she's going and never comes back again? And out of the blue, roysh – I don't know where the fock this comes from – I'm just there, 'I'll come,' and she's like, 'What?' and I go, 'I'll come with you. To whatever-it's-called. There's nothing here for me now. And I don't want to say goodbye to you,' and she just stares at me blankly, roysh, trying to work out whether I'm ripping the piss out of her, then her face breaks into a smile and she goes, 'I'm on the seven o'clock flight to Heathrow, then the eleven o'clock to Jakarta. This better not be like four summers ago when you told me you were coming over to the States to see me, then didn't show up.' So just to show her how much I've changed since then, roysh, I flip open my mobile and ring the travel agent that Knob Features uses and I book my ticket on his account roysh in front of her.

Then I tell her I'm going home to pack, roysh, and I'll meet her at the airport and she says she doesn't want to sound, like, mean or anything, but she'll, like, believe it when she sees it. So I basically peg it home, roysh, lash a few threads in my bag, watch the double episode of 'Judge Judy' and get a Jo to the airport. She nearly passes out when she sees me at the check-in desk, gives me this big hug and tells me she's SO glad I'm coming because it was me who basically got her to cop onto herself.

I get a text message as we're heading through duty free. A joke from Oisinn: **What's d only tng tht separates humans frm animals? D Liffey.** I feel bad, roysh, because I've put a bit of distance between myself and the goys since what happened at Christmas. I'll make it up to them when I get back. Sorcha's there, 'How did your parents take it?' and I go, 'Er, they don't know,' and she's like, 'You *can't* go away without—' and I'm like, 'Sorcha, they're out playing golf,' but I see the look she's giving me, so I tell her I'll ring them now and, like, explain everything. She goes off to buy perfume or something and I find a quiet corner and text Penis Head. It's like, **Goin off wth srcha to save sinatra tiger. Dunno when ll b bak or if. As if u2 giv a shit NEway.** I'm about to hit send, roysh, then I think better of it and go back into the message and add the word, **LOSERS!** onto the end, then send it. What I've done doesn't really hit me until about seven hours later when we're on the plane, roysh, and Sorcha's, like, fast asleep on my shoulder. I pick up a leaflet that's on the little table in front of her. It's all, 'Tigapuluh Hills. Illegal trade.

Deforestation. Urban expansion. Poachers.' She wakes up and goes, 'You really *are* here. I thought for a minute it was a dream.' I ask her what's the difference between a tiger and a leopard and she just smiles and tells me to get some sleep.

✱ ✱ ✱

According to Sorcha's *Lonely Planet* guide, Sumatra is Indonesia's island of plenty, in which case I'd hate to see the rest of the country, roysh, because basically there's fock-all here. I wouldn't have agreed to come on this trip if I'd known where we were going to be staying. I wasn't expecting the Hilton, roysh, but nobody said anything about a focking hostel. Or dorms. Communal focking dorms as well. OH MY GOD, it's just like being a Castlerock boarder, except we're not up until four o'clock in the morning doing things with digestive biscuits, or sleeping with one eye open in case someone gives you, like, an atomic wedgy.

I wouldn't even mind if it was like that. We're basically sharing the dorm with, like, twenty other Save the Animals losers, and me and Sorcha are in, like, separate beds. I follow a girl to practically the other side of the world and I find out there's basically no chance of getting my Andy Cole off her while I'm here. What focking star sign is that? Think she must have copped my face when we arrived as well, roysh, because she gives me one of her looks – as in, do NOT embarrass me – and when I went, 'There must be a Holiday Inn we can check into,' she was just like, 'I'll pretend I didn't hear that.' Oh and there's no telly in the gaff either, so the only thing there is to do in the evening is to sit around listening to the rest of the group, like, blab on about nothing and at this stage, roysh, my head is, like, SO full of useless information, like Sumatra is the sixth largest island in the world. It's home to forty-one million people. It's divided by the equator. Like I GIVE a fock?

We're actually staying in a place called Bukit Lawang. I asked Lee – this Australian, basically wanker, who's in charge of the whole gig – where it was exactly and he goes, 'It's not a million miles from Medan,' which is, like, loads of help. We *have* got a pretty good view of this, like, mountain, if you're into that kind of thing, 'the majestic Gunung Leuser' as he calls it, the twat. He's one of these Friends of the Planet knobs who wears sandals with, like, hiking socks, never washes his hair and only eats, I don't know, plants and focking shrubs. It's like, GET a life. Of course, Sorcha has fallen for him big-time. It's like, 'Lee said this,' and 'Lee said that,' and I'm there, 'Have you ACTUALLY smelled the goy?' and she ends up just, like, ripping into me, going, 'At LEAST he has beliefs,' one of which just happens to be smelling like a baboon's scrote, though I manage not to mention it. So later on, roysh, there we all are sitting around having our dinner, our *communal* dinner, of course, and Caitlin, this English bird who does nothing for me – whoever sold her those shorts should be focking arrested – she produces this, like, guitar, and I'm thinking, it's always the same with these focking hippy types, there's always a focking guitar handy. Caitlin's big boast – aport from having legs like a snooker table – is that she knows the words to every song that Simon and Garfunkel ever recorded, which makes me wonder why we have to listen to Lie La focking Lie twenty times.

I do make the mistake of saying this to Sorcha and she just, like, looks me up and down and goes, 'Did you know that Sumatra is home to the world's largest flower?' and there's no answer to that except, 'And this affects me how?' but she just looks at me sort of, like, spitefully and she goes, 'You haven't got a romantic bone in your body. If you were a *real* man, like Lee, you'd go and pick one for me.'

I actually didn't like that Lee reference, roysh, so I decide to show her just how romantic I can be if I, like, put my mind to it. I tell her I'm going off to drain the lizard and I head out to the porter – Dr Kananga, I call him, because he's basically a ringer for the goy out of the Bond movie – and I'm just there, 'What's this, like, massive flower everyone's banging on about. He goes, 'Aha, *rafflesia arnoldii*. Velly big,' and I go, 'I'd be prepared to pay top focking shekels to anyone who can get their hands on one.' I pull out 5,000 rupiahs, which I think is about five squids, tuck it into his shirt pocket and I go, 'Do you know what I'm saying?' He says thank you velly much and tells me that you can only basically get them between, like, August and November, then he taps his pocket and winks at me and goes back to what he was doing, without giving me my sponds back. I head back to Sorcha and I'm there, 'It's not actually in season at the moment,' and she looks me up and down and goes, 'Typical!'

I can understand her being stressed out. She came here to save the animals and we're here four days, roysh, and we still haven't seen one. We're supposed to be going to this, like, sanctuary where they have all these tigers, rhinos and orang-utans who've been injured by, like, poachers and we're going to help nurse them back to health, release them back into the wild again, blah blah blah, big focking yawn.

First, though, Lee – I even hate the dickhead's name – he says we have to take port in what he jokingly called a brief education programme. It's like, oh great, back to focking school again. It's like, five hours of classes a day for the first week, then on the last day, roysh, he shows us this slideshow. He warns us beforehand that it could be, like, distressing, but of course Sorcha has to watch it, roysh, and it's basically photographs of, like, tiny monkeys who were packed into these boxes to be shipped to America and they all, like, suffocated basically to death.

Then there's this one of, like, ten elephants who were poisoned by these farmers because they kept invading their palm oil plantations. And then this one of these three tigers who had their, like, brains blown out? Of course, Sorcha doesn't cry during the slideshow, because she doesn't want the others thinking she can't handle it. But later on she bawls for, like, two hours straight and it's muggins here – not focking Lee – who has to try to, like, pick up the pieces and console her.

I actually must have strong feelings for this girl to put myself through this shit. That's what I'm basically thinking to myself as she goes off to sleep in the bunk below me and I'm lying there, staring at the ceiling, that focking Lie La Lie still going around and around in my head, wondering whether she'd notice – would anyone notice – if I chanced a quick Allied Irish. Like I said, it's just like being a Castlerock boarder.

✱ ✱ ✱

It's absolutely roasting over here. I'm sweating like a mugger in a line-up and the last time I was bitten this much was when I was fifteen and going to Wesley disco on a Friday night. I'd actually prefer a dirty big Denis on my neck to all these focking mossie bites, but then to cap it all, roysh, Lee has storted cracking onto Sorcha big-time and we *are* talking big-time here. I *had* actually noticed the way he was, like, looking at her, roysh, but I just presumed she'd have basically no interest in him in *that* way, except maybe as a way to make me, like, jealous and shit. He's not the type she usually goes for, with his focking Ecco sandals and his stupid goatee and that hair that looks like dreadlocks but is actually just focking filthy. I turned around to her two nights ago, roysh, while he was giving us some boring lecture on, I don't know, Species Management, and under my breath I went, 'Do you reckon somebody told him that shampoo and water harm the environment as well?' and she actually laughed, roysh, and the tosser obviously knew it was something about him because he went, 'Can I have *everyone's* attention, please?' while staring straight at me.

Anyway, roysh, this particular night we get our first look at a real-life tiger. We're basically sitting around, eating our dinner – crap, before you ask – and suddenly *he* bursts in and tells us that – strewth, mate, stone the crows, G'day, G'day – a few locals have, like, rescued a tiger from a gang of, like, poachers and shit. So there's about ten of us, roysh, and we all peg it down to the hospital wing and there he is, laid out flat on an operating table, this big fock-off tiger and, bent as it sounds, roysh, even I have to admit the thing was basically beautiful. Couldn't get over the size of it. Its paws were, like, twice the size of my hand. Lee – dickhead – goes, 'There's nothing to be frightened of. He's been tranquillised,' and then he shakes his head, all sort of, like, sad, roysh, and he goes, 'Even in the national parks, they're not safe. This one was shot in the Gunung Leuser. Middle of the night. That's when they come out to hunt deer and wild boar.'

The goy thinks he's that focking crocodile hunter twat off the telly. He goes, 'It's an adult male. He's got a bullet wound in the leg, back left. But the good news is ... it's operable,' which *is* good news, roysh, but not so good as to justify Sorcha's reaction, which was to burst into tears and stort, like, kissing the thing's forehead, going, 'You're going to be alright. Hang in there, baby boy,' making a complete tit of me.

I genuinely didn't know where to put myself. Avril, this Scottish bird, who, I have to say, has the major hots for me, I catch her eye, roysh, and sort of, like, throw my eyes up to heaven and she sort of smiles and then Lee turns around to Sorcha and he goes, 'The surgeon's on his way, Sorcha,' the slimeball.

Of course when the surgeon arrives, roysh, she doesn't want to leave the thing, but in the end Lee has to persuade her to wait outside while the operation, like, goes ahead, and she's there, 'Okay, but I'm staying right here,' and she sits down right outside the focking door and Lee pulls up a chair beside her and, like, takes her hand and goes, 'We'll be here together when he wakes up,' and I get this urge to basically punch the focker's lights out.

I head back, roysh, to finish my dinner – if you could call it that – and then, like, three or four hours later, Sorcha bursts into the dorm and tells us that – *whoopee!* – the operation was a success. I'm there, 'Whatever,' under my breath of course, while she's going, 'It was a bit more complicated than we thought. The bullet completely shattered the tibia, but he's going to be okay,' like she's on focking 'ER' or something. I'm there, 'I'll make sure to send a Get Well Soon cord,' still a bit put out by her and Lee freezing me out of the picture, but she's so excited it goes totally over her head and she's there, 'He's still under the anaesthetic. If anyone wants to see him, come now. Before he wakes up.'

I'm actually trying to read *Loaded*, but, of course, I've got to, like, drag myself out of the focking scratcher and follow everyone back to the hospital wing. We get there, roysh, and we all crowd around the table where the focking thing's still laid out on its Ned Kelly and his leg is, like, all bandaged up and shit. Lee's there going, 'It's going to be two or three months before he can be released back into the wild. He'll do his recuperating here, at the sanctuary. You guys are going to help nurse him back to full health,' and while he's saying all this, roysh, Sorcha's there stroking the thing and kissing its head, going, 'It's okay, my brave boy,' and I'm about to tell her to stop making a total orse of herself, roysh, but, when I look around, I notice that pretty much everyone in the group has got, like, tears in their eyes, and then I'm sort of, like, jealous that I'm not feeling whatever it is they are. Lee goes, 'And if he's going to be spending three months with us, well, he's going to need a name ... Sorcha?' and she looks up, roysh, and she goes, 'You want *me* to name him?' He goes, 'He might not have made it through without you,' – yeah roysh, the surgeon had fock-all to do with it, of course – and Sorcha just, like, stares into space for a while, then goes back to petting the thing with this big smile on her face, and she goes, 'Falkor.'

I'm about to go, 'What kind of a focking name is that?' but Lee – the smelly, dreadlocked focker – he just storts smiling, roysh, and he goes, 'Falkor? Like the Luck Dragon in *The Neverending Story*?' and suddenly everyone's there, like, nodding their heads in agreement, as though it's an amazing idea. Sorcha goes, 'You know that movie?' and Lee's like, 'Are you kidding? It's my favourite movie of all time.' I'd actually tell the goy that I like his style, if he wasn't moving in on basically my bird. And the way they look at each other in that moment ... Well, I just decided there and then that I was going to have to do something to sort the dickhead out once and for all. No better man.

✳ ✳ ✳

Sorcha's been spending every hour of the day with that focking flea-bitten, half-dead animal – Falkor, not Lee, although he's still hanging around like a bad smell, literally actually. The two of them are feeding the focking thing and, I don't know, bringing its focking wind up or whatever. Wasn't being jealous or anything, but basically I decided it was time to say something. So I turn around to her, roysh, and I go, 'Some holiday this is turning out to be,' and of course straight away she storts having a knicker-fit – a total one – going, 'WHAT did you just say?' I'm there, 'Come on, Sorcha. You saved your tiger. Let's fock off to Bali and live a little,' and she totally loses the plot then, giving it, 'WHO SAID THIS WAS SUPPOSED TO BE A HOLIDAY?' and, not unreasonably, I go, 'I didn't pay good money to sit around in some jungle watching you play Rolf Harris,' trying to inject a bit of humour into the conversation, but there was, like, no talking to the girl.

She had such a strop on after that, roysh, that for the rest of the day I ended up having to keep out of her way, and basically ended up hanging out with Tim and Steve, these two Canadian goys, totally Stoke the two of them, but still sound. Anyway, roysh, the two of them are banging on about some stupid group they're in – Global Justice, or some shite – and Tim's going, 'What Steve has difficulty understanding, Ross, is that neo-liberalism doesn't begin and end with the World Bank and the IMF,' and Steve goes, 'So burn down a Starbucks, then,' and Tim's like, 'Ooh, you are SUCH a bitch,' and it's like watching an episode of 'Will and Grace', roysh, except I haven't a focking bog what they're going on about, even though I crack on that I do, laughing whenever they do and, like, shaking my head to pretend I understand, basically just like school.

So eventually, roysh, Lee sticks his big, ugly, nit-ridden head around the door and asks me can he have a word, so I follow him to his office and we both sit down on either side of this, like, desk. He scratches his head – Five Hundred Head Lice

Killed In Freak Earthquake; Death Toll Expected To Rise – and goes, 'She's quite a girl, Sorcha. Your ... *friend?'* and straight away, roysh, I know what he's getting at. I go, 'You didn't bring me in here to tell me that,' and he's suddenly all businesslike, roysh, going, 'Have you any idea what we're up against here, Ross? The Sumatran tiger is almost extinct. In the wild there are less than four hundred remaining. Yes, it's important for zoos to work together to increase the captive tiger population. But initiatives like ours are even more important, to preserve their natural habitat in the hope that more can be released into the wild.' I go, 'And your point is?' but he ignores me and just, like, carries on with his little speech. He's there, 'Don't think for one minute that trafficking is the only thing we're up against. For centuries traditional tribespeople relied on the forests here in Indonesia for their livelihood, taking only what they needed. Not anymore. Urban expansion, uncontrolled logging and slash-and-burn agriculture are destroying the habitat of a number of already endangered animals. Not just the tiger either. The two-horned rhino, the elephant, the honey bear, the orang-utan ...'

I'm like, 'Sorry, I'm kind of busy. If there's a point, I'd like to hear it before I need to shave again.' He goes, 'I'd like to know if anything's going on between you and Sorcha,' straight out with it like that, and I actually feel like decking the goy. I go, 'What's that got to do with you?' and he's there, 'Ross, I want Sorcha to stay here. I've never seen anyone with the kind of passion she has for the work we're doing. She's a natural. And, well, I wanted to find out first whether she had any ... ties.' I go, 'Well she has. We're actually engaged. And we're thinking of focking off to Bali, maybe next week. For a holiday and shit,' and he looks at me all, like, confused and he goes, 'That doesn't quite compute,' the stupid tosser. He goes, 'She seems so ... at home here.' He thinks for a bit and he goes, 'We want to become more active in the eastern lowlands, especially in the Tigapuluh Hills. We want to set up a proper captive breeding programme there and, well, I want Sorcha to head it up ...' I get up and I'm like, 'You're wasting your time,' and he's there, 'You know, I often wonder whether I am. Working out here in the jungle, battling against impossible odds, it often crosses my mind that I'm wasting my time. And when it does, I open my top drawer here and I look at this ...' and he whips the drawer open and plonks this focking thing on the table, roysh, it basically looks like a monkey's hand. He cops my boat and he's like, 'I took this from a poacher. Orang-utans are worth more to them alive than dead. Thirty thousand dollars they fetch in the States. But accidents happen. When they die, like this one, they chop their hands off and they make ashtrays from them. And when people tell me that my work here is a waste of time, I look at this ... I'm going to talk to Sorcha myself.' I just go, 'You're some focking sap,' and walk out, SO determined to fix that focker it's not funny. So that night, roysh, I'm playing cords with Will and Grace and in storms Sorcha and she storts, like, screaming at me, going, 'You are SUCH an ORSEHOLE!' I'm like, 'Hey, chill, babes,' trying to steer her out of the room before she makes a show of me again. She goes, 'WHY DID YOU TELL LEE WE WERE GETTING MARRIED? DO YOU *REALLY* THINK I'D WANT TO BE MARRIED TO *YOU*?'

I manage to get her outside, roysh, and calm her down and I go, 'Sorcha, I did it for a reason,' and she goes, 'DON'T, Ross,' and I'm like, 'I did it to protect you.' She looks amazing. A Peter Pan always suited her. She's like, 'Protect me?' and I'm there,

'He's not what he pretends to be, Sorcha. He's basically a phoney, if that's the roysh word.' She looks into my eyes, roysh, like she's going to find out whether I'm lying by looking in there. I'm there, 'Wake up and smell the coffee, Sorcha. The goy's working with the poachers,' and she shakes her head, like it's too terrible to believe. I go, 'This afternoon, he tried to sell me an orang-utan's hand to use as an ashtray. Five hundred bills, he asked for it. I told him, Sorcha, I said, "It's not just those poor defenceless animals that I feel sorry for, it's all the people who believe in you and what you're doing",' really laying it on thick to her. Suddenly she's got, like, tears in her eyes. She goes, 'We've known each other for a long, long time, Ross. We've been through so much together. There isn't a single person in the world I'm closer to than you. If you're lying, please tell me now,' and I look her in the eye, roysh, and I go, 'Look in his top drawer if you don't believe me. He's not in his office. Go in and have a look.' And she must do, roysh, because later on at dinner she's, like, really quiet. I can tell from her eyes that she's been, like, crying. And Lee comes in all of a sudden and he goes, 'Hey, Sorcha. You want to come and feed Falkor with me?' and she looks up and goes, 'I don't THINK so, do you?' And I look at Lee, roysh, totally clueless as to what's happened, and under my breath I go, 'Nobody focks with Ross O'Carroll-Kelly.'

CHAPTER FOUR
For Better or Worse

I said I didn't want to go into the gaff, roysh, didn't want to take my shoes off, if the truth be known, and anyway I was happy just mooching around outside – big swinging mickey. But Caitlin, roysh, the English bird with pins like Keith Wood, she just can't leave it, she shakes her head and goes, 'You can't tell your friends back home that you went to the Mesjid Raya and just waited around outside,' which goes to show that (a) she doesn't know my friends and (b) she doesn't know a pair of Hugo Boss loafers when she sees them. Steve, one of the Canadian blokes, he sticks his oar in then, giving it, 'Ross, it's a *mosque*. No one's going to steal your shoes if you leave them outside,' and I go, 'They cost nearly two hundred lids,' and Sorcha just, like, throws her eyes up to heaven, makes a sort of W with her fingers and goes, 'WHAT-ever,' and they all fock off inside and leave me out on the street, roysh, breathing in motorbike fumes, which Sorcha later says will do my brain no horm at all, though I basically ignore this.

We didn't come to Medan to go sightseeing anyway. We're supposed to be here for the trial of these two local dudes who are up for plugging, I don't know, eleven tigers in some national pork or other, illegibly, if that's the roysh word, because we don't know yet if they did it or not, though I suppose the fact that they've pleaded guilty means they probably did. Anyway, roysh, Lee says it's pretty much an open-and-shut case and will be done and dusted in, like, one day, but it's important that we turn up and sit in court so the judge sees that the eyes of the international community are watching, blahdy blahdy blah. I hear him going to Steve and Tim as they're leaving the temple, or whatever you'd call it, 'Anyone found guilty of killing an animal from an endangered species can be jailed for five years under Indonesian law. But the sentences handed down are often light. That's why it's important for groups like ours to keep the pressure on.' Steve and Tim are his new best mates now that Sorcha thinks he's a snake.

So we hit the court and we're all sitting there, roysh, and it's like focking 'Judge Judy' or some shit. The two goys are led in and I can see Sorcha and the other birds in the group giving them, like, total filthies, and at one stage I think Avril, the Scottish bird – fit as fock, a ringer for Renée Zellwegger – is going to hop out of the public gallery and deck the two goys. She's there, under her breath, going, 'Look at they moddering bastids,' in the, like, Scottish accent and I'm there, 'Chill,' because I've seen enough of Sorcha's Amnesty whatever-you-call it newsletters over the years to know that they shoot you for acting the mickey in countries like these. I actually feel a bit sorry for the dudes in the dock, having been in court myself that time when me and Oisinn were done for pouring Heino into an ATM on Grafton Street, basically right under the noses of the Feds, the night of the Loreto on the Green debs last year. The public gallery was packed for us as well. The goys found out about it, of course, and they all turned up and storted shouting, 'HANG THEM!' basically for the craic, roysh, and the two of us couldn't keep straight faces, and that only pissed the judge off and he ended up fining us, like, a grand each, which I can tell you the old man was not a happy camper about paying.

I'd enough difficulty understanding what was going on in our trial, roysh, but at least it was in English. This one's in, I don't know, whatever focking language they speak over here, though Lee's got some wanker friend of his in to translate for us. Basically the suss is that the two goys are saying they're sorry – which is fair enough – and they're asking the judge to take into account that they weren't killing the tigers to sell their skins, but to grind up their bones, teeth and claws for use in a traditional Chinese remedy for the relief of rheumatism and arthritis, which, for me, puts a whole new spin on things. But Lee's not impressed. I hear him turning around to Steve and going, 'I hope the judge treats *that* with the contempt it deserves. The guy on the right's been up before, for shooting two white-horned rhinos. The other one's one of the best-known poachers on the island. He gets up to $5,000 apiece for these poor animals in the States.' But the judge, roysh – I don't know whether he suffers with his knees or what – but he sentences them to, like, two months, which causes total uproar in the court, and we're talking *total* here, although the two dudes seem pretty pleased about it themselves. Steve shouts, 'SHAME ON YOU, INDONESIA! SHAME ON YOU!' like a focking twat, and Sorcha and Avril and the English bird with the fat legs all just, like, burst into tears. Lee's giving it, 'TWO-THOUSAND-AND-TEN! TWO-THOUSAND-AND-TEN!' which leaves pretty much all of us clueless, but it turns out afterwards that that's the year that conservationists predict this particular type of tiger will become extinct, though this didn't seem to cut much ice with anyone, especially the two goys, who were hugging and high-fiving their families.

Of course, me and my big mouth, roysh, I make the mistake of telling the rest of the crew that you have to, like, see both sides of the story and I tell them about Christian, who played centre for Castlerock and had, like, pain-killing injections in his knees roysh the way through school and now he's basically focked with arthritis and we're talking both knees here, and what good are tigers to him? And everyone just, like, sits there, staring at me, roysh, and Sorcha apologises to them for me. As the judge is leaving the court, Lee shouts out, 'JUSTICE INDONESIA-STYLE,' and the cops are giving us serious daggers, roysh – told you, these goys don't mess around – and to be honest, I'm glad just to get the fock out of there without being lagged off to Harcourt Terrace, or whatever the equivalent is over here.

✳ ✳ ✳

Sorcha hadn't been herself ever since the court case really and, well, since I told her that stuff about Lee to basically get the lech off her case more than anything. Very funny, roysh, but she went up to him outside the court, after his whole, 'INDONESIA'S SHAME!' bit, and she goes, 'WHAT a performance! You know, for a minute there you almost had *me* fooled,' and he's there, 'Sorcha, for the millionth time, what have I done?' but if he knew the girl as well as I do, roysh, he'd know that that's a question she never answers, she just goes, 'Leave it.' So she's been a bit, like, I don't know, disillusioned, if that's a word, ever since that day and spending even more time with Falkor, who has pretty much made a full recovery and is nearly ready to be released back into the wild, probably for some other focker to pump him full of lead, though you wouldn't say that to Sorcha. Though I did; it was four days before Ice Queen melted. Anyway, roysh, this particular day she's suddenly all lovey-dovey with me, probably for the first time since we arrived in this shithole, and at first I think it's because she copped me flirting my hole off with the Scottish bird, roysh, flashed the old abs at her when I went for a swim in this local lake and she was basically eating out of my hand.

So Sorcha's all, '*Ooh Ross, you're the person in the world I'm closest to,*' and '*Ooh Ross, you're my soulmate,*' and there I am thinking that I've cracked the nut with her when I finally find out what's going on. She goes, 'I'm getting out of here, Ross,' and at first, roysh, I think I'm actually hearing things, but then she goes, 'Falkor's strong enough to walk now without his splint. In a couple of weeks he'll be gone and, well, I just feel my work here is done.'

Of course, I'm like 'PORTY ON, BABE! Bali here we come,' but she just looks at me, roysh, and goes, 'Ross, I'm heading for Jakarta,' and even though it sounds like a bit of a focking dump, roysh, I couldn't give a toss as long as there's a nice beach and a happy hour in the hotel cocktail bor. Then it turns out that I've got the wrong end of the stick. It's *more* Save the Animals shite.

She goes, 'I've just become disillusioned' – yeah, it must be a word – 'especially with that ... HYPOCRITE!' I'm there, 'Yeah, there was something about that Lee goy that I never trusted,' and she goes, 'Thankfully, the animal hospital and the captive breeding programme are bigger than one man, Ross. And their work will continue. But I can't stand by while the work of all those good people is being undone be poachers. People like Lee's friends. And it's clear to me now that there's no political will there to do anything about it.' I haven't seen her this emotional since the day Mandela got out. Of course, I still haven't copped where she's going with this. I'm like, 'But you can't just give up,

Sorcha,' actually hoping that's *exactly* what she's going to do, but she looks at me like I've got two heads, roysh, and she goes, 'I'm not giving up, Ross. I'm going to try to cut off the trade in these animals from the consumer side,' and I'm like, 'Whoa, whoa, whoa, give that to me in English,' and she goes, 'I'm going to Jakarta to confront the people dealing in the sale of these animals.'

She's lost the focking plot. *Confront them?* These, like, dangerous criminal gangs? As if she's back in Mount Anville challenging them to a debate in Irish. I'm there, 'I am NOT letting you go there. It's too dangerous a place for you to go on your own,' suddenly feeling all, I don't know, protective of her. She just throws her orms around my shoulders and she goes, 'I *knew* you'd come with me. OH MY GOD, I SO knew.' And even though I know it's completely insane, roysh, maybe it's the fact that she's not being a total bitch to me, maybe it's the *Issey Miyake*, but I don't say anything and she's taken it for granted that I've agreed to go, which I probably just have.

So she focks off then, roysh, to book the flights on the internet and to check her emails and she comes back an hour later and says that it's sorted. I ask her how everyone at home is and she says she got a message from Sophie, who has apparently lost seven pounds in two weeks by just eating apples and kiwi fruit, and one from Erika who said, 'OH MY GOD! you will not BELIEVE what Claire turned up at the tennis club wearing last weekend, we're talking Ug boots, and – HELLO? – when *did* Pamela Anderson go from slapper to style guru?' She tells me all of this, roysh, and then she goes, really, like, sadly, 'Oh my God, my friends are SO shallow,' and then she's like, 'I'm SO glad I have you,' and this makes me feel good, better than good, totally amazing, in fact. Then she gets into the bunk below and she doesn't say anything for ages, roysh, and then when I think she's asleep she says that when she gets back to Ireland, she is SO getting a juicer.

✱ ✱ ✱

The Holiday Inn in Jakarta offers a choice of twenty – *twenty* – movies of, shall we say, an adult nature. Sorcha says she's planning to have a really long soak in the bath and she asks me if I mind watching the telly on my own for a couple of hours. I'm there, 'Does Jordan sleep on her back?'

✱ ✱ ✱

There I was, roysh, racking my brains trying to come up with an idea to, like, cheer her up, roysh, what with all this cruelty to animals vibe going on around us, and then it hit me, we're talking total inspiration here – buy the girl a monkey. So I get up pretty early on Thursday morning, roysh, tell her I'm going off to see if there's a Starbucks in Jakarta – she gives me a filthy and goes, 'You are SUCH an orsehole' – and I get the old boola into town. There I am, roysh, sitting down the back, wondering where the fock I'm gonna find a monkey going cheap in this dump, when all of a sudden we stop at this, like, intersection and this mad Chinese-looking dude with one leg hops over to the window next to where I'm sitting. In his hand, roysh – the one that's not holding the crutch – he's got this, like, box and he holds it up to my window and goes, 'Tigah penis. Tigah penis,' and of course I'm just there, 'What are you talking about, dude?' He thinks for a minute, roysh, and goes, 'Afflo dizzyak,' and I'm like, 'I'm fine in that deportment. Never any complaints. I want to buy a monkey though,' and his eyes light up and he goes, 'Pramuka Market. Come now,' and sort of, like, gestures at me to get off the bus. So

I hop off, roysh, probably taking my life into my own hands at this stage, and he's there going, 'I show. I show.' So there we are, roysh, me practically coughing a lung up what with all the shite that's in the air in this kip, and Hop-Along Cassidy up ahead, leading me down what could turn out to be Jakarta's version of, like, Sean MacDermott Street. But, fair focks to him, roysh, he takes me to this morket, and it's focking humungous, we're talking the size of a rugby pitch, and I'm thinking I can pretty much find my own way from here. So he turns around to me, roysh, and he's there, 'Engrish?' and of course I'm like, 'No, Irish,' and his face lights up, roysh, and he goes, 'Ahhh, Enyaaa!' which is basically my cue to try to lose him, which I was planning to do anyway, before the focker storted looking for a tip from me.

So I'm wandering around on my own for ages, roysh, but I can't see any monkeys, it's all, like, birds and shit, which are pretty boring, and tortoises and stuff like that. So this other goy sort of, like, sidles up to me – this dude is Burt Reynolds – and he goes, 'Finest maket in oro south-ee Asia for lare animal. Wha you like?' I cut straight to the chase, roysh. I'm like, 'I'm looking for a monkey,' and he nods sort of, like, thoughtfully I suppose you'd call it, rubs his chin and goes, 'You wan Siamang gibbon?' which sounds like a monkey to me, so I'm there, 'Cool.'

So he brings me out this side entrance, roysh, out onto focking Sheriff Street basically, and leads me down this laneway where there's this, like, lock-up garage. He disappears inside and I'm there basically crapping it, expecting a load of heads with baseball bats to come out and smash me into little pieces, but instead he comes out and he's got this, like, brown monkey thing in a cage, a really cute thing it is as well, a baby by the looks of it.

He goes, 'Siamang gibbon. Velly lare. Only tweny tousan left. Special pri for my flend. Tirty tousan,' and I'm there, 'Rupiahs?' getting ready to haggle with the dude, but he goes, '*Dorrar!* Amelican!' and now he knows from my reaction that I'm basically small fry and he gives me this filthy for wasting his time. He goes, 'Where oo stay?' and I'm like, 'Holiday Inn,' and he's there, 'More money at hotel?' I'm like, 'Not that amount. Could stick it on the old man's cord, I suppose. Do you take plastic?' and he goes, 'Prastic?' and cracks his hole laughing, and I laugh as well, cracking on it was just a joke.

He disappears into the lock-up again and this time he comes back with this little focking rabbit thing, which he says is called a cuscus. He goes, 'Marsupial. Two hundra fity tousan rupiahs,' which is, like, twenty-five bills and I'm there, 'Hey, it's cute. I'll take it,' and as I'm walking away he goes, 'Where from?' and I'm like, 'Ireland,' and he's there, 'Ahhh,' and he's clicking his fingers, roysh, racking his brains, and I manage to get the hell out of there before he thinks of Enya's name.

Anyway, roysh, I bring the thing back to Sorcha and she has a knicker-fit, that's how basically unpredictable she can be at times, she's there going, 'How COULD you, Ross? Have you not been listening to me? How could you give business to these people?' I thought she LIKED animals. She's bawling her eyes out, going, 'These poor little creatures. They pack hundreds of them into tiny boxes for shipping and only half survive the journey. Ten dollars is all their lives are worth,' and I'm thinking, That focker robbed me.

So to cut a long story short, roysh, I tell Sorcha that I didn't buy it and I make up this story about me passing by this morket and catching a goy packing these stupid-looking yokes into boxes. I basically ended up decking the focker for what he was doing to the animals, but I only managed to save one of them. I made my voice all wobbly so it sounded like I was going to cry. So suddenly she's seeing me in a new light, roysh, but now she wants to go back to the morket herself to confront the traders. She's going, 'That's what we're here for, Ross. Remember, I said that to you before we left Sumatra – cut off the demand from the consumer side. I'm going, Ross, with or without you.' So we end up hopping in a Jo and heading back to the morket and I'm hoping Burt Reynolds is, like, on his lunch break or some shit, but no – sod's focking law – he's the first person we see when we walk in. He's got this monkey in his hand, roysh, the same one he showed me and I can see Sorcha getting all, like, worked up and shit. I'm there, 'Let's play this Kool and the Gang, babes,' but no, she morches straight up to the goy and goes, 'THESE ANIMALS ARE PROTECTED UNDER THE CONVENTION ON INTERNATIONAL TRADE IN ENDANGERED SPECIES!' and you actually have to admire the girl's balls.

The goy, he hasn't a clue what's going on, roysh, but then he spots me and you can see the, like, recognition in his face and he goes, 'Ha ha, yes! Enyaaaaaa!' and he is SO about to blow my cover, roysh, that I've got no choice. I walk straight up to him and land one on him – BANG! – and the goy is just decked, it's lights out, and I stand over him and I go – and I'm pretty proud of this – I go, 'YOU HEARD THE LADY. ANIMALS HAVE RIGHTS TOO.' Then I turn around to Sorcha and – probably wise, this – tell her we should get the fock out of there. In the back of the Jo she tells me that I'm the bravest person she's ever met and she's, like, SO proud to know me. I tell her we should probably think about checking out of the Holiday Inn, though not until the morning. I know she's going to want to be with me tonight.

✳ ✳ ✳

Not being big-headed or anything, roysh, but after decking that goy, Sorcha's basically fallen head over heels in love with me again. She even said the word in the throes of passion last night and probably for the first time in my life, roysh, I'd no problem with her saying it. Anyway, roysh, there we are in the sack the next morning and I'm wondering whether I'll have poached or fried eggs for breakfast, when all of a sudden she turns around to me and goes, 'Ross, what did you actually do with Biko?' which was, like, her name for that little cuscus thing I bought her. It was actually pretty cute, roysh, I don't know why she didn't want to keep it, but she told me yesterday to go out and find a home for him. She goes, 'And don't just go out and release it onto the street,' and I'm thinking, sometimes this girl can read me like a focking book.

She says he wouldn't be able to fend for himself. I don't know what she thinks is going to happen, roysh, he's not going to get, like, mugged at a focking ATM, but just to keep her happy, roysh, and because I'm a nice goy, I go for a wander and look for an old pet shop that might be interested in buying it. I'd only walked, like, two hundred yards from the hotel, roysh, when all of a sudden this dude walking past me asks what's in the cage and I show him. I tell him I'm trying to get rid of it and he tells me his brother is a vivisectionist and would love it, and I'm thinking, happy days, that's great, the little goy's going to end up in, like, a puppet show. So I just, like, handed over the cage.

So when Sorcha asks me the next morning what happened to Biko, roysh, I can't actually remember the word vivisectionist. I go, 'He's gone to a very loving home, Sorcha. What do you call those guys who talk without moving their lips?' and she looks at me like I'm off my cake or something and she goes, 'A ventriloquist?' and I'm thinking, Oh FOCK, what have I gone and done? I'm there, 'A ventriloquist, that's it. Looks like Biko's headed for stordom,' and she goes, 'Once there's no cruelty involved, Ross. He's not going to be working in a circus, is he?' and I'm there, 'Of course not. What do you take me for?' It's only then, roysh, that I remember the word vivisectionist, still not having a bog's notion of course what it is. So I give it, like, five minutes, roysh, and then very subtly slip the word into the conversation, just to try to, like, get her reaction, see if it's a good thing or a bad thing. I'm flicking through the channels, roysh, and I tell her there was a programme on last night about vivisectionists and she goes, 'OH! MY! GOD! I couldn't have watched it, Ross. Did they actually show them dripping perfume into the animals' eyes,' and I'm thinking, so *that's* what a vivisectionist is. Poor Biko. He'd have been better off taking his chances on the street.

Sorcha goes, 'So Biko has a new home. And now I think it's time *we* went home, Ross,' and of course when I hear this I'm as happy as a northside bird with Velcro knickers, though I don't crack on. I'm there trying to sound all, like, disappointed, giving it, 'We can't leave now, Sorcha. Our work here isn't done,' while at the same time struggling to keep a straight face. She goes, 'What you did yesterday, Ross, it was amazing. But it has SO put us in danger,' and I'm like, 'The tigers and the, I don't know, penguins and those monkey things, they live in *permanent* danger,' and I don't know where I'm coming up with this shit from. She goes, 'That's why it's important that we get out. So we can continue the fight.'

I ring room service, order the poached, and forget to ask

Sorcha if she wants anything, though she doesn't, like, cop it. She goes into the bathroom and I've pretty much packed before she's got the top off her Lancôme Flash Bronzer. I'm still giving it loads, going, 'Just feels like we're running away,' and she sticks her head out of the bathroom, roysh, with that gunk all over her face, and she goes, 'We're not running away, Ross. It's a tactical retreat. It's important for the survival of so many species that we spread the word back home about the awful things we've seen here.' I'm there, 'Yeah, once it gets around Annabel's and Reynord's, the Indonesian government will have to do something,' though she doesn't hear this, and I'm kind of glad.

I go downstairs to pay the bill, roysh, basically not wanting Sorcha to find out about all the blueys I watched, including three that night she was downstairs in the bor talking to two bet-down American birds about the threat to the mangrove estuaries. The bird behind the counter, we're talking Lucy Liu here – she basically can't keep her eyes off me; I feel naked – she prints out the bill and I, like, hand her the old man's gold cord and she swipes it a couple of times and goes, 'This card has been cancelled, Sir.'

I'm there, 'That's impossible,' even though I know it's not, and I go, 'I just need to make a call,' and she hands me the phone and I dial the number and it's obvious from the dickhead's voice when he answers that he's half-asleep. He's there, 'Kicker? Kicker, is that you?' and I'm like, 'Wake up, will you? What the FOCK is the story with your gold cord?' He goes, 'Oh, had to cancel it. It was stolen. I think that new cleaner of ours took it. Turns out she's from Ballybrack. Where have you been, Ross?' I'm like, 'Drop the concerned parent act, will you? How the FOCK am I supposed to pay this hotel bill?' I can hear the other one waking up then, going, 'Where is he? Does he know it's three o'clock in the morning?' and the old man's going, 'It's half-past three now,' and I go, 'Sorry, have I rung the focking speaking clock or something?' The old man goes, 'Sorry, just trying to get my bearings here. When are we going to see you again?' and I just go, 'PROBABLY FOCKING NEVER!' and slam down the phone, which I regret doing because I was kind of hoping he'd pick us up at the airport.

I'm about to hand the bird behind the counter my own credit cord, roysh – last resort – when all of a sudden Sorcha arrives down and asks me what I'm doing. Turns out she already settled up last night and I was, like, trying to check out of someone else's room. We're heading back up in the lift to grab our bags and I go, 'So you knew we were going home last night?' a bit pissed off that I wasn't consulted, but quick as a flash, roysh, she just goes, 'What's *Pornomedics?*' and I can feel my face getting hot. She goes, 'I know it's a movie, but what's it about?' and I'm there, 'I thought it was a, er, nature film, like *Gorillas in the Mist* or something,' and out of the corner of my eye I can see her smiling because she knows she's basically caught me in the act. But, fock it, a few hours later we're on the plane home and while she's watching *Chicago* for the two-hundredth time, I'm sitting there wondering what the future holds for us, while at the same time trying to read this stunner of an air hostess's name badge without her thinking I'm scoping her rack. Sorcha takes off her headphones, roysh, puts her head on my shoulder and goes, 'Is this it, Ross? After all those years of prologue, are me and you ready to have a proper, adult relationship at last? One based on respect and honesty?' and I'm there, 'Sure, Sorcha. I want that more than anything in the world.' The air hostess's name is Nicola.

✱ ✱ ✱

Back home, roysh, sitting at the kitchen table, browsing through the *Sunday Indo*, trying to make up my mind in which order I'd, like, do the 03 Team, when in comes the biggest tool in the universe, giving it, 'Kerrigan's still at it, with his questions and what-not. It's anyone who has money with that man. I don't know why I keep bringing that paper into the house.' I'm thinking, Julia Moloney, then Siobhán O'Connor, no, maybe Sonia Harris next. No, actually, Emma Blain. It's a toughie.

The old man goes, 'Your mother loves it, you see. Bertie Stadium and his women,' and I give him this, like, filthy and I go, 'Just because I haven't told you to shut the fock up yet doesn't mean you can stort getting pally-wally with me.' Of course, he ignores this, fills up the percolator and storts banging on about Hennessy. He's going, 'They're trying to send the man to jail for something he didn't do,' and I'm like, 'Pay his taxes, I know' and the old man goes, 'Don't split hairs, Ross. Due process is all he's asking for,' which is why the goy focked off to Brazil, I'm sure.

I missed all this while I was away, roysh, but I got the full SP off Christian in the M1 last night. Turns out, roysh, that Hennessy Coghlan-O'Hara isn't even the dude's real name. He's called, I don't know, Frank Awder, which actually makes Christian's bird Lauren Awder, something her old man is not big on, as Fionn pointed out.

The dude was up to his nads in iffy shit basically. Don't know what half of it means, roysh, but when he was Frank Awder he was, like, borred from being a company director for life. So – get this – the goy took on a dead man's identity, studied law and came back as a dodgy solicitor. For twenty years he didn't pay any tax because, according to the official records, he was, like, toast.

Then on top that, roysh, he's got, like, six or seven offshore accounts and fock knows what else. Christian reckons it's a focking miracle it took the Feds so long to catch up with him, especially with him walking out of the tribunal every day, pointing at the cameras, going, 'The go-getter generation is being hounded by you, the media, and the bastarding police.'

It's truly shocking that Lauren sprung from that man's loins. But then, look at me and my old man. I *have* to have been adopted. Dick Features pours his coffee, then has the actual cheek to sit beside me. He goes, 'The man stood by me, Ross. Even during my own travails in front of Mister Justice Produce-The-Documents-Or-Go-To-Jail, thank you very much indeed. Poor Hennessy. God knows what he's going through.' I'm there, 'Half-a-pound of cocaine and a couple of Brazilian hookers would be my guess,' and he goes, 'Hookers are no subject for the breakfast table, Kicker. Brazilian or otherwise,' then he lights this big turd of a cigar and just, like, stares off into the distance.

I go, 'Fair focks to Frankie,' – I keep calling him this just to piss the old man off, because he knew fock-all about his, like, shady past until I told him – and then I'm like, 'bet he's buried conkers deep in some cracking bird, having the time of his life,' and the tosser loses it then, roysh, which is unlike him. The cracks are beginning to show. Must have a secret or two himself. He goes, 'Time of his life, my eye. He's being hounded by the likes of your chap there on the back of your paper. Mister Conscience of the Nation. I've a good mind to pick up and the phone and–' and I'm there, 'And go to jail? Isn't that what the beak said?' He goes, '*Stalking!* How could I be guilty of stalking a man I've never even met?' I'm there, 'You sent him twenty-eight letters and phoned him eighty-seven times in six weeks,' and he goes, 'I sent your mother twenty-eight letters and phoned her eighty-whatever-it-was times. We ended up married. Happily, too. I pay my €1.80, I'm entitled to my view. And next time I see Shane Ross I'll tell him. The man has to be stopped, with his rules and regulations, yes indeed thank you very much, M'Lud.'

Actually, Emma Blain's just jumped a position or two. He goes, 'Some of the chaps are popping by tonight. We're going to stort a campaign to clear his name.' I'm there, 'So why did Frankie peg it then? And why doesn't he come back and face the music?' and the dickhead takes the turd out from between his teeth and he goes, 'Couldn't get a fair trial. I'm not sure you've noticed, Kicker, but the law in this country is an ass. It's certainly not on the side of the law-abiding, revenue-generating classes.' My head is throbbing, basically telling me that I've reached my bullshit limit for the day. As I'm leaving the table the old man goes, 'I so do enjoy our chats, Kicker. Father and son, debating the great issues of the day. Like it should be.' I'm there, 'Give me a hundred bills. I'm going out on the lash tonight.'

✳ ✳ ✳

There I am, roysh, in Sorcha's gaff, doing the whole boyfriend-girlfriend bit, listening to a few sounds, some focking miserable tosser she's into at the moment. Of course, I'm only hanging around to see if there's a chance of my Swiss tonight, or am I going home with a loaded gun again. She's glued to 'Big Brother' these days and she's giving it, 'OH! MY! GOD! That Tanya is SUCH a bitch!' 'Hey, what does it say on the label of a northside bird's knickers?' That's what I say to her to, like, get her attention and she turns to me and goes, 'What?' like she's already pissed off, even before she's, like, heard the answer. I'm there, 'NEXT.' She goes, 'Some of my best friends are from the northside. Are you saying Gwen's a slapper?' and I'm there, 'Gwen's from, like, Sutton. It's hordly the northside,' and anyway she *is* a slapper, she tried to hop me in Reynord's last weekend while Sorcha was up at the bor talking to a few of her college mates about Iran or Iraq or whatever, not that I was exactly fighting her off.

Anyway, to cut a long story short, roysh, 'Big Brother' is over and we end up lying on her bed, listening to a CD of some mopey focker banging on about some bird he's just phoned up after, like, forty years and, of course, naturally, I'm like, 'What is this shit?' and Sorcha goes, 'It's Tom Waits.' I'm there, 'Sounds like Old Man River. When did you get into this muppet?' and she goes – get this, roysh – 'Recently. *Fionn burned it for me.*' I'm like, '*What?*' and she goes, 'Fionn said I'd like him. He put some of his best stuff on a blank CD for me. Ross, what's your problem?' I'm trying not to come across all, like, possessive, roysh, but for some reason this has really bugged the shit out of me. I go, 'He made you a tape?' and she's like, 'A CD, Ross.' I'm there, 'Same difference. Look, taping someone an album is fine. But making someone a tape, actually sitting down and picking out songs, that's boyfriend-girlfriend stuff.' She goes, 'Really? Funny, you've never done it for me,' and I'm like, 'I've never been good with technology, you know that. He's trying to move in on you, Sorcha.' She's like, 'He's just a friend,' and it's unbelievable, roysh, I'm shaking I'm so angry. I go, 'He's not roysh for you. He's got glasses,' and she goes, 'Will you get it into your head, I'm not interested in him. I love *you*. OH MY GOD, this is SO September tenth.'

But nothing she says can calm me down, roysh, and I tell her I have to go out to get some air, but she knows damn well, roysh, that I'm going outside to ring that penis, him and his moany focking tapes. The focker actually has the cheek to play it Kool and the Gang with me. He goes, 'Alroysh, Ross? Stuck in traffic. Harcourt Street's a mare. When's the Daniel Day gonna be finished anyway?' I'm there, 'What's your focking game?' and he's going, 'My *game*?' and I'm like, 'Making Sorcha a tape?' He goes, 'It's a CD, Ross. Did she like it?' His specs are SO going up his orse when I see him. I'm like, 'Don't play the innocent with me. You made her a tape. I know what that means. You make someone a tape and it's like … she's *my* girlfriend, you … glasses head.'

He's so focking smug, of course. He goes, 'Is she really, Ross? Well, who was that bird you were playing tonsil tennis with last Saturday night? She was doing a very passable impression of being your girlfriend,' and I'm like, 'You're bang out of order,' and he's giving it, 'Was her name Gwen? Isn't she one of Sorcha's friends?' I try to change the subject. I go, 'Get it into your thick head, she has no interest in you. She goes for looks,' and I hang up before he can say anything back. I'm still shaking. I can't believe the effect that this has had on me. I storm back into Sorcha's gaff and peg it up the stairs. She's on the phone to, I think, Aoife. She's telling her she SO hopes Tanya gets focked out of the house because the girl has got SUCH an attitude problem. I rip the CD out of the CD player – he drew a love hort on it, the steamer – and just, like, fock it out of the window. She goes, 'WHAT ARE YOU DOING? ARE YOU OUT OF YOUR MIND?' Then she goes, 'Aoife, I'm going to have to ring you back. Ross is being, like, SO weird.'

She hangs up and I just stort babbling. I'm going, 'I'm sick of it, Sorcha. Sick of all the messing around. Not saying what I mean,' and she goes, 'Have you been drinking?' I'm like, 'Sorcha … let's get married,' and she doesn't say anything for ages. I'm thinking, I can't believe I just focking said that and I think her answer is going to be, I don't know, getting married in your early twenties is SO working class or something, but instead, roysh, she just looks at me and she goes, 'The ring HAS to come from John Farrington's.'

❋ ❋ ❋

I'm going to look up the word 'simpering' in the old man's dictionary when I go home because I'm pretty sure, roysh, that's what Sorcha and her old dear are doing. Her old dear goes, 'It's going to be a wedding *no one* will ever forget,' and then she gives me a look that basically says, If you don't fock it up, that is.

Sorcha's like, 'I've already decided the theme is going to be cranberries,' we're talking ten minutes after I proposed to her. She goes, 'I'm going to have cranberry-coloured flowers woven into my dress. Ross's tie will be cranberry and the bridesmaids' dresses will have some kind of cranberry trim, as will the invitations and the placenames. And the menus.'

Her old dear's just looking at her, roysh, shaking her head, like she's struggling to take it all in. Sorcha goes, 'OH! MY! GOD! Mum, we HAVE to go away to shop,' and her old dear goes, 'Paris for the dress, Milan for the underwear,' and Sorcha shakes her head and goes, '*New York* for the dress.' Her old dear's there, 'Wait a minute. I know that look. You're thinking Vera Wang, aren't you?' and Sorcha nods and goes, 'Absolutely! OH! MY! GOD! Can you ACTUALLY picture Erika's face when she finds out I'm, like, going to New York to buy my dress?'

HELLO? I'm still here, people. Not that you'd know it. Sorcha's old dear storts, like, fussing over her, fixing her hair, like she's walking up the aisle in five focking minutes. She goes, 'I take it Erika's going to be one of your bridesmaids?' and Sorcha looks at her in, like, total horror and goes, '*No way!* I was thinking Orpha and maybe Claire.' Her old dear's like, 'Claire's *very* plain, bless her,' and Sorcha goes, 'I know. A girl doesn't like to be upstaged on her big day, Mum,' and her old dear just, like, nods her head, as the penny drops, and she goes, 'You should ask her to lose some weight though. Give her those Weight Watchers books.' Sorcha goes, 'I think I might even have cranberries on the wedding cake.'

The next thing, roysh, I hear someone coming in the front door and it's, like, Sorcha's old man, who wouldn't be my number one fan. You can't blame the dude either. I couldn't tell you how many times Sorcha's bawled her eyes out in this house over shit I've done. He was in the George in Dún Laoghaire having a few scoops. The old dear pretty much rugby tackles him as he walks into the kitchen and goes, 'Edmund, wĕ have the most wonderful news,' and I can see him eyeing me, roysh, and I know I make his flesh crawl.

Sorcha goes, 'Dad, I'm getting married,' and he doesn't need to say the words, 'Who to?' roysh, because they're written all over his face. Sorcha links my orm and she's there, '*We're* getting married. Ross and I,' and it's ages before he says anything, roysh, and the first words that come out of his mouth are, 'When did this happen?' The old dear goes, 'Oh yes, Sorcha, you still haven't told us how he proposed.' She goes, 'Yeah, we were up in my room ...' and straight away the old man's like, 'What the hell were you doing in my daughter's bedroom?' and the old dear goes, 'Oh, Edmund, they're practically married. You can't play that heavy parent routine anymore. Continue, Sorcha.'

Sorcha goes, 'Well, we were up in my room, just talking about how, like, close we'd become while we were in Indonesia and I was like, 'If only we could always have the fantasy,' and he was there, 'Why can't we,' and then – OH MY GOD! – he just, like, got down on one knee and I was like, 'OH! MY! GOD!' and he was like, 'Sorcha, will you make me the happiest goy in the world by marrying me?' and I was like, 'OH! MY! GOD!' which is total bullshit, roysh.

I'm not going to, like, contradict her, of course, because I actually come out of the story looking pretty good, it has to be said. Her old dear is *actually* crying and her old man is just, like, nodding furiously with this, like, stern look on his face, but at least he's not looking like he wants to tear my focking fingernails out with a pliers like he did a minute ago. The dude even offers me his hand, which I decide to shake. He goes, 'My wife is much easier-going than I am. I've never liked you from the first day I clocked eyes on you. But if you're what makes Sorcha happy, then as a father it's my job to ensure you continue to make Sorcha happy. Do you understand me?' It's one hell of a handshake he's got there. I'm like, 'Yes, Mister Lalor.'

Sorcha goes, 'Let's go tell your mum and dad,' and the old dear goes, 'Hurry back, Sorcha. We can get planning. Agent Provocateur have a website,' and Sorcha goes puce and she's there, '*Mum!*' and I haven't a focking bog what they're talking about. I go, 'I was just, em, thinking, Sorcha, we don't actually need to *call* to my old pair to tell them. Can we not just text them?' and she storts giving it, 'ROSS! O'CARROLL! KELLY! Their only child is about to get married and you want them to read the news in a text? OH! MY! GOD! You have got some strange ideas.'

So of course we've got to drive all the way up to Foxrock just to let the two biggest tools in the world know. In the cor, roysh, Sorcha had this idea of how she was going to tell them, dropping hints, 'Do you ever wish you'd had a daughter?' all that kind of shit. But, of course, the second the old dear opens the door, Sorcha can't hold her piss, roysh, and she blurts out, 'We're getting married, Fionnuala,' and the two of them fall into this, like, embrace, big-time amateur dramatics stuff, then the old dear actually goes to hug *me*, roysh, and my whole body stiffens up and I'm there, 'Just a congratulations will do, thanks very much.' She brings us into the kitchen and of course the old man's heard everything from inside the study and suddenly *he's* in on the act. It's all hugs and kisses and handshakes. He's going, 'Well, Sorcha, it's one way of getting you to come back and work for me. Because one day you and Ross are going to inherit the business,' and it's, like, false laughs all round.

He's going, 'Absolutely tremendous news and I mean that with a capital T. I have to tell you, Sorcha, Fionnuala and I always hoped that you'd be the one. You're a wonderful person. Must say, Ross, you're a bit of a dark horse. Didn't come looking to your old man for advice on this one?' and I'm there, 'I wouldn't ask you for advice on how to wipe my orse.' He goes, 'Sorcha, have you told your parents?' and she's there, 'OH! MY! GOD! They are, like, SO happy,' and Dickhead goes, 'Let's them over here. This calls for a celebration. We got that bottle of Bollinger that we picked up in Paris, darling. I'll pop it in the fridge for half-an-hour and then I'll ring Edmund.'

The old dear turns around to Sorcha and she goes, 'Has your mum decided what she's going to wear yet?' and Sorcha's there, 'Something black and white, I'd say. Pastels put ten years on you, that's what she always says,' and I can tell from the old dear's reaction, roysh, that she had black and white in mind as well and it's, like, may the battle of the mothers-in-law commence. The old man dials the number, roysh, and while he's waiting for an answer he goes, 'I suspect Edmund and I are going to play *quite a bit* of golf between now and the big day.' Then he goes, 'Hello, Edmund, old chap. It's Charles ... my congratulations to you, too. Both of you. We're delighted. Not a hint of it from Ross here beforehand. Played his cards close to his chest on this one. Yes, your daughter is a wonderful girl. Fionnuala and I loved her the very first day Ross took her home. He is one lucky man. What? Yes, he can be. But I think those days are behind him now,' and he just, like, winks at me.

Then he's like, 'Just wondered if you both fancied coming over. This calls for a celebration. I've been pretty busy lately, you've probably heard, but if my son getting engaged to a beautiful girl isn't reason enough to take an evening off from my efforts to clear an innocent man's name, then I might as well go and live in North Korea. Terrific! See you in half-an-hour.'

I'm just there thinking, This wedding's gonna be more focking trouble than it's worth.

CHAPTER FIVE
For Richer or Poorer

'So you're really taking the plunge?' Oisinn goes to me in Kiely's the other night and I'm there, 'Totally,' trying to sound a bit more enthusiastic than I basically am. He's there, 'Makes sense, Ross. No point in holding out for the dream. Luykx is gone. It's over, I tell you,' and we all just sit there staring into space for, like, ten minutes.

Eventually, roysh, Christian goes, 'I've been making some notes. For the best man's speech,' because, like, who else would I choose, and he goes, 'Want me to run some of them by you?' and he pulls out this, like, sheaf of paper, maybe ten pages. I'm there, 'As long as there's no *Star Wars* shit in it,' and he just, like, stares at me, like he's about to burst out crying, then he slowly puts the pages back into his pocket and I feel kind of bad, roysh, but the last thing I want is all that Obi Wan Kenobi shite on Sorcha's big day, and mine as well I suppose.

Maybe I'm just a bit uptight. December nineteenth is the date we've set. I say *we*, but I've got basically fock-all to do with this wedding. Sorcha, her old dear and my old dear have basically hijacked the whole thing. I'm being frogmorched into town next week to spend ten thousand lids on some Art Deco engagement ring the three of them saw while shopping for dresses, and after that, roysh, my only involvement in this wedding is showing my face on the day and, at this rate, it'll be a focking miracle if I do. I do love Sorcha, roysh, bent and all as it sounds, but I was hoping for a long engagement, three or four years maybe, keep putting it around Annabel's, Dublin Four Fanny Central, happy days. But no sooner have I popped the old question, roysh, than Sorcha's telling me that the choice of storter SO has to be dried apricots with goat's cheese and pistachios, or smoked caviar and hummus on pitta toasts, and suddenly I feel like I'm being shoved up the aisle on focking casters.

All the craic has gone out of her as well. It's like the wedding's all she ever thinks about. We haven't had a bit of the other in the three weeks since we got engaged and, not being crude or anything, but I've a love truncheon on me that could beat a donkey out of a quarry. Of course, I'm trying to keep the romance going. There I am sitting in the M1 with the goys and my phone rings and I actually answer the thing, even though I know it's her. And of course straight away it's like, 'Your mum's right, Ross. I forgot so many of my friends are vegetarians. We'll have lemon-scented couscous timbale with cut sugar-snap peas and gingered Parisian carrots for those who don't want the grilled charmoula lamb and yukon potato croquets,' and I'm there, 'Sorcha, I love you,' under my breath I admit, so the goys don't hear, but she doesn't respond, just goes, 'Or maybe zucchini julianne,' and then she hangs up.

The next thing, roysh, who walks in only Erika, who's in a total Pauline at the moment, basically because Sorcha's sister – whatever the fock her name is – and Claire – as in Claire from Bray of all places – were asked to be the bridesmaids and *she* wasn't, and she's still steaming over this. She stops by our table and she goes,

'A *Christmas* wedding, I believe. Your little girlfriend's been hanging around Claire so long she's becoming a knacker herself.' She looks amazing. Now I can understand Sorcha's game. Claire wouldn't get kicked in a stampede. No bride wants to be upstaged on her big day by good-looking bridesmaids, and Erika would basically go out of her way to knock spots off her.

Oisinn sniffs the air and goes, 'The new *Issey Miyake*, huh? Its fragrant nature explores essences of peony, white lily and carnation, blended with notes of jasmine, sandalwood and oakmoss. Erika, I don't think I'm going to be able to keep my hands off you,' and Erika goes, 'If you want to keep them attached to your orms, I suggest you try,' and she focks off to the jacks. Me and Oisinn and Christian and JP, we sit there for ages, roysh, staring at the toilet door, telling our Erika stories. Every single one of us has tried to get in there in the past and everyone, with the exception of me, has crashed and burned.

Oisinn chanced his orm at the Traffic Light Ball and she told him – word for word, roysh – 'If me and you were marooned on a desert island with a tin of frankfurter sausages, I'd kill and eat you and keep the sausages for sex,' which, like all of Erika's put-down lines, left him pretty speechless. She took JP to the Mount Anville debs four years ago, let him think he had a chance just to see how many birds he knocked back to be with her, then red-corded the dude on the way home in the limo, which he paid for incidentally. I'm basically the only one who's managed to bail in there, even if she was only doing it to fock with Sorcha's head. Oisinn goes, 'Forget what I was saying earlier, goys. The dream's not dead. Not while that girl's still single.' Suddenly the door opens, roysh, and out she comes, big pouty face on her as usual, and she can't resist the temptation to stop by and have another dig. She goes, 'I must drop by *Argos* tomorrow, Ross. See if the wedding list's in yet,' and as she heads for the door, roysh, we all notice at pretty much the same time that she's got this length of, like, bog roll stuck to the sole of her shoe and she hasn't noticed it. Off she goes, collar up, nose in the air and this, like, streamer of jacks paper following her, basically ruining the overall effect. Doesn't look so high and mighty now. We all crack our holes laughing. It feels good.

✳ ✳ ✳

A choreographer? A focking choreographer? That's what I go to Sorcha the other night, roysh. I'm there, 'This wedding business is getting out of hand,' and of course, suddenly I'm the focking Grinch Who Stole Christmas. She goes, '*This wedding business?* Ross, this is supposed to be the happiest day of our lives. I want our first dance to be something everyone remembers. I want to see Erika's face.' I'm there, 'No focking way, Sorcha. If the goys find out I'm getting dance classes, I'm totalled,' and she loses it then, roysh, going, 'It's always what OTHER people think, ISN'T IT? What about what *I* want?' and I'm thinking, HELLO? Definite case of blob strop here, and it *is* her time, roysh, but of course I say nothing except, 'I don't want the goys calling me a benny. End of story,' and she's there, 'You are SO homophobic.' I'm like, 'I'm *hordly* homophobic. I just don't like goys cracking onto me. I don't like tomato ketchup either. Doesn't make me ketchup-aphobic. Just don't like it.'

Of course there's no talking to birds when they've fallen to the communists. She just, like, storms off out of the room, roysh, opens the front door of her gaff and tells me she thinks a short period of reflection would do me good, which means she's going to basically sulk for a few days until she gets her way.

But she was roysh – my period of reflection did me no end of good. It was, like, Friday in Bar Mizu and Cocoon, Saturday in The Bailey and Lillie's, Sunday in Ron Black's and Reynord's, basically getting shit-faced and throwing the lips on any bird that came into my line of vision, happy focking days. Monday night my phone rings, roysh, and I can see it's Sorcha's home number and I think she's obviously decided she's left me stewing long enough. But it turns out, roysh, it's not Sorcha ringing at all but her old man – he's a total penis, this goy – telling me he wants to have a bit of a chat – 'man to man,' he goes, like the dickhead that he is. So I call a Jo and I head back out to Killiney and he leads me into the study and he's giving it, 'I've a very fine bottle of Port here somewhere that I keep for special occasions,' and he opens the bottom drawer of his filing cabinet, whips out the bottle and pours two glasses of this stuff, basically pisswater.

He goes, 'And what could be more special than my daughter's happiness?' and there seems to be a bit of a, I don't know, threat in his voice. Then the lecture begins. He's going, 'We want the best for our daughter, Ross. We want the best for both of our daughters,' and of course I'm there thinking, I've actually *given* them both my best, and I have to bite my lip to stop myself laughing in the dude's face. He goes, 'Anything that upsets Sorcha, upsets me, do you understand? And sometimes it's necessary to make these small sacrifices to make sure she's happy. I think I've said my piece. Knock that Port back.'

Suddenly Sorcha appears, roysh, and she obviously knows the score because she's, like, dressed to go out and she's got the dance brochures under her arm and she turns to her old man and goes, 'We'll be back around ten,' and before I know what's happened, roysh, I'm standing in this room with four or five other couples – we're talking some tool with a frumpy bird who thinks he's John Travolta, some dickhead with curly hair who actually falls asleep mid-dance, and a big focking balluba of a bird who ends up nearly, like, suffocating her poor boyfriend in her airbags – and we're all taking orders from this tosspot called Trevor, we're basically talking Graham Norton in orange leggings. He's giving it, 'Our goal here is to make your first wedding dance a memory you will cherish forevermore by offering you simple, practical instructions. We're also going to learn other moves with which you can wow the rest of your wedding party during the evening, including Latin nightclub dancing.' He definitely has the hots for me, this goy, just from the way he keeps looking at me when he's saying all this shit. He goes, 'Now, I'm going to go around you individually and ask you what are your dance goals *vis-à-vis* the first dance,' and of course it's the birds who do all the answering. It's like, 'Come What May' from Moulin Rouge,' and, 'A Whole New World' by Peabo Bryson and Regina Belle,' and, 'Can You Feel The Love Tonight?' by Elton John,' who's actually probably a good mate of this dude.

When it comes to us, roysh, Sorcha goes, 'Kiss Me' by Six-pence None the Richer. It's from 'Dawson's Creek',' – surprise sur-focking-prise – and Trevor claps his hands like a focking child on Christmas focking morning and goes, 'Oooh, the sugari-est of pop confections for you two dears. Okay, why am I think-ing of a hybrid of waltz and foxtrot with twirls thrown in? Because I'm a genius, that's why! I want to start with you two be-cause I'm excited by this.' So he drags the two of us out into the middle of the floor, roysh, and he's got his hand on my shoulder, as he just, like, guides us into position. He's going, 'Before you can develop your partnering skills, you have to learn to improve your own individual posture and rhythm, as well as the self-confidence that's absolutely integral to the art of partner dancing. Anyone can learn to dance once they have the right coach.' He asks us our names, roysh, and we tell him. He goes, 'So sweet,' and then he shows us where to put our hands. His own hand is still on my shoulder and I can feel my face going red. His fingers are like hot coals.

He goes, 'Now, Ross here is dressed ideally. A well-fitting, leather-soled, medium- to low-heeled shoe. And loose trousers,' and maybe it's the combination of his hand sliding down my orm, roysh, and him saying the words 'loose' and 'trousers' together like that, but I just, like, totally flip, push his orm away and go, 'Don't touch what you can't afford.'

And of course there's focking silence then. It's like one of those movies where someone walks into some focking battle cruiser and, like, says something to someone at the bor and the music suddenly stops. And everyone's, like, staring at me and I've got a serious reddener on me. I don't even want to *see* Sorcha's face. Eventually this Trevor dude goes, 'Just because I'm gay, Ross, doesn't mean I'm interested in you. Frankly, I find that preppy college look SO eighties. And I didn't even find it attractive then,' and everyone just breaks their shites laughing at me.

Oh, so suddenly *I'm* the focking oddball?

✳ ✳ ✳

I'm on the can, roysh, when I get this text from Oisinn, who's been seeing this bird Emma for, like, six months now and she's still not putting out. The goy's put some spadework into the job as well. Paddy's weekend, he takes her to the Aran Islands for a few nights and it's no-go. The June bank holiday they head down to, like, Dingle and she still won't let the dude go beyond the old tonsil hockey phase, after him shelling out a hundred and fifty bills for the B&B. So when they come back from another jiggyless long weekend in Donegal on Monday night, roysh, Oisinn is totally bulling it and he sends me a text to tell me he's decided to write a book. It's called **Round Ireland With A Frigid Bitch**.

This actually makes me laugh out loud, roysh, totally forgetting of course that there's someone in trap two and trap three, but I basically don't care, it's been that long since I've had a good laugh. Sorcha's, like, wrecking my head. She turns around to me after dance class the other night – *dance class*, for fock's sake – and she storts giving it, 'I don't think it's a rhythm problem with you as much as a ... posture one,' and of course I'm there, 'Meaning?' and she goes, 'Ross, I think you need to lose some weight.' Now, I'll be the first to admit it, roysh, I've put on a few pounds since I gave up playing serious rugby and shit, but I am SO not going on a diet. I go, 'I'm not doing it, Sorcha,' and she goes, 'You don't even know what I'm suggesting,' and I'm like, 'That fat birds' support group you go to. Counting your points and walking the roads swinging your orms. I'm not doing it.' She has a face on her then, roysh. She tells me I wouldn't have the discipline for Weight Watchers and says she wants me to do the Atkins diet instead, and when I tell her to drop the subject, roysh, she tells me she is SO not marrying a blubbergram – *a blubbergram*, HELLO? – and I tell her that's basically fine by me.

So there we are, bombing down the Blackrock bypass, roysh, neither of us saying anything for, like, ten or fifteen minutes, when all of a sudden we stop at the lights outside Maxwell Motors and she lashes this CD into the stereo in the cor, we're talking her black Rav 4. Turns out it's that whining focker again that Fionn introduced her to when he was trying to bail in. *The night does funny things inside a man.* This is, like, emotional blackmail, if that's the roysh word. *These tomcat feelings you don't understand.* If she thinks that just by putting on that tape ... I go, 'Alroysh, I'LL DO IT! Just ... just turn that off.'

She turns off the music and I go, 'This Atkins thing, I'll check it out on the internet over the weekend,' and she's there, 'No need,' and she drops this, like, assload of papers on my lap and goes, 'My dad got all the information for you off the 'net.' I'm like, 'Your old man knew I was going on this thing before I did?' but she just stares at me. She drops me home, roysh, and I stort going through the stuff and I can't believe what I'm reading. It's not all carrots and vegetation and shit. You can eat, like, steak and sausages and bacon, we're talking chicken, we're talking pork, we're talking eggs, and I'm just there, Happy days. So I get up the next morning, roysh, and tell the old dear to fix me a huge fry – we're talking six sausages, six rashers, four fried eggs, two pork chops and a big fock-off steak – and she goes, 'Do you want beans?' and I read the stuff Sorcha gave me and I go, 'Nah, I'm on a diet.' I stort wolfing the thing down, roysh, and of course the old dear suddenly thinks me and her are, like, best mates or something. She goes, 'This campaign of your father's is going so well, Ross. He thinks he'll have Hennessy's name cleared by Christmas,' and I go, 'I ordered a fry. Don't remember asking for a side of bullshit conversation,' and she takes the hint and focks off.

Lunch is two portions of buffalo wings from, like, Eddie Rocket's, roysh, and dinner is another big fock-off steak and three fried eggs. So this goes on for four or five days, roysh. I feel as full as a focking banana but the weight is, like, falling off me and by Friday I'm buckling my belt a notch tighter. So that night, roysh, I meet the gang in Kiely's and Christian goes, 'Pint, padwan?' and of course I'm there, 'Hey, kool plus *hombres*.'

But Sorcha, roysh, she all of a sudden goes, 'Ross, you're not allowed to drink,' and I'm there, 'Ex-squeeze me?' and she goes, 'Part of the diet is that you abstain from alcohol.' Then she turns to Christian and goes, 'Just a Ballygowan for him, Hon. Still.'

And I'll tell you what, roysh, being sober really makes you realise what a bunch of tools your mates are. We're all sitting there, roysh – I'm actually wondering whether I've got constipation, it's that long since the turtle showed his head – when all of a sudden Erika storts going, 'Someone's walked in dogshit.' Of course, straight away we're all, like, checking the soles of our Dubes and one by one everyone's giving it, 'It's not me.'

Mine are clean as well, roysh, but then Erika's like, 'Well what IS that smell. It's like, OH! MY! GOD!' and Sorcha, roysh, calm as you like, goes, 'It's actually Ross's breath. He's on the Atkins diet,' and everyone just, like, cracks their holes laughing. I'm there, 'You never said anything about bad breath,' and she just, like, shrugs her shoulders.

Christian tells me I smell like a Bantha, whatever the fock that is. I ask JP if he's got, like, a mint and Sorcha tells me that I can't eat them, they're not on the diet. She sips her Bacordi Breezer and goes, 'And I am SO not kissing you until you've finished the programme,' which I take it means that a bit of the other's not on the menu either.

✳ ✳ ✳

I'm in the kitchen, making myself a fry, a *full* one, roysh, because I've decided, roysh, that no diet can be healthy if it hurts to drop a load so I've given up the whole Atkins bullshit. The old dear comes into the kitchen, clucking away to herself, roysh, going, 'I know I'm honorary secretary, Ross, but the Ban Poor People from Dún Laoghaire Pier group are going to have to wait for their fliers. Sorcha's mum just phoned. I've been given *a job*,' and I go, '*Whopee*,' real sarcastic, roysh.

She goes, 'Now, keep it to you yourself, Ross, but we're throwing a surprise bridal shower for her. Here in the house,' and I'm there, 'Why here of all places?' and she looks at me over the top of her reading glasses and goes, 'Well, it wouldn't be appropriate for the Lalors to have it at theirs, Ross. It would look like they were soliciting for gifts. Now, we're looking at the October bank holiday weekend,' and I'm thinking, Thank fock I'm going to be in Australia, and that reminds me, roysh, I still haven't told Sorcha about the World Cup. The old dear has her best note-paper and the Mont Blanc pen she got from her tennis mates for her fiftieth, the stupid bitch. She goes, 'I'm going to make the theme pampering. There's more than enough presents for the home on the wedding list. I'll mention it on the invitations. Now, I must get a list of Sorcha's pals off you and get addresses for them,' and I go, 'Shut up, you focking deranged old bag.' She totally ignores this and goes, 'Okay, first and foremost, we need a format for the evening. Important to put a structure on things. Okay, guests arrive and are introduced to one another. Games maybe. Handbag Bingo. Yes, they played it at Dearbhla's daughter's bridal shower, young Jessica. Each guest holds her handbag open on her lap while someone reads out items from a list – purse, lipstick and so forth – and the first person to have five items on the list wins a prize.'

I'm there, 'Sorry, who do you think is listening to you?' She goes, 'Oh, they did that thing with the photo album as well. Each guest was asked to bring along a picture of herself with the bride-to-be, then had to tell the story behind the photograph, then put it into an album. It's a way of bringing to mind wonderful old memories and then creating a beautiful souvenir of the night as well.'

I'm there, 'Who the fock do you think you are – Martha Stewart or something?' Sorcha's always going on about Martha Stewart. She goes, 'Then food. Finger food, I think. Oysters with raspberry vinegar. Ginger chicken cakes. Sugar-cured tuna salad on noodles. And wine, of course. Then the opening of the gifts. And to finish off, it's simply *got* to be cake and cocktails.' I put a forkful of beans into my mouth and go, 'I hope the focking house burns down.'

✱ ✱ ✱

After weeks of, I suppose you'd have to call it deliberation, Sorcha has decided that the bridesmaids' dresses are going to be black empire line with a fifties kick and tulle, and a cranberry ribbon under the bustline, and of course this goes totally over my head. 'Murder She Wrote' is on. She's on the other end of the phone, going, 'Now, I still haven't decided on a font for the placenames. I think Mum's right, Edwardian Script is a bit too fancy. I'm actually veering towards a mixture of French Script and Times New Roman, which was your mum's suggestion, or possibly even Franklin Gothic Demi, I'd have to see how they go together.'

I've been having some, shall we say, strange thoughts about that Jessica Fletcher recently. I know, I know, there should be a national register for people like me. Suddenly Sorcha's going, 'Are you even listening to me?' and I'm there, 'Yeah, of course,' and she's like, 'What was the last thing I said?' and I've gone,

'Franctomatic Demi?' and she's there, 'I *asked* you what you thought of pew-end bows.' What kind of a focking question is that to ask a bloke anyway? I'm there, 'I can take them or leave them.' She lets rip then, giving it, 'OH! MY! GOD! You haven't done a tap for this wedding. It's like you don't give a damn. I've booked the caterer, ordered the cake, chosen the flowers, booked the honeymoon, sent the save-the-date cords, arranged the transport, booked the calligrapher for the stationery, arranged the announcement, booked the hotel, drawn up a provisional menu and seating-plan, booked the priest, decided on the service, chosen the readings, written the vows, scheduled the rehearsal and dinner afterwards, ordered the programmes, AND I still have to break in my shoes.'

I'm there, 'Chill out, Sorcha, there's months to go yet,' and there's this, like, silence on the other end of the phone and I know what's coming, roysh, the dam's about to burst. She goes, 'There isn't months to go, Ross, because there isn't going to *be* a wedding. I've decided I don't want to marry someone who doesn't support me,' and blahdy blahdy blah. I'm there, 'I asked you, like, ages ago if I could do anything to help and you went, "Yeah, stay out of my way".' She *will* marry me. The girl's in love with me. She goes, 'I *asked* you two weeks ago to book the DJ and you haven't, have you?' and I'm there, 'I was going to have a word with him in Lillie's last Friday, but I ended up getting hammered. I swear to God, Sorcha, I couldn't even order a focking doner kebab with garlic and cheese fries, never mind discuss the playlist for a wedding.'

Doesn't see the funny side of it at all. I'm not a psychiatrist, roysh, but I think she's sort of, like, channelling all the anger and, like, frustration she feels over the whole tigers-and-monkeys business into this. She goes, 'What are you doing now?' in a real, like, basically pissed off kind of way. Obviously, roysh, I can't tell her I'm flaked out on the sofa, playing the old Japanese helicopter pilot while looking at Angela Lansbury, so I just go, 'I was - *actually* thinking of going to see that DJ. His brother was actually on the S with me. I don't have the dude's number, but he lives in Stradbrook. I know the house and everything.' This seems to, like, please her, just the idea that I'm not at home just scratching my orse. Or other things. I go, 'Only thing is, Sorcha, like I said, the dude lives in Blackrock and, well, I lost my licence as you know,' and she goes, 'You want a lift? I suppose I should be grateful you're showing at least *some* interest in this wedding. I'll be there in twenty minutes.'

Of course, it's an hour-and-a-half before she arrives, roysh, dressed to kill, still a little bit of puffiness around the eyes from where she was crying. I get into the cor and she gives me a hug, roysh, and tells me she's sorry for over-reacting the way she did, letting things get on top of her, blah blah blah. She storts up the engine and she tells me she's decided to go on a course of Perfectil, which I naturally assume is something bird's take when they've got a blob strop on, like vallium or some shit. Turns out it's – what did she call it? – an advanced cosmetic supplement? She goes, 'It's, like, OH! MY! GOD! amazing for your hair and your nails. And your skin. I am going to be SO stressed and I don't want to walk up the aisle looking like a pizza.'

I'm there, 'It's here on the left,' and we pull in, roysh, outside this massive gaff where Karl lives, as in kid brother of Kenny, who was on the S with us. We knock on the door, roysh, and it's actually Karl who answers it. Small dude, spiky blonde hair, eyebrow ring, more into music than rugby, but still sound. He goes,

'Hey, Ross, come on in. And you must be Sorcha. Kenny's told me loads about you. What are you doing with this loser?' and he sort of, like, throws his thumb in my direction and I'm tempted to go, Loser? Who's the only person in this room with a Leinster Schools Senior Cup winner's medal? But I don't, roysh, because I have to learn to take a joke. He goes, 'So, I guess you goys are here to talk about the music for the wedding?' and I'm there, 'Shit the bed, Karl, are you, like, a mind-reader or something?'

He's like, 'A mind-reader? Ross, do you not remember the conversation we had in Lillie's last Friday?' and I don't answer, roysh, but I can feel Sorcha giving me this really hord stare. Karl laughs and he goes, 'You were fairly horrendufied alright. Don't worry, Sorcha. I'm his alibi. He was a good boy that night,' and I'm thinking it's a good job he didn't see me in the queue for the cloakroom later on.

'So,' he goes, 'what kind of music did you have in mind?' and he automatically looks at Sorcha, roysh, obviously picking up on the vibe that, as far as this wedding goes, she's wearing the pants. Out of the blue, roysh, for the first time since this whole wedding lark storted, she turns around and goes, 'What do *you* think, Ross?' and of course I'm just, like, speechless. I go, 'Em, I don't know, whatever *you* want,' and she goes, 'No, Ross. Look, I realise now how badly I've been acting lately. It's, like, OH MY GOD, I've turned into some kind of wedding Nazi or something. You shouldn't have to keep reminding me that this is *our* wedding, not *mine*. You choose the music.' So Karl all of a sudden turns his head to me, roysh, and he's sitting there with, like, pen and paper at the ready and I'm, like, just on the point of opening my mouth, roysh, when Sorcha goes, 'No synchronised numbers.' Karl's there, 'Sorry?' and she goes, 'No songs you can do a routine dance to. No 'Macarena'. No 'Saturday Night'. No 'Rock the Boat'. No 'Locomotion'. No 'Timewarp'. No 'Conga'. And no 'Friends in Low Places'. No Garth Brooks period, and nothing you can line-dance to. No 'Achy Breaky Heart'. No Pop Idol winners. No boy bands. No girl bands. Nothing by S Club Seven. No Abba, Jackson Five or *Grease* medleys.'

I look at her, roysh, and it's like something's possessed her, like in *The Exorcist* or some shit. She goes, 'No 'Summer of '69'. On pain of death, no 'Everything I Do, I Do It For You'. No 'I Will Always Love You'. No 'Love is All Around Me'. No 'Stand by Your Man'. No 'The Lion Sleeps Tonight'. No 'I Say a Little Prayer'. No 'Can't Take my Eyes off of You'. No 'Blame it on the Boogie'. No 'Celebration'.'

Karl's just there with his mouth wide open. She goes, 'No 'Staying Alive'. No 'Night Fever'. No Bee Gees at all. No 'Dancing Queen'. No 'Zorba's Dance'. And no karaoke favourites. No 'Sweet Caroline'. No 'Delilah'. No 'New York, New York'. No 'My Way'. No 'Like a Rhinestone Cowboy'. No 'Lady in Red'. No 'Green, Green Grass of Home' and *definitely* no 'Sex Bomb'. No songs you can do air guitar to. No 'Black Betty'. No 'Layla'. No 'Living on a Prayer'. No 'Jump' ...'

I'm about to interrupt, roysh, but she goes, 'No 'I'm Too Sexy' and no 'Deeply Dippy'. No 'Barbie Girl'. Nothing by the Vengaboys. No 'Don't Stop'. No 'I'm Horny'. No 'Jive Bunny'. No 'Love Shack'. Nothing Irish. No 'Fields of Athenry'. No 'In a Country Churchyard'. No *Riverdance*. No 'Irish Rover'. No 'Siege of Ennis'. No 'Fairytale of New York'. No 'Dirty Old Town'. No 'Fiesta'. Definitely no 'Ireland's Call'. And no national anthem. It's terribly working class ...'

I'm about to tell her, roysh, that she's bang out of order saying that about 'Ireland's Call', but I can't get a word in edgeways. She goes, 'No novelty songs. No *'Aon Focail Eile'*. No 'Mister Blobby'. No 'Frog Chorus'. No Christmas songs by Wizzard, Mud or Shakin' Stevens. No 'Respect'. No 'Red Red Wine'. No 'Stuck in the Middle with You'. No 'Relax'. No 'Reet Petite'. No 'You'll Never Walk Alone'. No 'Walk like an Egyptian'. No 'Walking on Sunshine'. No 'Pretty Woman'. No 'Shiny Happy People'. No 'Dancing on the Ceiling'. No 'Summer Loving'. No 'You're The One That I Want'. No 'Club Tropicana'. No 'Wake Me Up Before You Go-Go'. No 'Copacabana'. No 'Could This Be Magic?'. No 'Living Doll'. No 'Summer Holiday'. No 'Respectable'. No 'Feels Like I'm In Love'. No 'I'm in the Mood for Dancing'. Nothing by the Nolans, in fact.'

I sort of, like, get up, roysh, as if I'm about to go, but with a look she orders me to sit back down. She goes, 'No 'Let's Twist Again'. No 'Oh Carolina'. No 'Uptown Girl'. No 'Baggy Trousers'. No 'Land Down Under'. No 'Break my Stride'. No 'Like A Virgin' and no 'La Isla Bonita' either. No 'Rivers of Babylon'. No 'Rasputin'. No 'Yes Sir, I Can Boogie'. No 'Twist and Shout'. No 'Come on, Eileen'. No 'Moon of Love'. No *'Chanson l'Amour'*. No 'Five Hundred Miles' and no 'Letter from America'. No 'That's Amore'. No 'Bad Boys'. No 'What A Feeling'. Nothing from *Footloose* and nothing from *Flashdance*. No 'Pass the Duchie'. No 'I Don't Wanna Dance'. No 'Total Eclipse of the Heart'. Nothing by Bob Marley. It's poor people's music. No 'Perfect Day'. No 'Lust for Life'. No 'Don't You Want Me?'. Outside of that, everything's fine. Come on, Ross,' and she gets up to go. And Karl, roysh, he just shoots me a look that says, basically, you know, you have my sympathy, mate.

✱ ✱ ✱

So there I am, roysh, strolling down Grafton Street, taking in the sights, copping an eyeful of the scenario, when all of a sudden I nearly fall orse over tit over this stupid bitch begging outside, like, Bewley's. Of course, I was going to do my usual thing, which is, like, boot the cup down the street and then, when she's, like, scrambling around on her hands and knees trying to pick it all up, go, 'Good to see you're prepared to work for your money,' which always cracks the goys up. But this time, roysh, I didn't do it and the reason was that I recognised the bird who was begging. Or at least I thought I did. I'm there, 'Claire?' and she looks at me in, like, total shock and we're talking *total* shock. This is Claire as in Sorcha's bridesmaid, as in Dalkey wannabe, who actually comes from Bray of all places. I'm there, 'What the *fock* are you doing? I take it that summer job in USIT fell through?' and she goes, '*Ssshhh!* Pretend you don't recognise me,' and of course I'm there, 'With focking pleasure. Wouldn't do much for my street cred to be caught talking to a pile of focking gorbage.'

So I'm about to walk away, roysh, but I just have to turn back, roysh, and I go, 'Okay, the curiosity is killing me. What's the focking Jackanory?' She goes, 'If you MUST know, Ross, this is part of my thesis. I'm doing, like, social studies? I'm doing it on the plight of the poor in our society and I'm trying to find out how little these beggars have to get by on.' She SO wants to be Sorcha it's not funny.

There's about three euro in change in the little Wrigley's box in front of her. I'm like, 'Not doing very well, are you? Do you the think the cappuccino there is putting people off?' She's *actually* got a big frothy coffee from, like, Butler's on the ground beside her. She goes, 'HELLO? I'm entitled to a coffee break, you know.'

I'm just there cracking up, going, 'This I've *got* to tell the goys,' and I'm just turning around to, like, walk away, roysh, when who do I literally bump into only the one person who always seems to, like, materialise – if that's the roysh word – whenever you're in a really embarrassing situation. We're talking Erika. For the first time basically ever, roysh, she actually looks pleased to see Claire.

She goes to me, 'When I saw you talking to a vagrant, Ross, I really thought Princess Diana was storting to rub off on you.' That's, like, her name for Sorcha. I try to, like, deflect the heat away from me, roysh, pointing at Claire and giving it, 'What's she focking like, huh?' and Erika just gives her this – I think the word is, like, withering – look and goes, 'Going back to your roots, Claire?' and Claire, roysh, storts going, 'It's ACTUALLY for my thesis? It's on the plight of the poor in our society. Not that you'd know anything about *them*?' and Erika goes, 'I'm proud to say I don't, dear. Still, I'm sure I'll get to meet your family one day.'

Of course Claire's trying to come up with something clever to say back, roysh, but you never can with Erika because she's a last-word freak. The next thing, roysh, she whips out her mobile phone which has got, like, a camera on it, hands me her Pia Bang bags, takes five steps backwards and takes a picture of Claire, huddled up in the doorway under a blanket like a tramp. As she's checking the picture, she's going, 'Wonder what Sorcha will think when she finds out about her bridesmaid's double-life,' then she looks at Claire and storts giving it, 'It's amazing how at home you look.' So at this point, roysh, Claire does basically the worst thing you can do with Erika and that's, like, show weakness, except she actually shows more than weakness, she just, like, bursts into tears. Erika goes, 'I think you'd be a lot happier, Claire, if you just accepted what you are. *This*. Anyway, must dash. Meeting a gorgeous man for lunch in Shanahan's. Owns half of Kildare,' and off she saunters, full of herself, and I'm there thinking, I got off pretty lightly there. I go to walk off myself, roysh, but Claire's there blubbering away and, being the nice goy that I am, I turn back and ask her is she, like, alroysh. She's there, 'Why is she SUCH a bitch to me?' and I go, 'Come on, Claire, you *know* why.' She's like, 'Do you think if I could change the fact that I come from Bray, I wouldn't?' I'm there, 'Doesn't make it roysh, though,' and she goes, 'I know. And it's something I'm going to have to live with for the rest of my life, Ross. But it doesn't help when people keep rubbing your nose in it every day.'

I don't answer, roysh. I'm on Erika's side on this one and I don't want to be, like, two-faced. Claire goes, 'What time is it?' and I'm there, 'Four o'clock,' and she's like, 'Been out an hour. Think I'll call it a day,' and she whips off this blanket thing she's got around her, roysh, and underneath she's got on what she usually wears, we're talking pink Ralph, blue jeans and Dubes. She goes, 'Do you want to go for a drink?' and I say yes, roysh, because, well, the girl was upset, needs a shoulder to cry on, blah blah blah, and you know me, roysh, I'd drink with basically anyone. So we end up hitting The Bailey and I get a round in, pint of Ken for me, vodka and Diet 7-Up for her and it's not long, roysh, before she storts pouring her hort out to me, telling me how Sorcha has *totally* lost the plot over this wedding and I'm there, 'HELLO? I'm marrying the girl. You think I don't know?' She goes, 'OH! MY! GOD! She ACTUALLY told me I needed to go to Weight Watchers. I'm like, HELLO?' I'm there, 'No way,' wondering is she going to get a round in tonight at all. She goes, 'I'm, like, eight stone, Ross. I'm there, "If you want me to lose weight, Sorcha, I will. Oh my God, I SO will." So I, like, signed up to the same Weight Watchers she goes to. I am going to lose SO much weight, it's going to *totally* wreck her head.'

So I suddenly find myself telling her a few of my own Sorcha stories. How she's sending out a reminder to all guests over the age of forty that she doesn't want them wearing pastels because they look cheap. How she told her grandmother – her *own* grandmother – not to smile in the photographs unless she gets a job done on her teeth. I'm there, 'Now she's signing up for some focking diamond course. Won't choose the engagement ring until she knows everything there is to know about diamonds.' Claire goes, *'The four Cs – Clarity. Cut. Colour. Carat.'* It's not a bad impression actually. She goes, *'OH! MY! GOD! I am SO getting a cold sore. Claire, am I getting a cold sore?'* She says Sorcha's a total Bridezilla and I go, 'Yeah, and we're talking totally here,' and she's like, 'I have to say, though, I love how you proposed,' and I'm there, 'Really? What did she tell you?' She goes, 'How you took her to the place where you first ... you know.' I'm like, 'JP's old Daihatsu Charade?' and she goes, 'No. Where you first, like, kissed. Where the Forum cinema used to be in Glasthule. You got down on one knee, in the middle of a rain-soaked street, and said, "I want to have that first night together every night for the rest of our lives. Sorcha, will you marry me?" That is, like, SO incredible,' and I'm thinking, Where is Sorcha getting this shit from? Anyway, roysh, you can pretty much guess where this is going, three or four drinks later Claire's storted, like, flirting her orse off with me, the hand-on-the-knee bit and everything. Even though I've never actually found Claire attractive, roysh, what with her being a mutt and everything, four or five pints later, with the old beer goggles on, I've pretty much decided I'm going to bail in there, bridesmaid or no bridesmaid.

I swear to God, roysh, getting engaged is the most surefire way of getting your end away on a regular basis. Before I asked Sorcha to marry me, roysh, I was sitting at home most nights watching the Tracey Shaw aerobics video and strangling Kojak. Now every bird and her sister wants to get it on with me. Even Sorcha's friends. No, *especially* Sorcha's friends. Birds are like that, basically always trying to prove something by getting one over on each other – *Oooh, Ross is marrying Sorcha, so I have to prove that I could have him if I wanted him* – and I'll tell you something for basically nothing, that's fine by me.

There's no discussion on the subject, roysh, it's basically taken for granted that me and her are getting it on the second we leave here, though the only problem is where. She lives in Bray obviously, but her old pair are in her gaff at the moment and she says they wouldn't approve of me and her doing the bould thing under their roof, especially given that they know I'm marrying their daughter's best friend. They might think I'm a bit of a dirtbag. Of course my gaff is out for pretty much the same reasons, so Claire comes up with this idea, roysh.

She looks after this old biddy who lives in some focking sheltered housing scheme in Bray – *wants* to be Sorcha, I told you – and it turns out the stupid wench is in hospital at the moment, getting a new hip or some shit. She goes, 'I've got the keys. We won't be disturbed there.'

Course I'm Kool and the Gang with this, roysh. It's, like, forty focking bills in a Jo, but I'd spend that in an average night in Annabel's and not be guaranteed my Nat King, so it's, like, happy days, fock it if the gaff is cold and smells of cats and focking stewing beef.

One thing I didn't like, roysh, was the idea of doing it in some old dear's bed, but of course when the passion takes over you couldn't keep me away with a focking cattle prod. Don't need to paint you a picture I'm sure, but basically I did the business and then dozed off, as did Claire, who had a big smile on her boat and kept going, 'I can't believe I just slept with Sorcha Lalor's fiancé. That is, like SO cool.'

And it was, roysh, until – old story – the next morning. Seven o'clock, roysh, I wake up and she's screaming the house down, going, 'GET UP! GET UP!' and of course the first thing that crosses my mind, roysh, is that Miss Marple's back, taking the new hip for a test drive or some shit. But that's not it. She's going, 'What the FOCK is that smell? OH MY GOD, I think I'm going to puke,' and fair enough, roysh, the pen in the room is Padraig alroysh and I'm finding it hord to a take a focking breath.

So I hop out of the bed, roysh, lash on the light and it turns out the whole room is just full of, like, steam. Claire pegs it out the door and storts, like, borfing her ring up in the jacks because all of a sudden, roysh, she's copped what it is. But of course she lets me stand there breathing it in for another ten minutes before she tells me. Cut a long story short, roysh, Claire turned on the electric blanket before we hopped in the sack. It turns out this old biddy has problems with her plumbing, if you know what I mean. Course Claire forgot there was a focking incontinence sheet on the bed. Don't need to explain the rest to you. Didn't do physics, but I still understand it. Claire's still blowing chunks when I head into the bathroom and tell her I'm hitting the road. She goes, 'You're not leaving me like this are you?' – vom all over her chin – and I'm just like, 'Yeah. I think I can take it for granted that neither of us will be telling Sorcha about this?'

✳ ✳ ✳

This one night, roysh, me and Sorcha were supposed to be learning the foxtrot or some shit, but I basically couldn't be orsed with these stupid classes anymore, so I told her my knee was sore, an old rugby injury, and she was there, 'OH! MY! GOD! That's like, *Aaaahhh!*' and I was just there giving it, 'Yeah, it's a total bummer. Means I can't go dancing tonight, which is a bitch,' and she's going, 'OH my God, you take care of yourself, Chicken.' Didn't expect her to take it so well, and I actually thought about breaking the news to her there and then, roysh, that me and the goys are focking off to Australia for the World Cup and I'm not going to be back until basically four weeks before the wedding, but in the end I decided not to, like, push my luck and that I'll tell her closer to the date. The main reason I didn't want to go, roysh – aport from feeling like a complete tit in front of a roomful of strangers – was because the old man was holding his first Press conference to support that tool of a solicitor of his. The whole thing's a total joke. We're talking, like, totally as well. The stupid dickhead had two thousand posters printed up with, like, **FREE HENNESSY** in big letters on them, and of course people were, like, ringing the gaff, asking where they could collect their brandy, basically ripping the total piss.

Oisinn rang one night putting on this, like, skobie voice and I was on the other line listening in to the old man going ballistic, giving it, 'Don't try to guilt-trip me, they have hostels for you and your ilk. Free brandy? The very idea of it! You'll get no handouts from me,' and of course I'm doubled up on the floor at this stage.

So me, Oisinn and JP, roysh, the three of us end up getting pretty tanked up, we're talking eight or nine pints here, and we hit the Berkeley Court for the Press conference, cracking our shites laughing when we see Dick Features there in his best tin of fruit with a dirty big cigar between his fingers. He's chatting away to some bird from RTÉ, but the second he sees me, roysh, he's straight over, shaking my hand and giving it, 'Kicker! You and your pals have come! I knew you wouldn't let me down,' and I'm like, 'Get a focking life. I'm here to rip the piss.'

He just ignores this, roysh, and storts, like, scanning the room, going, 'Don't see Kerrigan here. Scared to come along, I expect. Afraid he might learn something.' Then it's like – and I swear, these are his words – he goes, 'Time for the kick-off I think. There's an innocent man out there tonight, languishing in the misery of not being allowed to see his family. Excuse me, chaps. I have a fight for justice to attend to.' I reckon I could get the focker certified. So he heads up to the top of the room, roysh, sits down at this table with two of his asshole mates from Portmornock – Eduard is one, only know the other dude to see, a tosser like him – and there's this, like, banner behind them and it's like, Bring Him Home. All of the, like, journalists I suppose, they take their seats and the old man storts going, 'It's nice to see that in these days, when there's so much sensationalism in our newspapers, that some of you have managed to tear yourselves away from the tribunals and what-not to write about a real scandal that is affecting real lives. Hennessy. Coghlan. O'Hara ... The name will mean nothing to most of you. To others, he is a husband. A father. A golfer.'

And before he gets a chance to finish, roysh, this one dude stands up and goes, 'You've called your campaign the Bring Him Home campaign, which implies that he's being held against his will. The truth is, he absconded from Ireland to avoid serious fraud and tax-evasion charges. Surely if he wants to be brought home, all he needs to do is to go to the airport in Rio de Janeiro and buy a ticket?'

The old man, roysh, he's focking bulling at this. He goes, 'And face the Star Chamber up at Dublin Castle? *Can you remember this?* and *Can you remember that?* People like yourself digging up the bones of the past – how many bank accounts does he have? How much money does he have in Bulgaria? How many times has he changed his name?' All of a sudden, roysh, JP shouts at the top of his voice, 'THE MAN SHOULD HANG FOR WHAT HE'S DONE!' and everyone turns around, but of course the old man – he's blind as a focking bat – he's straining to see who shouted it, but he can't.

Then this bird from TV3 gets up and she goes, 'Have you spoken to Frank yourself and if so, how is he?' and the old man's like, 'HIS NAME'S HENNESSY NOW! He made a mistake when he was younger and he didn't want to spend the rest of his life paying for it. And yes, I have spoken to him. He's bearing up okay. Of course he misses his beautiful wife, who sadly couldn't be with us here today – her Irish Countrywomen's Association night and so forth, but her apologies will be duly noted in the minutes. And their lovely daughter, Lauren. But he's, em, let's just say he's putting a brave face on things.' Too roysh he is. I was the one who took the call the other night. The dude was coked off his tits and I could hear at least two birds giggling away in the background, fair focks to the dude.

All of a sudden, JP shouts, 'IF THAT HOMEY COMES BACK HERE, I'M GONNA POP A CAP IN THE MOTHER'S ASS,' and me and Oisinn crack our holes laughing and, like, high-five each other. The old man goes, 'Can we ignore the hecklers at the back. They're obviously plants. I would have thought Bertie Stadium had enough to worry about what with his women and their carry-on. The point I want to get across here is that this campaign against Hennessy is part of a wider conspiracy against the revenue-generating classes to try to get us to apologise for who we are.'

Oisinn stands up and shouts, 'I WON'T REST TILL I SEE THAT MAN SWINGING FROM THE GALLOWS,' and the old man, who still can't make out who it is, goes, 'Tell your boss we all thought the wedding was wonderful. Very classy.' This goes on for, like, twenty minutes, roysh, and when it all breaks up, a few of the Press people come down to where we're sitting and stort chatting to the goys, and I actually have to move away, roysh, because JP's telling them that his name's Toby and Hennessy conned his old dear out of her life-savings, which is total bullshit, and Oisinn – Eddie, he calls himself – is telling them his grandmother died homeless and basically on the game because the dude took her house away. I'm sitting there down the back, roysh, texting Sorcha, telling her I'm in bed, resting the old knee, when the old man comes over and goes, 'Think that went rather well. And you can take that woe-is-me expression off your face, Kicker. I'll have the man's name cleared inside six weeks. Quote-unquote.'

✳ ✳ ✳

'Well, what did *you* have in mind?' That's Sorcha's answer, roysh, whenever I raise even the slightest objection to basically anything. We're in her room, roysh, doing the table plan, for which, incidentally, she's got her cousin, who's an architect – and also a total focking tosser, but that's another story – to draw up a plan of the ballroom of the Berkeley Court and she's, like, photocopied this maybe two hundred times and she's trying out different combinations of people at different tables. There's, like, forty or fifty of these plans crumpled up on the floor, that's how much thought is going into it. She's there, like, sucking on the top of her pen, roysh, when all of a sudden she looks at me, roysh, and she goes, 'What? I can tell from your face that you're pissed off about something. What is it?' I'm like, 'They're our *grandparents*, Sorcha. You've put them as far away from the top table as it's possible to be. Behind a pillar,' and she goes, 'I've told you before, Ross. They're just going to have to understand that the theme of the wedding is youth.' I'm there, 'I thought it was cranberries?' and she shoots me a filthy and goes, 'It's cranberries *and* youth. It'd look a bit stupid, Ross, having all these young and beautiful people all around here,' and she sort of, like, sweeps the pen across the page, 'and then this table of old fogies bang in the middle. It's them I'm thinking of, Ross. I don't think they'd be comfortable.' I go, 'How does your old dear feel about her mother having to sit next to the emergency exit?' and she goes, 'She's *actually* with me on this one, Ross. She knows how noisy old people are when they eat. Oh I know it's not *their* fault they have dentures. I mean, when Gran grew up there was no fluoride in the water.' I don't answer, roysh, and of course then Sorcha gets in a total snot with me, pushing the page across at me and going, 'Let's see *you* try then,' and I grab the pen off her, roysh, and get to work. One of the things I noticed about her table plans – this *had* to be intentional – was that she put all of the good-looking birds out of my line of vision, we're talking Amie, Sophie, Melissa, Emer, Chloe, Emma, Melanie. And the single ones, roysh – as in Sophie, Melissa, Emma and Melanie – she's put sitting next to complete tossers, mostly her cousins who she wants to, as she puts it, fix up.

So I redo the plan, roysh, putting all the best-looking honeys at one table, roysh at the front, where I can see them. Then I put all the goys – we're talking JP, we're talking Oisinn, we're talking Fionn – roysh in front of the top table, within high-fiving distance of me. Then, working off the guest list, I find places for everyone else while Sorcha just, like, tuts and shakes her head. When I pass it back to her, roysh, she throws her eyes up to heaven before she even looks at it, but then she does look at it and she goes, 'Where are your mum and dad?' and I'm like, 'Oh, did I not put them in?' She's there, 'You did. But you have them at the back of the room. Ross, it's traditional for the parents to sit at the top table with the bride and groom,' and I go, 'But they're orseholes, Sorcha.'

She goes, 'And why have you got all the girls lumped together at one table. I want Sophie next to Simon. OH MY GOD! They would look SO cute together. He is earning a *fortune* in architecture. And Melissa. Why would she want to sit next to Emma and Melanie? She, like, sees them every day of the week. She wants a man, Ross.' And she storts, like, scribbling away, basically undoing all of my suggestions, as in, you've had your chance to say what you want, now we'll do it my way. She's there, 'I'm *supposed* to be going to the States in the morning.' She's going to New York for the weekend with her old dear and her sister to, like, buy the dress, some Vera Wang number she saw in a magazine.

She goes, 'Probably would have got through this in – HELLO? – *half* the time if you were, like, a bit more supportive?' and she carries on scribbling, roysh, in a way that says, I don't know, Do Not Disturb, Bridezilla At Work. Ten minutes later it's finished, roysh, and it's exactly the same as the one she showed me to begin with, we're talking oldies at the back, parents at the top table and all the quality scenario sitting next to some of the biggest wankers in the world. Strawberries to a donkey. Then I cop something, roysh. Someone's missing. I'm there, 'You haven't got Erika down here,' and she goes, 'I have. Look again,' and I do, roysh, and I cannot focking believe it, there is GOING to be World War Two – or wherever we're up to – when she finds out. She's put her at the table, roysh, with the grannies, worst seat in the house basically, behind a pillar, with her back to the top table. I go, 'Sorcha, she'll go ballistic,' but Sorcha's just like, 'It's *my* day, Ross, not hers. She's *supposed* to be turning up in some Maria Grachvogel number. Not a Debenham's one. She's going *away* to buy it. It'll be white, naturally. Let's see how good it looks next to Gran's Marks & Spencer's suit in peach.'

CHAPTER SIX
In Sickness and in Health

I know if I don't go and get fitted for my tin of fruit, I'll never hear the end of it, roysh, so I go in on Saturday afternoon – still making the old man pay for Jo Maxis for me everywhere – hit BTs and end up getting suited-up in less time than it takes to talk an Orts fresher into the old Margaret Thatcher, in other words fifteen minutes. Saw what I wanted straight off, roysh, an Armani tux, we're talking two-and-a-half focking Ks here, lashed it on the old man's cord and that was it.

The dude who was, like, measuring me up, roysh, I actually know him to see, basically from the circuit, we're talking Cocoon, Ron Black's, Lillie's, Reynord's. Fancies himself as a bit of a player on the ladies front and you can see, roysh, as he's measuring my neck, he's thinking, There goes the competition, and I'm thinking, Don't count on it, dude. He storts, like, asking me about the wedding, roysh, really rubbing it in, and I end up telling him I'm only doing it for tax reasons, making sure he knows I'm not out of the game yet, but he thinks I'm joking. He goes, 'Will you be needing a dicky bow with that?' and I'm there, 'Certainly will.' He goes, 'Black?' and I'm like, 'No, er, cranberry,' and he sort of, like, smirks to himself, roysh, obviously thinking, This goy is totally pussy-whipped.

So I hand over the cord, roysh, to pay for the lot and when I've signed the receipt, I pick up my bags and I go, 'Don't get *too* complacent, that's all I'm saying,' and he looks at me, roysh, like he hasn't got a bog what I'm talking about. I'm there, 'Don't, that's all I'm saying.' I go back out onto Grafton Street and it's true what JP says, roysh, there's nowhere in the world like it for scenario. I give a few birds the old mince pies, roysh, and the Ross half-smile and I get a few long looks back and it's nice to know that the magic's still there. I don't know if I'm having what you'd call pre-wedding jitters. It's just that Sorcha's putting so much of herself into organising *the* social event of 2003, she doesn't have any time for *us* anymore. Then totally out of the blue, roysh, the solution hits me – get hammered.

So I saunter up to Stephen's Green, roysh, put the tin in the back of a Jo, give the driver the address and thirty sheets and tell him that if he thinks of it to tell the goy who opens the door that I said he's the biggest penis who's ever lived and then I give him another ten bills for that. All I need now is a portner in crime. Usually, I'd ring Christian, roysh, but him and Lauren have gone to focking Brazil to see her old man. JP's at the opening of some new housing scheme in middle of bogland, the sales pitch for which is, 'Tullamore – the commuter belt just went up another notch!' I text Oisinn, but he texts me back saying he's up to his ears in jasmine and amber accords and as a last resort, roysh, I give Fionn a bell, but he's helping some cracker from first year Orts with some 'extracurricular work', the jammy focker. So there's nothing else to do, roysh, except get hammered on my own. I hit The Bailey, roysh, and knock back two pints of Ken so fast that I'm half expecting a tap on the shoulder from Norris McWhirter, except he's dead. I do get a tap on the shoulder, though, and I hear this real, I don't know, faggoty voice go, 'Well *heeelllo*,' and I spin around quickly, roysh, and who is it only Trevor, this dance teacher Sorcha has us going to. He goes, 'Hey, don't look so shocked, Ross. I said, "Hello", not, "I wanna bum you",' and I'm like, 'Oh. Em, yeah, sorry Trevor. Look, can I get you a beer? Or a white wine?' and he laughs and goes, 'Beer is fine. Might make a man of me, huh? Budweiser. And not a glass, before you ask,' and I'm thinking, this goy's a focking mind-reader. I go, 'What's the story with you? You meeting someone?' and he's like, 'No, looks like I've been stood up. Was supposed to meet the girls but they're missing – presumed spending – in BTs. You know what we're like with a credit cord. Hey, how's Sorcha? Did she get a dress?' I put the pint in front of the dude and I go, 'She went to New York yesterday. Haven't heard from her yet.' He goes, 'Oh and I bet she has them tearing their hair out in Vera Wang! She's an amazing girl, Ross,' and I'm there, 'Amazing.' He goes, 'Such a sweet, caring soul,' and I'm there, 'Caring, yeah.' He goes, 'But when she gets that bit between her teeth ...' and I'm like, 'Unstoppable. Yeah, when she takes something on, it gets all her attention. She doesn't, like, see anything else.' He goes, 'But you like that, right?' and I'm there, 'Sometimes.'

The goy sort of, like, pulls back and looks at me, roysh, and goes, 'Am I hearing the teeniest, weeniest bit of doubt in your voice, Ross?' and never having realised before how easy these kind of people are to talk to, roysh, I end up going, 'It's just that I used to be the centre of her world until I asked her to marry me.' He goes, 'Ross, I'm fortunate enough to meet maybe three or four hundred couples a year in the same boat as you and Sorcha. Setting out on the great turbulent adventure that is marriage. Let me tell you, what you're feeling is normal. You love her, right? I mean, how could you not? She told me how you proposed. *Oooh* you little Lothario.'

I'm there, 'What did she tell you?' and he goes, 'The whole nine yards, baby. You took her up in a hot-air balloon and just as the sun was setting you fell to one knee and said, "Be with me forever, Sorcha, marry me".' Where is she getting this shit from? He goes, 'I don't blame her for saying yes. The bitch! I'd have taken your hand off myself.' I sort of, like, shift in my seat, trying my best not to look uncomfortable. He goes, 'Ross, you've got nothing to worry about from me. You rugby boys have got far too much testosterone to be my kind of fag. Do I scare you?' and I'm there – again, really easy to talk to – I'm there, 'Not *scare* as such. It's just that I don't *get* what you do. I mean – I don't know the roysh word here – bumming each other?' He just, like, shakes his head, roysh, and goes, 'There's a sign on my butt, Ross, that says Exit Only. We're not all into *that*. There are other pleasures. You want I educate you?' and I'm there, 'Educate me?' He goes, 'Let's go to The George,' and I'm there, 'I take it you're not refer-ring to the Royal St George Yacht Club in Dún Laoghaire?' He's like, 'You know what I'm referring to,' and I go, 'Trevor, no offence, roysh, but it's for, like, steamers.'

He just, like, drains the rest of his pint, roysh – he can stick them away, Stoke or not, fair focks to him – and he goes, 'Come on, drop that rugby jock façade for an hour and you might just enjoy yourself,' and he gets up, roysh, and again I don't know why – they're very, I don't know, persuasive, aren't they? – I end up following him and the next thing I know, roysh, I'm walking into Dublin's very own Blue Oyster, thinking if anyone sees me I'm going to end up having sixty or seventy thousand broken-horted birds on my conscience.

Don't know what I'm expecting, roysh, maybe blokes in droopy moustaches and leather waistcoats and caps, and even though there a few of *them*, roysh, it has to be said that most of the people in there actually look quite normal. Trevor introduces me to some of his friends, roysh, some who are obviously a bit ... funny, and some who you'd never know it to look at them. He goes to everyone, 'Girls, this is Ross O'Carroll-Kelly, the worst dancer I have *ever* seen,' and all the goys crack their holes laughing, roysh, and high-five each other, a bit like me and the goys do.

I hadn't actually realised this, roysh, but for the first half-an-hour in there I sort of, like, subconsciously had the cheeks of my orse tightly shut. I mean, you basically couldn't have swiped your focking Visa cord between my butt cheeks. But after a while, roysh, I actually storted to relax and basically enjoy myself. So the next thing, roysh, there's goys coming from everywhere to talk to me, in other words try to chat me up. I could see them checking me out, especially the old bod, because I actually have a serious set of pecs on me at the moment. They're asking me all about my rugby, blah blah blah, and not being big-headed or anything, roysh, but I think I actually became a bit of a gay icon, the fact that I'm, like, unattainable probably adding to the attraction. Despite myself, roysh, I actually end up having the best night I've had in ages. Not exaggerating here, roysh, but not one bloke felt my orse. I even felt comfortable enough to go to the can on my own. So the end of the night, roysh, me and Trevor are there just, like, vibing off each other. I'm, like, pointing out blokes and asking him if he fancies them, roysh, and if so what it is he likes about them. I point out one dude – we're talking make-up, the lot – and he shakes his head and goes, 'Oh, no! Too much of a queen!' and I look at him as if to say, you know, that's a case of the pot calling the kettle an asylum-seeker.

He goes, 'Hey, I'm as camp as a field of pink tents, I know. But guys like that make *me* homophobic,' and I end up nearly spitting beer all over the place. I'm there, 'What about that goy over there?' and he's like, 'Him? He's straight,' and I go, 'I don't know, that T-shirt's very tight, Trevor.' He's like, 'Take it from me, Ross. He's too self-conscious. He might be a little confused, but trust me, he's straight. We can pick up on these things. Why do you think no one's tried to chat him up all night?' and I'm there, 'But I'm straight and loads of goys have tried to chat me up,' but he doesn't answer, just smiles.

Then he goes, 'Okay, Ross, you've had your education, now run along. This is a pick-up joint, not a circus,' and I stand up and I go, 'I'd a good night tonight. I'm probably a bit, I don't know, wiser.' He goes, 'If you're talking to Sorcha, tell her from me she's one lucky girl.' And as I'm walking out of there, roysh, I know – not being a dickhead or anything because I don't mind – but I know the goy is checking out my orse.

✳ ✳ ✳

I'm sitting in, roysh, watching, of all things, 'Coronation Street', when the phone rings and I end up answering and it turns out it's, like, Sorcha, phoning from New York. I'm there, 'Hey, how's things in the Windy City?' and she just goes, 'We're about to go into Vera Wang. OH! MY! GOD! I am SO dreading it,' and I'm there, 'Why?' and she's like, 'Had dinner at the Waldorf Astoria last night – Mum's treat – and I feel like SUCH a whale.' I'm there, 'You'll be fine,' thinking that Candice has actually blossomed in the last few months, roysh, to the point where she's knocking spots off Sarah Louise. Sorcha goes, 'Anyway, haven't got time to chat. The reason I'm ringing – will you phone the Berkeley Court and tell them I've settled on the napkin folds I want?' and I'm there, 'Right,' obviously only half-listening. She goes, 'For the top table, I want a flower tuck, and if they don't know what that is, you fold the napkin in thirds and position it with the open edge at the top. Then you fold the top layer down by about an inch, then fold again by the same amount, so that the napkin edge is now tucked underneath. Then you turn the napkin over, fold one end in halfway to the napkin's centre and repeat with the other end. Then fold both ends in again so they meet in the middle, trim the stem of a gerbera daisy – no, an orchid, cranberry-coloured – and slip the flower into the gap in the centre. Did you get all that?' and I'm there, 'Every word.'

That Peter Barlow's some lad, giving it to Shelly and the bird in the florists. Reminds me of myself in my heyday. Sorcha's like, 'Now, for the rest of the tables I want cutlery pockets and, in case they ask, you fold the napkin in thirds and position it with the open edge at the top. Fold the top layer down by about one-and-a-half inches. Turn the napkin over, fold the ends over to meet in the middle, then fold the napkin in half so that the ends are inside. Slip the silverware inside the pocket and tuck the place card under the cuff.' I'm there, 'Okay,' and she's like, 'Did you write all that down?' and I'm there, 'Of course,' and she goes, 'Read it back to me then,' and I'm like, 'Em. Hello? Hello? Sorcha, you're breaking up. Hello?' then I blow into the phone four times and then – childish, I know – hang up.

✳ ✳ ✳

Talk about stepping down memory lane. I'm in – of all places – Hilper's with a couple of the goys, and I'm not sure if it's my imagination, roysh, but the birds in Orts actually seem to be getting better-looking. There's two of them hanging off Fionn, who it has to be said has a lot more honeys hanging off him these days now that he's in a position to decide whether they've passed or failed their exams. Swear to God, roysh, these two birds hordly even look at me. They go off and when JP asks me what I think, roysh, I shrug my shoulders as if to say, I could take them or leave them.

Oisinn arrives back from the can and goes, 'I think it's going to be ready, Ross. *Eau d'Affluence.* I'll have it finished in time for the wedding. Have to say, the sandalwood and the citrus accords are working better than I thought they would together. All I need now is one more secret ingredient, which I should be able to pick up in Australia.' Fionn's there, 'Speaking of which, have you told Sorcha that you're going to Australia yet?' and I'm like, 'I'm picking my moment. What business is it of yours?' and he goes, 'Chillax, Ross. I was only asking,' and he's trying to make it look like I'm totally over-reacting, roysh, like he's *not* trying to get in there himself? I go, 'I'm telling her when she gets back from the States. Stop trying to make an issue out of it Fionn,' but he just, like, laughs in my face.

Oisinn goes, 'Will you two faggots give it up?' and I'm there, 'Oisinn, do you have to use words like that?' He's like, 'What? Faggot?' and I go, 'Yeah. Look, I'm not saying I agree with what these people do, roysh, but some of them are, like, normal blokes,' and the two of them look at each other like I've suddenly storted talking Greek or some shit. Fionn goes, 'This *is* the same Ross O'Carroll-Kelly who, when I brought one of my friends from the Gay Society into this very bor, refused to go to the toilet on his own in case he followed you in?' I'm there, 'That was, like, two years ago.' He goes, 'And asked Christian to keep an eye on your drink when you were gone in case he slipped something into it?' and I'm like, 'Can we drop the subject? I was just making a point that they can't help it if they were born a bit ... funny.'

Oisinn goes, 'Hey, have you heard from Christian?' and I'm there, 'He rang last night. Said they're staying on another week. Hennessy's very depressed apparently. Wants to come home,' and Oisinn goes, 'He thinks he's depressed now? Wait'll he sees the room they've got reserved for him in the Joy,' and I'm there, 'Totally.'

So we carry on sitting there, roysh, knocking back a few slow ones, when all of a sudden my phone rings and of course my first instinct is that it must be Sorcha, checking did I go to the florists to get them to order in the Birds of Paradise that she's going to, like, present to her old dear at the reception. I didn't, of course. But it's not her at all, roysh, it's JP and he's having a major knicker-fit, and when I say major I mean total. I'm going, 'Slow down, slow down, I can't hear you,' and he's going, 'Apologies for not making myself understood, dude. Just wondered whether you'd had the chance to peruse today's *Irish Times*,' and I'm there, 'I'm not much of a reader, JP. You know that.' He goes, 'I'll distill it for you then. They're upsizing Donnybrook,' and I'm there, 'The ground? Cool,' bluffing, of course, because I haven't a focking bog what upsizing means, though it sounds like it could be a good thing. He goes, 'And they're knocking down the Bective Pavilion.'

That I understand. I'm just there, like, frozen to the seat. He goes, 'Say something.' Oisinn and Fionn have copped my face, roysh, and they're giving it, 'What's wrong, Ross?' I'm like, 'Bective? You mean Bective disco's going to be ... *gone*?' and the two goys' jaws drop as well. JP goes, 'Direct hit, Ross. Got it in one,' and I'm like, 'But that's where I got my first ...' and he goes, 'Me too.' I'm like, '*And* that's where I got my first bit of ...' and he goes, 'Same for all of us, Ross. The place should have a preservation order slapped on it. It's a shrine to our coming of age.' I just shake my head and I go, 'Presumably they'll put some kind of plaque up, just to say this is the spot where thousands of goys—' and JP loses it, roysh, and storts going, 'A plaque? Is that all it was worth? Are you going to settle for that? Or are you and the rest of the goys going to fight this thing with me?' I'm there, 'You've got me on your side, JP, you *know* that. And judging from Fionn and Oisinn's faces, they're on board, too,' and he goes, 'With ticket for passage. Ten-four, Ross. You're coming in loud and clear. Look, I know you've got a lot on your plate with the wedding. Must be pretty stressful. But I'm proposing a picket of Donnybrook in two weeks' time.' I'm there, 'Who are they playing?' a bit pissed off that I'm going to have to miss an actual match. He goes, 'No, we're not picketing it during a match. It'd be unfair to take it out on Drico, Victor and the goys. No, we'll choose a quiet Tuesday afternoon or something, when no one's around.'

* * *

Get a text message, roysh, and it's from, like, Trevor and he's just there, **Hope u gt hme alrite. Remembr d secrt 2 gr8 dancin is relxation. Ur goin 2 b fine.**

* * *

'You're what?' she goes. How could I have thought she'd be cool about it? She goes, '*Australia?*' and I'm there, 'For the rugby World Cup.' She goes, 'I don't care what it's *for*, Ross, it's out of the question,' and she goes, 'and stop making faces.' How the fock did she know that, she's on the other end of the phone? I'm there, 'It's not fair. All the other goys are allowed to go,' and she goes, 'All the other goys aren't getting married in fourteen weeks' time, Ross. There's things to do.'

I'm there, 'Yeah, the goys said this would happen,' and she goes, 'What would happen?' suddenly all concerned. I'm there, 'No, just leave it,' and she's like, 'No, Ross, if someone's saying stuff about me, I'd like to know.' I'm there, 'Okay, they just said that you were a bit possessive, that as soon as you got a ring on your finger, you'd have me under the thumb,' all total bullshit, of course.

She actually sounds a bit more upset than I expected, roysh, there's this, like, quiver in her voice, and she goes, 'But that is SO not the case.' I'm there, 'You know that, Sorcha. And I know that. But that's how it's going to look if I'm the only one who doesn't go. I'm thinking about *you* here as much as me.'

I count the seconds. One. Two. Three. Four. Five. Six. Seven. Eight. Nine. Ten. She goes, 'OH MY GOD, I am being SUCH a self-ish bitch. If Lauren's cool about Christian going, why can't I be cool with the idea of you going? I mean, *I'm* going to Paris with Mum and the girls for the underwear and you didn't complain. I'm, like, SO sorry, Ross.' I'm there, 'I'm sure you are,' making her feel like a shit for a few minutes longer, and she goes, 'I can be, like, SO hord on you at times. I'm SO sorry,' and eventually I'm there, 'Apology accepted.'

✳ ✳ ✳

The old dear comes into my room, roysh, totally uninvited, and goes, 'Oh, Ross, your father and I have bought the most wonderful Newbridge Jewellery neckpiece for Sorcha. It's inset with Swarovski sparkling ice crystals. It may or may not go with her dress, but her mother thinks she might well wear it with her going-away outfit.'

❋ ❋ ❋

Call out to Sorcha's gaff on Wednesday night. Sister answers the door, roysh, Orpha, or Aifric, or whatever the fock her name is, all I know is she's done a lot of growing up since that time I was with her, nice rack, brace gone from her Tony Smeeth, and she's basically flirting her orse off with me, roysh, I'm like, 'Is Sorcha in?' and she's there giving it, 'How come you never call to see *me*?'

I just, like, walk straight past her, roysh, but I can feel her mince pies following me up the stairs and into Sorcha's room and there's Sorcha, roysh, lying on the floor doing, like, sit-ups. I'm there, 'Didn't get a chance to ask you on the phone last night, how was the States?' and she goes, 'Make it quick, Ross. I've got Weight Watchers tonight,' and she's obviously in another Robbie. I stand at the door and I'm like, 'You didn't return any of my texts,' and she goes, 'I am SUCH a whale. I should have known better than to go to America. The portions are like, *Aaarrrggghhh!*' I'm there, 'Three times I texted you,' and she carries on doing her sit-ups, giving it, 'OH MY GOD! I bet Claire lived on air while I was away. I am going to have to seriously get my act together if I'm going to fit into my Vera Wang. It's like, *Duuuhhh!* I think I'm getting a cold sore.'

She gets up, roysh, and she picks up her cor keys and I go, 'I'll come with you,' but she's like, 'No, you are SO not coming. Not after last time,' and as we're heading down the stairs, roysh, her sister's on the way up and she turns around to me in this real, like, flirty voice and she goes, 'Ross, you can stay here with me and help me with my homework. Do you know the difference between a stalactite and a stalagmite?' and Sorcha laughs out loud and tells me she'll be back in an hour and under her breath I hear her go, 'I swear to God, if Claire has lost more weight than me ...'

Not even going to tell you what happened next, roysh, because you basically know. I'm a bad person. Snap the bracelets on me and sentence me on Tuesday morning. She basically wouldn't let it go. Hand on my knee. Full eye contact. Asking me to smell her neck. You can fill in the dots yourselves, roysh, but suffice to say that everyone got what they wanted and it's a good job I'm quick because we were pretty much dressed again by the time Sorcha walked back in the door, totally focking steaming.

She goes, 'OH! MY! GOD! That FOCKING BITCH. Phenola has it in for me.' She's basically the bird who puts them on the scales and writes down their weight on this, like, cord they have to bring every week. She's not exactly Calista Flockhart herself, it must be said. Sorcha goes, 'She CLAIMS that I stayed the same. I KNOW I lost weight,' but I know that's not what's really eating her. I'm there, 'How did Claire get on?' and she just, like, stares me out of it. She goes, 'OH! MY! GOD! She was SUCH a bitch to me. We were standing in the queue for the scales and I went to take off my docksiders. And she was like, "That's cheating." And I was like, "Sorry, girl?" And she was like, "You had them on when she weighed you last week. Of course you're going to be lighter this week if you take them off." She thinks she's great just because she's only a pound off her target weight.' I go, 'So how much did she lose?' and she's there, 'Ross, we can *all* lose three pounds in a week by storving.'

I'm there, 'So what did you get for penance? Two Hail Marys and a stick of celery?' just trying to cheer her up, roysh, but she stares through me and goes, 'I should have asked Erika to be my bridesmaid instead. Anyway, what have you two been up to?' and at exactly the same time, roysh, I go, 'MTV,' and Orpha or whatever her name is goes, 'Geography,' but Sorcha's having too much of a knicker-fit over Claire to notice our basically guilty faces.

✳ ✳ ✳

I spent the afternoon bet into Oisinn's new bird, and before you stort getting all, like, high and mighty about it, roysh, I have to tell you that the dude knew what was going on. Cut a long story short, roysh, he storted seeing this bird – Haley – and she's quality, roysh, we're talking Kristin Kreuk except taller. But her problem – and there's always a problem with birds if you stick around long enough to actually know them – her problem was that she was a bit too Roy for Oisinn's liking. Met her in the old Club d'Amour, scored her two or three times and the next thing she's telling all her mates about her new boyfriend, we're talking boyfriend after, what, three or four dates? HELLO?

So she's ringing and texting the dude, like, six or seven times a day. I told him to get a focking barring order out against her, but of course Oisinn, roysh, he doesn't want to hurt the girl. He's a bit like me really, too nice for his own good sometimes.

He wants to finish it, roysh, but at the same time he wants to, what does he call it, maintain the moral high ground. So basically, roysh, he asks me to bump into her somewhere – we're talking accidentally-on-purpose – give her the old silver-tongued chormer act and then, hopefully, bail in. Then he can ring her later on, tell her I've confessed everything, turn on the old water-works – 'I never thought you'd hurt me. I thought you were the one' blah blah blah – then hang up. And Bob's your auntie's hus-band. He gets her off his case, she gets the best night of loving she's ever had, I get five hundred lids from Oisinn's trust fund, and nobody gets hurt.

So this particular Friday night, roysh, the night before the Italy game, Oisinn bells me and he says that Carolina Herrera – that's what he calls her – is going out that night with a few of her mates – a birds' night out in the old Club of Love – so I lash on the best threads, splash of *Gio Aqua Di* and the next thing I know I'm in a Jo, cruising out to Leopardstown, orm out the window, and running through the bullshit lines I'm gonna give her.

I've got Christian with me for back-up, roysh, and we both end up at the bor, five or six pints of Ken in us, getting fairly steamed, and there I am listening to him giving it, 'Lauren's really upset about this business with her old man. He wants to come home. Face the music. But the papers are saying he's facing ten years. I told her if he gets ten years it'll be the biggest injustice since Bib Fortuna kidnapped the Twi'lek to be Jabba the Hutt's mistress. But nothing I say seems to help.'

Of course, I'm cracking on to be interested while looking over at Haley and her mates, one or two of whom aren't bad. One of them I think is called Sarah and I was with her sister at, like, JP's twenty-first. Wouldn't mind getting stuck in there, but there's five hundred sheets riding on this, roysh, and I have to, like, stay focused.

That song 'Dilemma' comes on and I make my move, roysh, mooching over to her and going, 'Haley, how the hell are you?' and she's like, 'OH MY GOD, you're Ross, Oisinn's friend,' and I'm there giving it, 'Guilty as charged. And where, pray tell, is that boyfriend of yours tonight?' hoping I'm not coming across as too smarmy. She goes, 'Oh he's busy. He does volunteer work at this hostel for homeless blind people with HIV.' I nearly crack my hole laughing in her face. The goy's got class, you have to give it to him. She goes, 'He is SUCH a nice goy,' and I go, 'That's our Oisinn.'

So it's like, '*No matter what I do, you know I'm crazy over you*', and I give her a few lines, shit she wants to hear about what a good dancer she is, how I can't believe she got that tan out of a bottle, how she doesn't look anything near twenty-six, how Oisinn would want me to take care of her, blah blah blah.

Then I make my move. We're out on the dancefloor, roysh, my hands are getting busy and she's saying fock-all and the next thing I go, 'If you were *my* girlfriend, I wouldn't want you coming out on your own,' and she's like, 'Oh my God, why?' and I go, 'In case this happened,' and I throw the lips on her.

And, well, you only need to look at my track record to know what happened next. No details. Let's spare everyone's dignity by just saying, HOME RUN! So anyway, roysh, we're in her gaff and about two o'clock in the afternoon I decide to get up, maybe catch the second half of the Italy match in Kiely's, and before I leave I happen to mention to her that I'm going to tell Oisinn everything. She took this a bit more, I don't know, philosophically than I expected. I mean, you could have knocked me down with a feather, roysh, when she turned around and went, 'There's no need. I rang him this morning, while you were asleep.' I was there, 'And?' and she went, 'I mustn't have loved him if I let this happen.' I go, 'So, all's well that end's well, huh?' and she's there, 'I said, I mustn't have loved *him*, Ross.' I'm like, Oh no. Please don't let this be happening. I make some excuse to go, roysh, and hit the battle cruiser for the game. Two hours I was in there, max. I left my mobile in Christian's cor, roysh, and when I finally check it, the screen said I had fourteen – *fourteen* – missed calls. And I don't remember even giving the psycho my number.

✳ ✳ ✳

Kiss me. Blah blah the bearded barley. Bit of a twirl here. *Nightly. Blah blah the green, green grass.* Think it's a kick now. Yep. No filthy from Sorcha. *Swing, swing. Swing your something-something. You wear those shoes and I can wear that dress.* Stand close. One hand on her waist. Grab her hand with the other. *Kiss me, under the milky twilight. Blah blah along the moonlit shore.* And waltz. *Something something something. Raise your open, strike up the hand and blahdy blahdy blahdy. Kiss me.*

Everyone in the place gives us this huge, like, cheer, roysh, and I'm just there, 'Thanks, fans,' and Trevor's clapping his hands together and giving it, 'Ross, I think we're going to make a dancer out of you yet,' and Sorcha, roysh, she's secretly steaming because there I am getting all the attention. Trevor goes, 'Don't forget to keep looking into Ross's eyes, Sorcha. This is the man you'll have just married remember?' Trevor turns to me and winks and goes, 'You see what wonderful things can happy when you relax,' and what can I do but high-five the dude.

✳ ✳ ✳

'I'm not going to tell you how to do your job,' Sorcha goes to the photographer, before she goes on to do exactly that. She storts, like, lecturing the dude about light, composition, framing, blahdy blahdy blah, basically shit she's learned off the internet. She's dangerous with a computer, that girl. Oh, we'll be getting the wedding photos taken in Herbert Pork, by the way. Sorcha and her old dear decided.

So Sorcha ends up giving this poor goy – supposed to be one of the best photographers in Dublin, roysh – a twenty-minute ear-bashing on what she does and doesn't want and all the dude can do is basically nod. At the end, roysh, she goes, 'And I want a

Brad and Jen,' and the goy goes, 'A what?' and Sorcha sort of, like, shakes her head like she's trying her best to be patient with him, then whips out this picture of, like, Brad Pitt and Jennifer Aniston, on their, like, wedding day.

She goes, 'This one's for the mantelpiece.' The goy looks at it, roysh, and he goes, 'You want something like this?' and Sorcha's like, 'No, I want *exactly* that. Ross looking at me adoringly while I'm looking in the other direction.' The goy goes, 'Okaaay. Em. See, I know what you want, but it's not just down to the man with the camera, if you understand me. I can't make you look like the people in the photograph. *You* can only do that.' So Sorcha turns around to me, roysh, and she goes, 'Ross, do you think you can look at me the way Brad Pitt's looking at Jennifer Aniston there?' and I look at the picture for a minute and, like, nod my head and I go, 'I'll give it a try.'

And she looks at me and then at the photographer, like she's about to rip both our heads off, and she goes, 'I *want* my Brad and Jen. And you two better not fock it up.'

✳ ✳ ✳

I'm in Sorcha's room, roysh, the two of us lying on her bed, when I realise there's one in the post, as in a serious fort. Sorcha made me go back on the Atkins, roysh (said she'd tell her old man that I'm acting the dick if I didn't), and it is making serious shit of my digestive system. I mean, without being crude, roysh, having an Eartha these days is either like giving birth to a focking elephant or it's like Chris Rea's little brother, Dia. And the pen is Padraig focking Pearse, I'm telling you. So I'm lying there, roysh, obviously thinking, do I subtly squeeze it out, or do I leave the room? And, of course, being the kind of boyfriend I am, I tell her I have to use the can and I'm out of there, just in time as well.

Talk about chemical weapons. I'd say the UN weapons inspectors would have been at the door if I hadn't opened the window. See, I always think of killer lines like that when there's, like, no one around to laugh at them. So I decide to text a couple of the goys – we're talking JP, Oisinn, Christian, maybe Fionn – to tell them, but then I realise, roysh, that I've left my phone on the bed and of course I'm like, 'FOCK!' I whip up the old tweeds, roysh, reef the door open and peg it into the room, but it's too late, Sorcha's got it in her hand and she's, like, scrolling down through my numbers, checking up on me, the paranoid bitch. She's going, 'There's an awful lot of girls' names in here, Ross,' and I'm there, 'Sorry?' trying to buy myself some time and hoping against hope that Sorcha will somehow lose interest. Fat chance. She goes, 'Who are all these girls?' and I'm like, 'What girls?'

She's there, 'Jessica. Medb. Tina. Sadbh ...' I'm like, 'I've never heard of them.' She goes, 'Rebecca. Beibhínn. Caoimhe. Leanne ... that better not be Leanne who I used to play tennis with?' and I'm like, 'Okay, okay. They're just friends, alroysh? *Old* friends,' and she looks into my eyes to see am I telling the truth – hah, that's a joke – then she carries on scrolling down through my numbers. She goes, 'Why have some of them got TD beside their names?' and of course TD is, like, TOUCHDOWN! I'm there, 'You're asking me why some of them have TD beside their names?' and she goes, 'Stop stalling for time, Ross. I want to know what TD means. *Now!*' and quick as a flash, roysh, I go, 'Too Dumb. It stands for Too Dumb.' She's there, 'Too dumb?' and I'm like, 'Yeah. Most of those girls, well they're nice and everything. They're probably very intelligent in their own ways. But I just end up comparing all girls to you, Sorcha. And compared to you, well, they're all TD. Guess that's what happens when you meet *the one.*'

She actually buys this shit. She goes, 'OH! MY! GOD! That is SUCH a nice thing to say,' and I go, 'Give me that phone here. I'll delete all those numbers,' right after I've written them out on a sheet of paper, of course. She tells me she loves me, roysh, and I tell her I have strong feelings for her too. We're not really watching the telly, roysh, but all of a sudden whatever programme's on gets interrupted by a news flash and suddenly we're looking at, like, Ann Doyle – yes, I would – and she's going, 'Hennessy Coghlan-O'Hara, the fugitive Dublin solicitor whom gordaí want to question over frauds involving several million euro, has been arrested in Dublin.' Sorcha goes, 'OH! MY! GOD! Poor Lauren,' and I'm like, '*Ssshhh!*' Ann's like, 'He was arrested by gordaí from the serious fraud squad at Dublin Airport when he returned to the capital voluntarily tonight. This report from Charlie Bird.'

Next thing they cut to the airport, roysh, and there's Hennessy with the old bracelets on, surrounded by Feds, and Charlie's giving it, 'There were scenes of pandemonium at Dublin Airport tonight as Hennessy Coghlan-O'Hara was taken into custody after returning from South America where he was in hiding for several months. There were tussles between gardaí and some of his supporters as he was arrested by gardaí investigating fraud allegations thought to involve some twenty million euro.'

The next thing, roysh – I nearly fell off the focking bed laughing – Knob Head himself is standing in front of the gordaí as they're hauling Hennessy's orse off to the slammer, and he's giving it, 'You call this justice?' then he turns around, roysh, faces the camera and goes, 'HAVE WE LOST OUR DIGNITY? ARE WE LIVING IN HAITI ALL OF A SUDDEN?' and suddenly this big ignorant bogger of a cop lets him have it with his baton.

It's like, WALLOP! right across the focker's head.

Sorcha – the drama queen – she puts her hands over her eyes and goes, 'OH MY GOD! Your poor dad,' and I'm there going, 'Follow up! Follow up!' knowing from my own experience playing rugby that a whack like that is enough to put someone down, but not necessarily to keep them there. Of course the old man's up about five seconds later, his eyes all over the place, his cigar all bent in his mouth and he's, like, giving out yords to Charlie Bird, going, 'You see, this is where it gets you, Mister Special Correspondent, thank you very much indeed. You and that Cooper chap with your questions answered and your answers questioned and your fellow in the *Independent*, not even going to say his name and give him the oxygen of publicity. Is this what you wanted? A police state?' He looks in the camera again and goes, 'WELCOME TO HAITI! LEAVE YOUR HUMAN RIGHTS AT THE CUSTOMS DESK IN THE BAGGAGE HALL!' and I can see from the dude's eyes, roysh, that he's, like, concussed basically – as in, all over the shop – and it's not going to take much to put him out and this bogger, roysh, fair focks to him, he obviously knows that too because the second whack he hits him isn't as hord. It's just sort of like, CRACK! but it's still lights out.

Good enough for the dickhead.

✳ ✳ ✳

Erika asks me to meet her in the Westbury Hotel for cocktails, roysh, and like a fool I end up getting a Jo there, thinking I might be on for my rock and roll. She'd only be doing it, of course, to get at Sorcha, but try telling that to the old one-eyed zipper fish – doesn't want to know. Turns out that isn't Erika's game at all, of course. No sooner have I put a drink down in front of her than she hits me with the bombshell. She goes, '*You've* been a naughty boy, Ross.'

I'm thinking, Obviously someone saw me going at it with Oisinn's ex in Club of Love last weekend. I'm there, 'Meaning?' and she goes, '*Both* bridesmaids? I've never had a very high opinion of you, but I have to say, Ross, even I'm surprised at you,' and every drop of blood in my body goes cold, roysh, and I'm thinking, how the FOCK could she possibly have found out? There's no point in me denying it, though, the guilt is written all over my face and we both know it. I go, 'Who told you?' and she sips her Cosmopolitan and goes, 'I worked it out. It was easy. Come on, you must have noticed the superior way that that little Bray *scrubber* has been acting, especially around your so-called fiancé. I thought, that sudden confidence hasn't come from nowhere. I knew, of course. It was just a matter of coaxing it out of her. I suspected it might have been that day I caught her begging on Grafton Street. So she was drunk the other night – Bulmers! the dear girl – and I storted at her, told her that Sorcha had one thing that she would never get her hands on. And that was you. And she was only too happy to tell me how wrong I was.' I just, like, nod and stare into my Slow Screw Against The Wall With No Questions Asked Or Numbers Exchanged. My whole life is flashing in front of my eyes here. I go, 'And what about, what's-her-name?' and she goes, 'Orpha? That was easy. I know where she keeps her diary.' I'm there, 'You actually *read* someone's diary?' and she goes, 'Spare me the moralising, Ross. *You* slept with your fiancé's sister. Sanctimony doesn't become you.'

I'm there, 'Are you going to tell Sorcha?' and she's like, 'Of course I am. Just haven't made up my mind when. It would be a shame if Claire never got to wear these. Picked her up a couple of little presents for her big day out,' and she storts rooting through her shopping bags, roysh, and whips out a pair of huge hoopy earrings and a bottle of cheap fake tan, which she's obviously bought in some pound shop. She goes, 'I've never actually been in Bray myself, but I believe these are all the rage out there. It'll be a shame if she doesn't get to wear them.'

I'm there, 'And you'd do that? You're going to tell Sorcha just to stop her being happy?' and she goes, 'Ross, I've never known what the girl sees in you. But I suspect that whatever I tell her, she's still stupid enough to go ahead and marry you. She handles private humiliation well. It's being publicly disgraced that she can't handle. So I think I'll keep my mouth shut. Until the reception. Then tell her everything.' I watch her stand up, dragging half of Nine West behind her. Then she disappears down the winding staircase without looking back once. Goddess. Bitch. Same thing.

✳ ✳ ✳

She looks at me, roysh, like she's just caught me knocking the fock out of a baby seal with a baseball bat. I'm there, 'I'm *going* to collect that Jasper Conran at Wedgewood teaset that your aunt Delma bought us. Just not now,' and she goes, 'Ross, you promised,' and I'm there, 'That was before the goys rang. Look, you know Delma. I'll be there half the night listening to her stories about the old biddies from Bridge,' and she goes, 'Fine! Don't bother, Ross. I'll collect it myself,' to which I reply, 'Kool and the Congregation,' give her a peck on the cheek and go, 'Later.' What was so important — not that she'd give a fock one way or another — is that the Leinster branch is basically pushing ahead with its plan to rebuild Donnybrook. Meaning, roysh, that they're going to end up totalling Bective disco, where me and most of the goys got our first bit of the other. It was actually

Fionn who rang me just as me and Sorcha were heading out the door. He goes, 'We're picketing the Leinster branch offices at two o'clock. Get your orse down here,' which of course I do. Fionn doesn't tell me, naturally, that all the goys are wearing their Castlerock jerseys and of course I look a basic tool in my blue Ralph. Still, I high-five the goys. JP tells me he's glad I could interface with them, Oisinn says we have the IRFU on the run and Christian – looks the part with the Peter Pan he got in Rio – asks me who I think would win in a fight between a wampa and a dewback lizard, if the fight was held on neutral territory, we're talking Dagobah.

I haven't actually seen enough of the goys lately, which is portly my fault, mostly Sorcha's, and I have to say, roysh, the craic is great, even if the picket is a bit of a waste of time. In the first hour we're there, not one single person goes in or out of the place. The biggest surprise of the day, though, is when Ryle Nugent shows up with a camera dude, saying he's going to do a piece on us for that programme of his. JP, who's, like, his cousin, tipped him off with the exclusive. After high-fiving us all individually, Ryle asks us to nominate a spokesman, which of course has to be Fionn, what with the glasses and everything.

So he does the interview, roysh, and fair focks to him he makes all the right noises, first time any of us played tonsil hockey was in Bective, first time any of us saw a set of melons, blahdy blahdy blah, and of course we're all in the background going, 'You liar, Fionn. You've never done it,' and they end up having to do it in, like, twenty takes because Ryle keeps cracking his nuts laughing.

So of course an hour later, roysh, there's still no one coming near the office and I suggest moving the picket more towards the

Kiely's end of things, which we do. It's pretty thirsty work, all that protesting, and it's a good thing we don't have any slogans to shout. It's while we're in Kiely's, roysh, having a few pints of Ken – of course Fionn's drinking Probably, just to be focking different – that JP produces this, like, bag, and out of it, roysh, he whips out this T-shirt and on the front of it, roysh, in big letters, it's got, **I Ended Up Being With Ross O'Carroll-Kelly In Bective Disco,** and on the back it's got, **And So Did Most Of My Friends,** and what can I do, roysh, but high-five the dude and tell him he's a genius. JP goes, 'That's a sample. I'm getting five hundred of them printed up. Try and do me up a list of birds you were with in there. This'll really put the squeeze on the IRFU,' and then he's like, 'Oisinn, show him yours,' and he's got one done up for Oisinn as well, roysh, and on the front it's got, like, two big black arrows and, not being crude or anything, but they're pointing to the top ten area, and in big letters it's gone, **Oisinn Wallace Groped Me Here And Here In Bective Disco,** and on the back it goes, **And Here,** and there's an arrow pointing down to the orse. He goes, 'They'll be available in Ross, Oisinn, Christian, Fionn and, of course, my good self. There's bound to be a lot of girls who'll want the full set, but we'll have to limit it to one garment per customer, making sure we maximise our exposure on the streets.'

✳ ✳ ✳

One Portobello full-length mirror. Two John Rocha champagne flutes. One Newbridge Paul Costelloe Amourette cold-forged, seven-piece, single-setting silver service. Two oblong Denby dishes. One box of Penfold Rawson's Retreat white wine. One Victoria Palace Double Quilt Cover in cream. Sorcha walks in blowing into two mugs of hot chocolate and straight away I'm like, 'What the fock is this?' She puts the mugs down on the dressing table and she goes, 'Our WEDDING list? HELLO? Nice to see you showing an interest.'

One David Campbell soup tureen in elm. One Louis Vuitton clutch bag in cherry blossom satin. One Louis Vuitton business bag in monogram glacé leather. She's dropping the marsh-mallows in when all of a sudden she's like, 'OH MY GOD! Have I put down a white goose down pillow?' and I'm there, 'No, but you have managed to find a salad fork for a hundred bills. Do you not think we need the essentials first like, I don't know, a kettle? Pots and pans? A Playstation?'

She gives me a total filthy, roysh, and she goes, 'I am SO not having Erika laughing at my wedding list,' and she says *Erika*, roysh, with this, like, edge to it. I pretty much know what's com-ing next. She goes, 'You are SO not going to believe the stuff she's been saying,' and I can feel myself getting hot and I'm wondering is my face giving me away. I'm there, 'Go on, this should be good,' and she goes, 'It's just, like, hints really. Trying to make me think you've been with both of my bridesmaids recently. As in the past few weeks?' The hairy Cyclops has no conscience, what can I say. I'm there, 'I hope you told her it was total bullshit,' and she's there, 'Yeah, I was like, "Nice try. You've been trying to break us up since the day we got engaged. Ross wouldn't do that to me".' I look her straight in the eye and I go, 'It's a good job you're such a good judge of character,' and it scares me how, like, gullible she can be at times. You wouldn't blame BTs for trying to get ninety bills out of her for a carafe, whatever the fock that is.

We lie there on the bed, roysh, watching 'Sex and the City'. Sarah Jessica Coathanger Slammed Into My Mouth Sideways

Parker. What's going on there? Steamy, they call this show. Have you ever noticed that nobody takes their bra off when they're at it? Men in New York must have no interest in top tens. Sorcha all of a sudden goes, 'Oh and I've made an appointment for us at the bank,' and of course the old alorm bells are ringing now. It's like, Whoa! Grown-up shit! and she must cop the look on my face, roysh, because she's there, 'We *need* a house, Ross. You didn't think we were going to get married and carry on living with our parents, did you?' I'm like, 'No, but I just presumed someone was going to, you know, buy us one.' She looks at me like I'm a pube in her caramel macchiato. She goes, *'Buy us one?'* and I'm there, not unreasonably, 'I just presumed that, you know, your old pair would stump up half. And I'd get the other half off Wank Features as, like, a wedding present and shit,' and she goes, 'OH MY GOD, do you know how much houses cost? We're talking half-a-million minimum. Unless you want to end up living in some hellhole. Mum and Dad say they'll give us the deposit.'

In a way she's roysh, there's no way I can ask the old man for half-a-million lids. It was hard enough getting twenty grand out of the dickhead for the World Cup. I go, 'Where is all this leading, Sorcha?' playing the innocent, knowing damn well that the word 'job' is heading in the direction of this conversation like Oisinn diving into a ruck. She goes, 'Ross, I can't pay a mortgage of that size on the money I earn.' She's just storted managing her old dear's new boutique in the Powerscourt Townhouse Centre. I'm like, 'I know where you're going with this and you can forget it.' She goes, 'If we're going to start a life together, Ross ...' – and her voice is all, like, high-pitched and shit? – '... you're going to *have* to work.' I'm there, 'I told you, I'm basically chilling until I get back from the World Cup. Maybe next year I'll see if any schools senior cup teams need a coach. You turn on the waterworks, and I am SO out of here.'

I'm not, she is. She just gets up from the bed and storms out. I watch the end of this pile of crap. Samantha's banging away like a barn door in a force-ten gale and then the credits roll. I get bored waiting for the stupid cow to stop sulking, roysh, and I pick up one of her magazines and it says that when Sting has sex, roysh, it goes on for, like, five hours, which means he mustn't be very good at it in my book.

The next thing, roysh, the door opens, but it's not Sorcha coming back in to apologise. It's her old man again. Big serious face on the focker. Looks like I'm back in the bad books. He goes, 'It's bad enough you leaving all the wedding plans to Sorcha. Now you've gone and upset her again. But the consolation for Sorcha's mother and I is that you've done it for the last time. This *is* going to be the happiest day of her life, whether you like it not. You need to learn to shut your mouth and go along with whatever it is she wants. Is that clear?' and instead of saying what I should say – which is, It's none of your business, you interfering focker – I just end up going, 'Yes Mister Lalor.'

On the way out the door, roysh, he stops and turns around and he goes, 'This friend of hers – Erika. These things she's been saying ...' and suddenly I'm giving it, 'Nothing happened, Mr Lalor, I swear,' before the dude's even focking accused me. He nods, roysh, real calmly and – there's no point in telling Sorcha this, roysh, because she'd never believe me – he goes, 'Make sure nothing does, Ross. I've got a length of rope and a spade in the boot of the car. Do you know how easy it is to dispose of a body?'

*** * ***

Trevor sends me a text and it's like, **Dont 4get, waltzing is jst 1-2-3. Keep saying it in ur mind wen ur sittin watchin telly - 1-2-3, 1-2-3. Tap it out on the kitchn table**, and I send him one back going, **U d man**, and he sends me one back and it's like, **X**.

*** * ***

Sitting in, roysh, all packed and everything, watching the Leinster match, having a few Britneys, when Sorcha rings, at half-time luckily enough. I'm there, 'Hey, whazzuuup?' and she's like, 'Hey, what are you doing, Chicken?' and I'm giving it, 'Having a beer. Watching the game.' Ding – TRUE.

She goes, 'Just wanted to say goodbye. I'm going to miss you SO much.' Ding – TRUE.

She storts, like, blubbering away, roysh, fock it, just as the teams are coming back onto the field. I'm there, 'Believe me, Sorcha, however lonely you're going to be without me, I'm going to be twice as lonely without you.' Beep – FALSE.

She goes, 'You mean that?' and I'm there, 'Yeah, like I'd lie to you about something like that.' Ding – TRUE.

She goes, 'I'm sorry. I am making this SO hord for you.' BEEP – FALSE.

I'm there, 'Come on, Sorcha. It's only Australia. It's hordly the other side of the world,' and she goes, 'OH! MY! GOD! I'm being SO selfish. Hey, did you just higher up the television?' and I'm there, 'No.' Beep – FALSE. I'm there, 'What do you take me for?'

I think deep down, roysh, I do love Sorcha, even if that makes me sound like a benny. And it's not that I'm having second thoughts about, like, marrying the girl, roysh. It's just that I want to marry Sorcha *and* keep my old life. Said it before, roysh, and I'll say it again – this wedding business has, like, taken all of the fun out of her. It's all, like, wedding lists and cappuccino machines and Hampshire rugs and sometimes, roysh, it feels like all of a sudden I'm living somebody else's life.

Shane Byrne's having a focking stormer. Sorcha goes, 'I love you, Ross.' Ding – TRUE.

I'm there, 'You know how I feel about you.' Beep – FALSE.

She goes, 'Were you listening to Lite FM tonight?' and I'm there, 'What?' Come on, Leinster, get your focking act together. She goes, 'I told you to listen to The Love Affair. They played our song.' I wasn't actually aware we had one. I'm there, 'Oh that! Yeah, I heard it.' Beep – FALSE.

She goes, 'And did you hear my request for you?' Fock's sake, if any of the goys heard that, I'm toast. I'm like, 'I heard it alroysh.' Beep – FALSE.

She goes, 'How did it make you feel?' Fock knows what she said. I'm there, 'I've got goosebumps just thinking about it, Sorcha. Goosebumps.' Beep – FALSE.

Suddenly she storts singing, roysh, we're talking Sap City, Wisconsin, here. *I used to think, I had the answers to everything. But now I know that life doesn't always go my way.* Don't know how that ended up our song. Never focking heard it before. Then the waterworks again. I'm not sure which I prefer, the singing or the crying. She's there, 'I'm really sorry. I shouldn't be making this horder for you.'

I'm there, 'You're not.' Ding – TRUE.

She goes, 'It's just ... I know I shouldn't listen to her, but some of the stuff that Erika's been saying. She comes over earlier and she's like, "Do you REALLY think Ross is going to stay loyal while he's travelling around Australia? You're delusional, girl",' and I'm there, 'She's jealous because *you* have me and she doesn't.' Beep – FALSE.

She's like, 'I know that. But it's just. She's relentless. That stuff about Claire. And my sister. HELLO? Then she tried to tell me the other night that you were with Stephanie Burton.' Burton – that was her second name.

I'm there, 'That's total bullshit.' Beep – FALSE.

She goes, 'She said she saw you talking to her in Club 92,' and I'm there, 'HELLO? I *am* capable of talking to a girl without wanting to hop her.' Beep – FALSE.

She goes, 'I know that.' Beep – FALSE.

She's there, 'That's what Fionn said. He told me I was being silly,' and I'm there, 'The dude's roysh. Wait a minute. Fionn? When were you talking to Fionn?' and she goes, 'He called out to me earlier. I was lending him my Elgar CD,' and all of a sudden, roysh, I lose the plot. I'm going, 'He's focking trying to get in there,' and she's like, 'In where?' and I'm like, 'In with you.' She goes, 'I don't know what you're talking about.' Beep – FALSE.

She's like, 'I've told you before there's nothing going on between me and Fionn.' Ding – TRUE.

She goes, 'I don't fancy him.' Beep – FALSE.

She's there, 'And he doesn't fancy me.' Beep – FALSE.

She's like, 'We're good friends.' Ding – TRUE.

She goes, 'But there's nothing more to it than that.' Beep – FALSE.

She's giving it, 'I didn't mean to make you feel jealous or insecure, Ross.' Beep – FALSE.

I'm there, 'It's Kool plus assorted hangers-on.' Beep – FALSE.

I'm there, 'Look, I better go. Got to be up early in the morning,' and she's like, 'I thought you and the goys would be going out tonight. Kick the holiday off in style,' and I'm there, 'Nah, I'm gonna stay in.' Beep – FALSE.

I'm there, 'Gonna try and get my head down.' Ding – TRUE.

She's like, 'Aoife and Sophie are heading into Reynord's, but I'm gonna give it a miss.' Beep – FALSE.

She goes, 'I love you.' Ding – TRUE.

I'm there, 'I know.' Ding – TRUE.

She's there, 'When you come back we are SO going to live happily ever after, aren't we?'

I'm there, 'True.'

First impressions of Australia? What can I say? The beer is basically piss, roysh, but the craic is unbelievable. Don't know what city we're in, I got that hammered on the plane. But there we are, me and the goys, having a few scoops, talking about old times, reminiscing, if that's the roysh word. The time we played Exes and Ohs. What a focking game that is. You've got a month, roysh, to see how many exes you can make go. 'Ohhh!' The winner was yours truly, of course, leaving a trail of broken horts in my wake. Most chicks are like that. Can't resist a pretty face. Even when they know they're going to be, like, treated like basically shit. Oisinn goes, 'What was that bird's name? Used to wear that *Contradiction*. Made a tit of herself in Pegs. *'I can't believe I let you hurt me twice.'* Threw a bottle of Smirnoff Ice over you.'

I'm checking myself out in the mirror behind the bor. Have to say, roysh, I'm looking pretty well at the moment. Stubble looks amazing on me. I'm there, 'I think it was Melanie,' and JP goes – all, like, dreamily, roysh – 'Meeelaniiieee. You hurt her, Ross. Hurt her like hell on wheaten toast. Word is she hasn't been with a goy since,' and we all laugh and, like, high-five each other. Of course Fionn's trying to, like, change the subject, roysh, never being comfortable when we're talking about previous scores, basically because he's had fock-all to speak of, he was still a plastic surgeon when he was nineteen and the only bird he's actually shagged in the past twelve months is that kipper in his class. He knocks back the last of his beer and goes, 'Better text Kathleen,' who's the ginger minger I'm talking about. He's *seeing* her, when he's not trying to worm his way into my bird, that is. He storts texting her, roysh, and he cops me making a face at the other goys, basically going, What a steamer, so he storts giving it, 'Sorry, Ross. Some of us believe that relationships are founded on mutual respect,' and I go, 'Yeah, that's why you spent all your teenage years in your bedroom, playing with the one-eared Space Hopper,' and he goes to grab me, roysh, but I lean back and I end up falling backwards – orse over tit – off the stool. I hop up and I go, 'If my mobile's broken, you are SO totalled,' and JP steps in between us and goes, 'All this aggravation ain't satisfactioning me, goys. I'm prescribing chill pills. To be taken instantly.'

My phone's not broken, roysh, because it storts ringing and Fionn is so steeped because if it was, roysh, I'd have shoved them specs so far up his ... I go, 'Y'ello,' and of course it's focking Ass Breath. He's like, 'Hey, Kicker. Where are you?' I'm there, 'Australia? Duh!' He goes, 'Australia? Oh. You've gone then?' and I'm like, 'What did you want, tears at the focking airport?' He totally ignores this and storts giving it, 'The World Cup, eh? It's well for you. You and your pals. Of course, as I told the chaps in Portmarnock, if it wasn't for injuries, bad luck and so forth, he'd be going as a player, not as a fan. Never mind your Humphreys and your O'Gara and your what-not.' I'm like, 'Is there much more of this bullshit because I'm trying to get seriously beered here?' He doesn't answer. I'm like, 'Good. I need another five grand. Transfer it into my account,' and straight away he's like, 'Five thousand, em, euro. I'll, em, do it this afternoon,' and I'm there, 'Make sure you do. Don't dick me around.' Then he goes, 'I went to visit Hennessy this morning, Ross. Locked up like an animal, but he's keeping his chin up. There's no need for you to be worrying about him,' and I'm there, 'Hennessy can rot in jail for all I focking care,' and I hang up.

Of course then I feel a bit guilty, roysh, what with Christian going out with the tosspot's daughter, and he suddenly goes all quiet and I wait until the other goys aren't listening and then I'm there, 'Christian, I didn't mean that. It's just my old man. You know how pissed off I get when he storts that whole old pals act,' and he goes, 'It's okay, padwan.' Oisinn sticks 'Beautiful Day' on the jukebox and suddenly we're all forgetting our jetlag. We all stort singing and we're getting total daggers from the borman. Or maybe it's a woman. I knock back the rest of my beer. They've got pots over here instead of, like, pints. I thought the focking Aussies could drink. I give the old nod to the thing behind the bor and I go, 'Five more Fisher Price pints when you're ready.'

✳ ✳ ✳

Get a text from Erika, roysh, and it's like, **Tought id let u no im goin 2 get proof tht u slept wit Claire n Orpha n giv it 2 ur darling wife on ur weddin day x**. She's bluffing.

✳ ✳ ✳

This SO better be the roysh place. I don't know what they put in those My First Lagers, roysh, but I'm totally hanging this morning and this is, like, the fifth focking house we've called to. Mister Brainiac took down the directions, roysh. We were in Darwin when we woke up this morning and we've been walking for so long that I'm, like, expecting to see Ayers Rock any focking minute. Fionn goes, 'This is definitely the place,' and we're all, like, 'Better be.' The house is a total dump. Wouldn't look out of place in Finglas or one of those shitholes. It's got, like, two or three broken windows, half the roof tiles are missing and there's, like, old fridges and mattresses just, like, dumped in the garden. Of course JP's giving it the whole estate agent bit under his breath. He's going, 'A mature, single-storey residence in one of the more desirable parts of Australia's northern gateway.' The dude can't switch off.

There's no bell, roysh, no knocker either, so Oisinn basically thumps on the door, roysh, and we hear this borking from around the side of the gaff and suddenly, roysh, this focking dog appears – we're talking, like, a Rottweiler here? – and before I can move, roysh, the thing makes a lunge for me, jumps up in the air, and he's about, like, two inches from my throat when all of a sudden he stops and I cop that he's on a chain. I'm, like, rooted to the spot. The goys are all cracking their holes laughing. I can feel the top of my leg wet. Not much, roysh, but there's been a bit of discharge and I *would* be wearing beige chinos as well, wouldn't I? They notice that and I'm totalled.

The next thing we hear this voice going, 'Wocha want, ya facking baggers?' and suddenly this fat old biddy's, like, storming in our direction, moustache and a sawn-off focking shotgun, which she's pointing right at us. Don't like the way her hands are shaking either. Fionn goes, 'We've come about the ad. In the local paper? For the caravan?' She goes, 'How do I know you're not doggas?' We all just look at each other, wishing we'd actually *listened* to 'Home and Away' when it was on instead of just looking at the school uniforms. She goes, 'Cops, ya mongrels! How do I know you're not flaming cops?' She keeps waving that focking gun. Fionn holds up the local paper and he goes, 'We come in peace,' like he's talking to a focking Martian. He's going, 'We mean you no harm. We are interested in buying the caravan. We have money.' She goes, 'How much money?' and Fionn's like, 'A thousand dollars. The asking price.' She lowers the gun and smiles for the first time. She's got teeth like one of them focking methadone addicts.

She goes, 'Follow me. And don't fack with me on the price. There's others facking interested.' We follow the crazy bitch around the back of the house. The dog's pegged it somewhere. Even *he's* focking scared of her. Christian goes, 'I've got a baaad feeling about this.' Actually, the van's not half as bad as we expected, roysh, one of those Winnebago jobbies, needs a lick of paint, roysh, but it's focking huge. The five of us could easily live in it, which is good because that's what we're, like, planning to do.

We hop in the back and there's, like, everything in there, we're talking cooker, fridge, beds, the whole shooting match. The old weapon gives JP the keys, roysh, and he hops in the front and storts the engine. Takes four or five turns of the key for it to catch, roysh, then it storts, like, spluttering before the engine comes to life.

'Purring like a kitten,' JP goes and Oisinn's giving it, 'Yes, this will certainly suit our needs, good lady,' then he puts his orm around her – he ACTUALLY puts his orm around her – he's flirting his orse off with her and then comes the inevitable, 'What *is* that scent you're wearing?' She goes, 'Scent?' and he's like, 'Your perfume.' She goes, 'Doesn't *have* a facking name. It's just in a bottle,' like it's the most obvious thing in the world.

Oisinn storts, like, sniffing her neck – I'm too focking scared to laugh – and he's giving it, 'Essences of orange, lemon and bergamot. Blended, unless I'm very much mistaken, with notes of rose, jasmine and oakmoss.' He looks down, roysh, and she's got the gun stuck right in his town halls. She goes, 'What did I tell you mongrels abaht the price? Don't try and flattah me. I know what I smell like.' Fionn just storts peeling off the notes. She turns back to the house and I can't resist, roysh, I have to ask. It's on my mind. I go, 'Why is it so cheap?' and she stops, roysh, and looks around at me, really slowly, and all of the rest of the goys just look away, the shitters. She goes, 'My husband died in it. And if you fellas *are* cops, you won't find anything on me in there. And by the way,' she goes, pointing to my trousers, 'you've pissed your dacks.' I don't need a translation.

* * *

I get a text from Sorcha. It's like, **Ur mum orgnsed a sprise brdal showr 4 me. So amazng. Goin 4 flwers 2moro. Hows Oz? Mis u hon. X X X.** No comment.

* * *

'Close your eyes,' Oisinn goes and I'm like, 'Come on, we're not kids.' JP's there, 'No, he's roysh, Ross. We want to see the surprise on your faces.' Oisinn and JP have been painting the Chick Wagon, as we've decided to call it. Me, Christian and Fionn were knocking back the old Jim Beams while the goys were busy at work. 'Come on,' Oisinn goes, 'play the game,' so we knock back the last of our drinks and the goys lead us outside, me, Christian and Fionn just there feeling our way with our eyes closed, like a three focking tools. They manoeuvre us into position and then JP goes, 'Okay goys, get an eyeful.'

I open my eyes, roysh, and I cannot BELIEVE it. The whole

thing's been painted green, roysh, and there's loads of shit painted on the side of it in, like, spray paint, things like, 'BABEMOBILE,' we're talking, 'LOVE MACHINE,' and we're talking, 'ROCK BOYS ON TOUR,' in huge letters on the sides. Then there's other shit like, 'EDDIE O'SULLIVAN'S GREEN AND WHITE ARMY,' except Eddie's spelt EDDY, which I'm sure is wrong, and then on the back there's like, 'CAUTION – LOVERS ON BOARD!' I'm like, 'It's absolutely, focking brilliant,' and I turn around and Christian and Fionn are just shaking their heads. Oisinn goes, 'Something like that, it'd be easy to make it look cheap and nasty,' and JP's there, 'But I think we've avoided falling into that particular trap.' We all hop in the back. Fair focks to them, roysh, they've even managed to find new sheets and everything. I'm like, 'Hey, those beds are going to be seeing some action between now and the time we hit Sydney,' and we all go, 'TOUCHDOWN!' and high-five each other.

Oisinn's there, 'Speaking of which. Fionn, have you drawn up the itinerary?' and Fionn pulls this piece of paper out of his pocket, pushes his glasses up on his nose – focking nerd – and goes, 'Yeah, I was thinking we might hit the road the day after tomorrow.' JP's like, 'Zero-nine-hundred hours?' and Fionn goes, 'Roger that. We'll hit Cookstown, then Cairns. Spend four or five days there, acquaint ourselves with the local female populace,' – that's a laugh in his case – 'maybe check out the Great Barrier Reef. Then we'll hit Townsville, Noosa, a few days in Brisbane, then into Sydney in time for the Romania match.' All the goys are like, 'Kool plus significant other,' and JP's giving it, 'Military-style precision,' but I'm like, 'The day after *tomorrow*? But this place is a kip. What's there to hang around for?' and wait'll you hear this, roysh, Fionn goes, 'There's the East Point Military Museum for storters. They've got actual real footage there of the Japanese bombing of Darwin in 1942,' and we all just look at him for ages, roysh, then I crack my hole and go, 'Lo-ser!' but then Oisinn goes, 'I actually wouldn't mind getting a look at that myself,' the fat bastard that he is, and JP goes, 'And that gallows they used for the last hanging in the Northern Territories, where's that?' and Bill focking Bryson's there, 'The Fannie Bay Gaol Museum,' all delighted with himself basically.

Quick as a flash I go, 'There's only one kind of fanny I'm interested in,' trying to, like, get the goys on my side. Oisinn's there, 'Well go on then, Ross. Off you go and find some.' I'm like, 'Roysh, I will. I'm off to do what I was put on this Earth for – to bring happiness to the lives of young ladies,' and I head out, slamming the door behind me, and I can hear them, roysh, I can hear them through the walls of the caravan, doing impressions of me, going, *'The name's Ross. Played a bit of rugby in my time,'* and they're all cracking their holes laughing, even Christian, my so-called best mate. So later on, roysh, I'm sat at the bor in Mulligan's – there's Irish bors everywhere you look here – and I'm there, 'Can I get another beer?' The bird or whatever it is behind the bor just goes, 'I told you half-an-hour ago the bar's closed,' and I'm like, 'Can I just stay for a bit longer? You won't even know I'm here.'

She gives this big fock-off Maori guy a nod and he comes over – ten foot focking six, roysh – and he picks me up, still sitting on the stool and everything, he carries me to the door and focks me out into the cor pork. I get up and check my watch. It's, like, twelve bells. Too early to head home. I head around the back of the boozer and sit down next to a wall. I'm a bit more hammered than I thought and I end up conking out. I wake up with, like, spit dribbling down my face. I wipe it off and check my watch. It's, like, four o'clock in the morning.

I head back to the Chick Wagon. No, we're calling it the Chuck Wagon now. Chuck is Australian for basically bird. I open the door, making loads of noise, roysh, making sure to wake the goys up and I'm there going, 'Sorry about that, goys. Met a couple of Sheilas. Talk about passion,' and Fionn goes, 'Funny that, we went out ourselves. We saw you passed out in the cor pork.' Then all I hear is all this sniggering. I wait until they've fallen asleep, then I take a dump in one of Fionn's shoes.

✱ ✱ ✱

I'm in the can, roysh, having a shave if the truth be told, when JP storts, like, banging on the door, demanding to be let in. I open the door and I'm like, 'What is it, you fag?' and he goes, 'I need to ask you something,' and straight away I'm there, 'Before you do, I just want to tell you I'm strictly into birds.' He goes, 'Ross, this is serious shit. I've got a strange feeling about this place.' He's talking about the Chuck Wagon. I'm there, 'What are you bullshitting about?' and he goes, 'Have you not noticed the way it's colder inside than it is outside?' I wipe the last of the shaving foam off my chin. I'm there, 'You're not making much sense, JP.' He goes, 'We had to open the windows the other night to let some heat in. Dude, I think the place is possessed.' I'm like, 'Possessed?' He goes, '*Ssshhh*, will you,' and he looks over his shoulder, as if someone might be listening. Then he's like, 'A man died in here, Ross. And we don't even know how.' I'm just there, 'You'd want to lay off the sauce, man.'

✱ ✱ ✱

There we are, roysh, on the open road, sun beating down on us, me – Lead Foot himself – at the wheel, which I shouldn't technically be, I suppose, because I don't have a licence, but no one's gonna know that out here. It's, like, the desert, roysh, and there's fock-all out here, just sand basically and the open road. The radio's blaring, roysh, and it's 'Sweet Child of Mine' and we're all giving it loads, air guitars, the lot. *She got eyes of the bluest kiiind.* Next thing, roysh, there's two birds behind us in a Ferrari and they must have the same radio station on as us because I can see them in the rear-view and they're, like, mouthing the words to the same song. Then they pull up alongside us, have a quick scope in at us, crack their holes laughing, put the foot down and leave us for dust. 'Let them go,' Oisinn goes, feeding his face as usual. Vegemite. Focking stinks. He's there, 'Save ourselves for the birds in Cairns.' He better brush his teeth. After a couple of hours, roysh, we lose the radio, so we strike up a few songs. We basically give them all an airing. We're talking 'Ring The Bell, Verger'. We're talking 'Ruck, Ruck, Wherever You May Be'. We're talking 'Teddy Bears' Picnic'. Then, roysh, I pull a cracker out of the bag. We're talking 'Bestiality's Best', which is, like, to the tune of 'Tie Your Kangaroo Down'. I'm giving it:

Bestiality's best, boys,
Bestiality's best (fock a wallaby),
Bestiality's best, boys,
Bestiality's best.

Then you've got to come up with, like, your own lines for the verses, roysh, like, 'Stick your lug in a slug, Doug. Stick your lug in a slug,' and, like, 'Slip your slew in a ewe, Lou. Slip your slew in a ewe,' and it's, like, totally amazing. We're all, like, high-fiving each other as we try to outdo each other with the lines and it's just like old times, like it was at school. Even me and Fionn are, like, hitting it off. So what if he wears glasses. He's into books and learning and shit, so what basically? We're laughing and singing and cracking one-liners and, like, reliving old times. And none of us even gives a shit when the focking gearbox suddenly falls out of the Chuck Wagon. We just, like, laugh at that as well. We walk the three miles to the next village – don't think it even has a name – and we find a mechanic, who tells us it'll cost a thousand bills to fix the heap of junk, which is, like, two hundred lids each, and we're like, 'We don't care. We're rolling in it, dude.'

We hit the town's only restaurant to get some nosebag. It's, like, twenty minutes since Oisinn last ate and bless him he's fighting that anorexia every inch of the way. We're looking down through the menu, roysh, and JP turns to the owner and goes, 'Is this roysh? They eat kangaroos here?' and quick as a flash, roysh, Oisinn goes, 'That's what we'll have. Five kangaroos. And five pints of Fosters.'

The grub arrives, roysh, and we're straight into it, just breaking our holes laughing between mouthfuls, and Oisinn keeps going, 'Well, Skippy, your old dear sure did taste nice,' and I can hordly eat I'm laughing that much. My phone rings, roysh, and who is it only Sorcha, sounding majorly pissed off. Checking up on me basically. She goes, 'You haven't returned any of my messages. You said you'd text me every day,' and of course I'm pretty horrendufied at this stage, and I'm like, 'Can't talk roysh now. I'm looking at the most magnificent animal I've ever seen,' and she's suddenly all interested, going, 'What is it?' and I'm, like, trying to keep the laughter in, going, 'It's a kangaroo, Sorcha.' I happen to know they're, like, one of her favourite animals. She goes, 'OH! MY! GOD! I never saw one outside of captivity. What's it like?' and I'm like,

'What's it like?' while the goys are, like, cracking their holes. I'm like, 'It's, em, medium rare, Sorcha,' and I hang up and high-five all of the goys in turn and tell them that these are going to be the best five weeks of our lives. And everyone just goes, 'Totally.'

✱ ✱ ✱

I'm in the sack, roysh, watching 'Home and Away' when JP barges in and goes, 'Seen the condensation on the windows?' and I'm like, 'What about it?' and he's like, 'It's on the *outside.*' I got an F in biology in the Leaving Cert. Is that supposed to, like, mean something to me?

✱ ✱ ✱

The big debate of the week, roysh, turns out to be whether we should actually go to the Romania match, which would mean, like, slamming the foot down all the way to Sydney and seeing Australia at pretty much ninety miles an hour, and in the end we were all, like, fock that for a game of soldiers. Didn't want to break our necks getting down there and plus, roysh, it took longer than expected to fix the gearbox on the Chuck Wagon, we're talking sixty-five hours, no fifty-eight – fock it, whatever three days is in hours – but we spend the time anyway hanging around, doing the whole goy thing, knocking back beers, having the craic, meeting Sheilas. Eventually, roysh, we get our wheels back and we hit the road again, the plan basically being to carry on rolling into these little outback towns that have never clapped eyes on five Irish stud muffins before and hit the road again when we've got the entire female population grinning from ear to ear. It's like, next stop Cairns. Takes us three hours to hook up with these three Septics, roysh, California they're from, total honeys, so hot you'd basically need oven gloves to get their focking bra straps open. We meet them in this bor, roysh, yours truly breaking the ice as per usual with a few cheeky one-liners, giving it, 'I must have died and gone to heaven – all I can see is angels.'

And they're loving it, roysh, they're telling me I'm, like, SO sweet, then one of them – image of Penelope Cruz – storts telling me that her great-grandmother comes from County Donna Gall and I manage to resist the temptation to go, 'And this affects me how?' because it's nice to be nice sometimes, roysh, and when you're away from home you've basically got to be, like, an ambassador for your country and shit.

We pair off pretty quickly. I bag off with Penelope, JP scores the Drew Barrymore lookalike and Oisinn ends up with the one who looks a little bit like Barbara Hershey, as in ten years ago. Christian, of course, is still going out with Lauren and has no interest in doing the bould thing behind her back – whatever you're into – and none of the birds has any interest in Fionn because he's an ugly focker.

Of course he's bulling it, roysh, because none of the birds has the slightest interest in the facts he's quoting about the annual rainfall in the Northern Territories – they're air hostesses, for fock's sake – and he leans over to me, roysh, and he goes, 'Bit dizzy, aren't they?' and I'm like, 'Whatever.' Just to try to hammer his point home, roysh, he turns around and goes, 'Remember those two planes crashed into the World Trade Centre? Does anyone remember what date that was?' and the three birds – The Flying Waitresses, we call them – they look at each other, totally focking clueless, and eventually, roysh, my one goes, 'I think it was around this time of year? Was it, like, September, or October?'

I give the goy a filthy, but it doesn't matter, roysh, because fifteen minutes later, me, Oisinn and JP are taking the porty back to test the suspension on the old Winnebago, leaving the glasses-wearing geek at the bor, listening to Christian spouting on about how Lobot was never the loyal courtier that Lando Calrissian thought he was.

The next morning, we take the whole show on the road again, the birds and everything, and we hit the Great Barrier Reef. They're actually mad into seeing coral and shit, so me, Christian, Oisinn and JP hit the nearest battle cruiser and leave them to it, although Fionn goes with them, with his guidebook and his focking glasses. As JP says, the goy lacks dignity at times. Me and the rest of the goys get talking about rugby. Don't know much about Romania really, except that wine we had at Odhran's twenty-first, Riesling or some shit, one-ninety-nine a bottle, ended up borfing my ring up all over the gaff. 'Crap jeans,' Oisinn goes. 'That's another thing you associate with Romania. Remember that whole Communism thing came to an end. All those stone-washed baggies pegging it into the west,' and we all break our holes laughing. JP goes, 'Hey, I can just picture your old man at this very moment in time, Ross. He's at the bor in Portmornock offering everybody in the bor his views on the match, whether they want them or not. *"The Romanians have contributed nothing to our society except that wretched accordion music"*.' Have to say, roysh, it's an unbelievable impression. He's going, *'"They've ruined the Blue Danube for Fionnuala and I"',* Oisinn goes, 'Hey, didn't your old pair try to adopt one of those Romanian babies, Ross?' and I'm there, 'Yeah. Till this social worker bird came around and heard some of the old man's views. He told her he thought everyone in Ballymun flats should be turfed out onto the street so they could be redecorated and used for student flats,' and we all crack our shits again and high-five each other.

The Flying Waitresses arrive back with Fionn in tow, bullshitting on about how the reef is the biggest structure in the world built by living organisms, pissing into the wind basically, and the birds tell us it was, like, SO beautiful and, like, SO amazing – they actually talk like Sorcha – then we suggest we all go out for dinner, roysh, which is, like, a farewell thing more than anything. Because we've had our fun basically and it's time to move on, though sadly the birds didn't see it that way. No bird likes being given the Spanish Archer, although we were probably wrong to break the news to them by phone. I was the one who did the dirty deed, ringing Penelope Cruz on my mobile. She goes, 'Where are you guys?' and I'm like, 'Em. Halfway to Townsville, if Fionn's directions are roysh.' She goes, '*Townsville*?' obviously not a happy bunny. I go, 'Hey, they're the rules of the road, baby,' not wanting a big emotional scene and shit, but her voice goes all sort of, like, quivery, roysh, trying to lay the whole guilt vibe on me by threatening to turn on the waterworks. She's going, 'But ... but you told me last night you ... loved me.' Oops. That focking Bundy rum.

✱ ✱ ✱

JP told Fionn and Oisinn he heard noises in the night. We're talking voices. He also said he woke up at one point and saw a figure standing over him. I'm pretty sure it was me getting up for a hit and miss. I did stand over his bed for a minute or two trying to decide whether I should shave the focker's eyebrows off or not. But the voices. Weird voices, he said. He's pretty much freaking us all out at this stage.

✱ ✱ ✱

We hit Sydney eventually and if you're asking me, roysh, it's not a moment too soon. JP's got this CD of Elvis gospel songs that he petty-pilfered off some – get this – forty-six-year-old bird he pulled in some kip on Leeson Street, and I swear to God, roysh, if I have to listen to it one more time it'll be JP walking that milky white way of the Lord one of these days.

The last two weeks have passed in a haze of nights I can't re-member and birds whose names I never bothered my orse ask-ing. Fabienne is the bird I'm with now, roysh, French chick, we're talking twenty-seven, hasn't put out yet, but she's a total lasher. Stick Courtney Cox on a drip, wean her slowly onto three square meals a day and you're in the same ballpork.

Fionn's pulled her mate, this Cork bird called Ciara, who's ba-sically cat, roysh, though not bad for an ugly focker like him, and she also has a head full of useless bullshit, which makes them per-fect for each other. As for Oisinn, he's pulled this, like, Aussie bird called Shona, and if I called her a dog, roysh, I'd have the ISPCA on my case for cruelty to animals. She puts the bet in bet-down.

Christian's still staying loyal to Lauren – each to their own – while JP's put the old broom-handle away for a few days after a bad experience in which he got totalled on Jim Beam and ended up giving some Irish bird he poked his real phone number. He's going, 'I'm a danger to myself and to wider society,' and we're all like, 'Totally.' So anyway, roysh, we pull into town – we're talking me, the goys, Fabienne and the Gruesome Twosome – pork the Chuck Wagon somewhere near Dorling Horbour and hit the the Pyrmont Bridge Hotel, which is basically a battle cruiser that's open all day and all night, we're talking twenty-four-hour lager frenzy for the Rock boys on tour here and high-fives all round.

The local piss we're drinking is called Toohey's New, though it doesn't matter a fock what you order over here, because the same urine arrives. I think that's why they drink those little pots instead of, like, pints, because it's so focking horrible.

We knock a few back and all of a sudden Ciara and Oisinn's hound, this Shona one, they stort banging on about how they have to go out to Bondi and check out the surfies and, Fabienne, roysh, she just goes, 'Mmmm,' as in, yeah, let's go check out those amazing bods, trying to, like, make me jealous and shit and it must work, roysh, because before I've even noticed it I've turned around and gone, 'I do the odd bit of surfing myself. Irish champion three times,' which leads to a bit of a debate, roysh, with Ciara – the focking hog – basically calling me a tin-roofer.

Out of the corner of my eye, I can see the goys and they're, like, trying to keep a straight face, but I'm looking at Fabienne and she SO wants to believe me. She goes, 'Ross, plees tell za troot to me,' because she's, like, French don't forget. She's like, 'This eez true, yes, what you say about ze surfing?' and I go, 'The record books don't lie, babes,' but Ciara's there giving it, 'Let's head out to Bondi and see you do it then,' the interfering cow. Seen better legs on a piano as well. I'm like, 'No can do. Might be going back playing AIL for Castlerock next season. Their insurance doesn't cover me,' and she goes, 'That's bullshit,' big bogger head on her, and then Shona storts giving it, 'Yeah, fair go, Ross,' and it's the look on Fabienne's face, roysh, the look of, like, disappointment I suppose, that makes me go, 'Roysh, I'll do it if someone gets me a board,' thinking in the back of my mind there's no way anyone's gonna lay their hands on one straight away.

Should have known, roysh, Fionn's straight out the focking

door and he's back like a focking boomerang, with a board under his orm, a cover on it and everything. So the next thing I know, roysh, we're getting the train out to County Bondi, as all the Irish here call it, and Fabienne has her orm around my waist and she's telling me she loves goys who are sporty and she can't wait to tell all her mates back in Frogland, blah blah focking blah. Of course I'm there thinking about the start of 'Home and Away', all those dudes giving it loads out on the waves, making it look a cinch basically, and I'm thinking, you know, how hord could it be?

We get there – the whole crew – and hop off the train. Bondi ends up being a dump, boggers everywhere, in their county colours, like the knackers that they are. Oisinn at this stage is really laying it on thick, telling the birds that I'm such a modest bloke I kept all this world-champion shit to myself. We hit the beach and Fionn hands me the board, roysh, and he tells me to do my stuff, and suddenly I'm totally kacking it, roysh, because I've only just remembered that I can't even swim. I'm looking out at the waves – we are talking twenty-foot-high babies here, I shit you not – and my knees are, like, totally shaking. I can't let Fabienne see that I'm a wuss, roysh, so I tell the whole crew that I need to be alone to, like, prepare myself mentally and shit, and I walk down towards the water on my own – Oisinn going, 'Knock 'em dead, champ' – whip off the old T-shirt, dubes and chinos and lash on the old shorts. CRAAASSSHHH!

The focking waves are getting bigger and I'm bricking it now. I unzip the surfboard and ... SHIT THE BED! I don't BELIEVE it. It's ... it's not a surfboard at all. Fionn – the focker – has just broken the legs off the focking ironing board and stuck the thing back in its cover. SHIT! I'm in trouble now. But what else can I do? I've got to go through with it or else they'll be giving it, I don't know,

'I wouldn't have thought the Irish champion would have cared what kind of surfboard he had,' or something to make me look a total tit. I can actually hear the goys sniggering behind me, obviously in on Fionn's little joke.

I just lash the board under my orm, roysh, troop down to the edge of the water, get in it up to my knees, lay the board down, lie face-down onto it and stort paddling my way out to sea, like you see them do on the telly basically. But you don't need to be Einstein to know what happens next. I see this wave coming from, like, fifty metres away and it's focking humungous even from that distance. It's focking massive and it's getting closer and closer. I look over my shoulder, roysh, and I'm a good bit out, definitely way over my depth, so it's too late to turn back, so I'm just there waiting for the basically inevitable. WHOOOFSSSHHH!!!

The next thing I know, roysh, I'm waking up, not knowing whether I'm alive or basically toast. But I can feel the sand on my back and I can hear the waves breaking and I can smell the sea air and maybe *Contradiction* by Calvin Klein. And I can feel someone's lips pressed against mine. Blowing, like, into my mouth.

Fabienne must have saved me. Fock the embarrassment. I'm enjoying the, I don't know, sensuality of the moment, if that's even a word. And I can hear voices – the goys – asking if I'm going to be alroysh. And I can feel ... fock ... I can feel someone's stubble rubbing off my top lip. I open my eyes quickly and – yuck! – it's ... it's ... *Shona*? I just, like, swat her away and sit up, roysh, and stort looking around for Fabienne, but she's nowhere to be seen. Unless that's her I can see in the distance, chatting to that dude who looks like a lifeguard. Then walking off with him ...

✳ ✳ ✳

I get a text from Erika and she's there, **Was in Orphas room 2nite readin her diary again. 4got sum of it from b4. Hilights – 'ross was so gentl wth me' and 'Srcha cant find out but I thnk im in lov wth hm.' Barf! Hav phtocpied relvnt pges. Hop ur njoyin urslf. x.** Now I know she's not bluffing.

✳ ✳ ✳

'I've got roots in Ireland,' this Aussie chick goes to me the other night and I look at her – straight face, roysh – and I'm there, 'I've got roots in Darwin, Townsville, Surfer's Paradise, Brisbane, Coffs Harbour and Sydney,' which earns me a stubby of Carlton Draught down the front of my shirt, as well as a slap in the face. As Oisinn says, though, there's nothing wrong with being a slave to the old one-liner. And fock it, there's a hell of a lot more fish in the sea. And basically, roysh, fish in the sea has been the, like, story of the last couple of days. We arrived in Adelaide after driving down from, like, Sydney after the Namibia game, and JP spent half the trip banging on about the Great Whites that swim off the coast and how coming face-to-face with one of them would be the ultimate hit – better than watching the look on the face of a Gick boy as you kick the winning penalty in the last minute of the Senior Cup final, then throwing the lips on his bird in front of him in Annabel's.

I remind JP – basically having the craic – that he hasn't had his Nat King since the millennium, roysh, unless you count those five-knuckle shuffles he's been enjoying when the lights go out every night in the Vengabus, and he tells me that when I go to sleep tonight he is SO using my blue Ralph as a jizz rag, we're talking the one I got as a Chrimbo present from Sorcha, and that gets me thinking about the whole Claire-and-Orpha situation, which just, like, depresses me.

We stick the Chuck Wagon down some sidestreet and hit the beach, where Fionn read in the local rag – *look at me, I'm a nerd and I can see thanks to Weatherglaze* – that you can get into this cage and be dropped down into, like, the actual water with the actual shorks.

I'm kacking it just thinking about it, roysh, and we're talking totally here, but the goys are determined to do it and I'm dropping orse biscuits to beat the band, so I decide I need a couple of straighteners first. So we hit the bor, roysh, and Specsavers can't let it go, storts going, 'You're not nervous, are you, Ross?' and I'm like, 'Nervous? Don't make me laugh,' and I end up ordering a quadruple Jim Beam with no ice, a bottle of Hahn Premium for Christian and My First Lagers for the rest of the goys. Oisinn knocks his back in one go, then tells us he has a little matter to attend to, which I presume means he's dropping the kids off at the pool, but he doesn't go near the jacks, roysh, he actually goes outside, but none of us thinks any more of it, roysh, and I don't even bother asking him where he's been when he comes back with a plastic bag from Coles, as in the supermorket. Another quadruple Jim Beam for me and the next thing the five of us are hitting the seafront. The goy in charge gives us this big lecture, roysh, don't do this, under no circumstances do that, blah blah blah, in one ear and out the other.

We lash on the old wetsuits and the oxygen tanks, roysh, and step into the cage, which is hung on these, like, heavy chains and then suddenly we're, like, lowered into the water. It's pitch black down there, roysh, and nothing happens for ages, but then all of a sudden we feel this, like, bump off the side of the cage and we all turn around – shitting ourselves basically – and there's, like, two big fock-off shorks circling us. Focking huge, we're basically talking Jaws's two older brothers here.

But we stort to relax, roysh, because they're not, like, threatening and shit, just massive and amazing to look at. They've got, like, eyes that just stare at you and never blink, and teeth like that bird Oisinn copped off with in Noosa.

Of course JP then storts acting the maggot, doing the whole haka thing. *Ka mate, ka mate, ka ora, ka ora.* And we all join in, giving it loads. *Tenei te tangata puhuruhuru.* Doing the actions and shit and it's, like, a total buzz, letting the shorks know who's the boss. You've met your match, goys. Castlerock boys on tour basically. Spread the word. *Nana i tiki mai whakawhiti te ra.* Anyway, roysh, where all this is going is that Oisinn all of a sudden whips out this Coles bag he had in the battle cruiser earlier and – OH MY FOCK! – I couldn't BELIEVE what was in it. I shit you not, roysh, the fat focker pulls out these three, like, sheeps' horts, roysh, and he storts, like, squeezing them? And suddenly there's all this, like, blood? We're talking floating around in the water?

Of course the shorks, roysh, from being really calm, suddenly stort going totally ballistic, basically headbutting the cage, trying to break their way in, obviously thinking it's dinnertime.

Ssshhhiiittt!!!

Castlerock boys on tour are suddenly Castlerock boys on toast. They're going mental. So are we. We're, like, screaming like a bunch of focking birds.

Fffoooccckkk!!!

Takes the dude in the boat about ten focking minutes to get the cage back up. At one point, roysh, I thought the shorks were actually trying to bite the focking chains off. We finally get out of the water, roysh, and out of the cage and Oisinn just falls on the deck, cracking his hole laughing. The goy in charge knows fock-all about the sheep horts and he tells us he's, like, really sorry and shit, that he's never known shorks to behave like that in all the weeks he's been working with them, and now he understands why he can't get insurance for this little project.

And this makes Oisinn crack up even more. He's on his back now and he's, like, kicking his legs in the air. The rest of us are just, like, sitting there, not moving, half in shock and half in fear of taking off these wetsuits and seeing the mess we've made.

✳ ✳ ✳

Get this, roysh, JP decides we need to have a sort of, like, séance, roysh, to see can we contact the dead dude who was offed in the back of the Chuck Wagon. He's going, 'His spirit is restless,' but I'm giving it, 'Don't *go* there, goys. You shouldn't fock around with things you don't understand,' and Fionn goes, 'Didn't stop you sitting the Leaving,' and quick as a flash – see, I'm always too quick for him – I go, 'You are one focking tool.' Anyway, roysh, I end up getting out-voted because Oisinn's up for it as well and, well, you know Christian, he's as easy-going as they come. He's probably going to ask the old dude to stick Obi Wan Kenobi on the line when we're finished talking to him. So the goys all stort accusing me of basically crapping it then, roysh, and I tell them they're talking through their orses and then they all stort making, like, chicken noises, so I pull up a seat and sit down beside them at the table.

The next thing, roysh, JP whips out this thing, roysh, which turns out to be, like, a ouija board, roysh, which he says he bought in some, like, morket or other this morning. Not trying to sound all, like, intellectual here, roysh, but *oui* is the, I think, Irish word for yeah and *ja* is the French word for roysh. Anyway, it's got, like, all the letters of the alphabet going around in a basic circle, roysh and then Yes and No in the middle. JP goes, 'Oisinn, grab that glass off the draining board, will you dude?' and Oisinn goes off into the kitchen and the next thing we hear him shouting in, 'Is this Heino in it?' and JP shouts, 'DON'T DRINK IT!' and you can hear Oisinn spitting it into the sink. JP goes, 'It's a urine sample, dude. I was a bit worried about that blue stuff in my piss, but it seems to have gone now.' Oisinn comes in wiping his mouth, going, 'Thank God it's only piss. Thought you were going to say it was Budweiser,' which gets a good laugh, then he goes and rinses the glass out and comes back to the table.

JP goes, 'My old dear has an aunt, mad as a wheelchair, smells of Marietta biscuits, but she's got, like, *the gift*. She's able to *contact* people.' Oisinn goes, 'She can contact my old man then, tell him to send me out another three grand. Haven't been able to get a signal since we hit Adelaide,' and we all crack our holes laughing, all except JP. He's there, 'The occult is no laughing matter, goys. I'm telling you. Auntie Melicent has the gift. And she told me once she saw it in me.' I'm there, 'Okay then, David Copperfield, let's get focking on with it,' and he gives me a filthy, roysh, then he puts the glass upside down on the table and he tells us all to place a forefinger on it. Then he makes his voice go all sort of, like, quivery, roysh, and storts giving it, 'Is there anybody there?' and nothing happens, roysh. He goes, 'Is there anybody there?' and again fock-all. He tries one more time, roysh. He goes, 'Is there anybody there?' and the next thing – I am *not* bullshitting you here – the glass storts to, like, vibrate under our fingers. Then, roysh – I swear to God, I nearly drop one in my kacks – it storts to focking *move*, we are talking *actually* move here. I'm there, 'Who the fock is doing that?' but all the goys are there, 'It's not me,' and it definitely isn't me. JP goes, 'It's a message from the spirit world, Ross. It's spelling something out.' H. E. L. – I'm shitting it here. Christian looks a bit freaked as well, but JP, Fionn and Oisinn seem fine about it – L. O.

I'm there, 'What do you think he's trying to say?' and all the goys just, like, groan and Fionn goes, 'Ross, you're slower than a wet weekend in Tullamore,' and JP goes, 'He *or she* said hello, Ross.' Oisinn goes, 'Couldn't be our man then,' and JP's there, 'Why do you say that?' and Oisinn's just like, 'Our man's an Aussie. He would have said G'day.' JP goes, 'There's no apostrophe on the board, though. And maybe he wants to converse in our language. Make sure we understand the message.' Fionn's there, 'I've always wondered about that. I mean, if you contact someone who was dyslexic in this world and they wanted to warn you that you were going to, say, get knocked down by a car, would they warn you to be *craeful corssing the raod*?' and Oisinn and JP crack their holes laughing and so do I, roysh, even though I haven't a clue what he's talking about, as per usual. I don't know how they're staying so cool.

JP goes, 'Can I just remind you goys that there *is* someone else with us in the room. As in a *spirit*?' and then he looks up at the ceiling, roysh, and he goes, 'How. Are. You. Feeling?' like the way you talk to people when they're, like, foreign. The glass storts, like, vibrating again, roysh, and moves really slowly across to the L, then to the O, then to the N, then it's to the, like, E, then to the S, then back to the O, roysh, then it's like the M, then back to the E. Then it's, like, the T, then it moves really slowly to the O, then to the N, then the I, then it's, like, the G, then the H and it stops, roysh, on the T. Fionn goes, 'Lonesome tonight,' and there's, like, silence and Oisinn goes, 'Shit the bed, we've contacted Elvis FOCKING Presley,' then he looks up and goes, 'Sorry, Elvis.'

Fionn goes, 'Let's ask him does he know anything about Roswell and Area 51,' and Oisinn goes, 'Fock that. Just ask him has he met some Aussie bloke up there with a head shaped like the back of a shovel.' JP's getting majorly pissed off with the goys. He goes, 'When you enter the spirit world, you don't ask questions. You listen. Do you not appreciate what's happening here? There's probably, like, millions of dudes out there who've tried over the years to get a message from Elvis from beyond the grave. And he's talking to *us*. Doesn't that mean something to you? It's *got* to be that CD. There's something, I don't know, spiritual about it.' He looks up, roysh, turns his palms over and, like, raises them in the air – he thinks he's a priest now – and he goes, 'Have. You. A. Message. For. Us. King?' and nothing happens for, like, thirty seconds, roysh, but then the glass storts, like, shaking and it goes to the W, then to the I, then to the S, then it's, like, the H. Then it goes I, then N, then E, then V, then E and then it's, like, R. We're going, 'Wish I never ...' and then after maybe thirty seconds, roysh, it storts moving again and it goes to the S and then to the U and then, like, the N and then the G. Then it's the D, then the A, then he gives it a bit of M, then a bit of N, then it's, like, S, then it's O, then it's N, then it's G and before it even gets to the S, roysh, we've all jumped up from the table, basically shitting ourselves.

We've all basically found our own corner of the room, roysh, and we're all there trying to catch our breaths and calm ourselves down. I'm there, 'Do NOT yank my chain on this – was one of you goys moving that glass?' but they're all, like, 'No,' and I go,

'JP, fock that *yeahroysh* board or whatever you call it out the window. I mean it.' He goes, 'What? Goys, we've made a success- ful connection to the spirit world. Our goy's probably waiting to talk to us next. We want to find out how he died, don't we?' and Fionn goes, 'I have to say, I'm with Ross here. I'm not even curi- ous anymore.' I tell the goys I'm going for a walk and, one by one, roysh, they all say they're coming with me. I'm there, 'Are you *sure* one of you goys wasn't acting the dick with the glass?'

✱ ✱ ✱

Get a text from Sorcha, roysh, and she tells me she's having SUCH an amazing time in Paris, where she's gone with her old dear and a few of the girls to get the lingerie. It's a weird thing to say, roysh, but I'm actually storting to miss her.

✱ ✱ ✱

There's fock-all great about the Great Ocean Road when you're suffering with the mother of all hangovers, that much I can basically tell you. And the goys are making me drive all the way to Melbourne, roysh, even though I'm, like, bleeding out my focking eyes here, and Fionn's wrecking my head, bullshitting on about how he's looking forward to the Twelve Apostles and I tell him it'll make a change from Pam and her Five Sisters and he goes, 'Says the man whose right bicep is twice as big as his left,' and quick as a flash I'm there, 'I'm not the one who's half-blind, Specs Xpress.' JP, who's, like, flaked out on his bed, shouts, 'It's like listening to Terence Stamp and Guy what's-his-name in that steamer film. Shut the fock up, I'm hanging here,' and Fionn focks off, roysh, and I lash a CD on, listen to a bit of U2 while trying to, like, concentrate on the road. Our last night in Adelaide, the night of the Argentina match, storts coming back to me. It was a good match, what I can remember of it. Six o'clock's a pretty crap time for kick-off because we were all basically horrendufied by the middle of the afternoon.

When we got the try, it looked like it was going to be pretty much plain sailing, roysh, and we storted having a bit of banter with this Argie crew who were there giving it, 'AR-GEN-TINA! AR-GEN-TINA!' and I was giving it loads back, going, 'You can shove your ...' and I turn around to Fionn and I'm like, 'What do they make in Argentina?' and he goes, 'Corned beef,' and I'm there, 'You can shove your corned beef up your orse ...' making pretty much everyone who heard it crack up.

Of course, when they went ahead, roysh, they were quick to point out that I'd gone, like, totally quiet, but in the end we kicked their orses and we all basically ported on good terms, Fionn picking up a couple of email addresses, so he can – his words, now – 'find out a bit more about the culture of Argentina', but more likely take his campaign of boring people to death to a brand new country.

We were heading out of the ground, roysh, and I stort shooting the breeze with these two Argie birds, I'm giving it, 'Are you enjoying Adelaide?' really laying it on thick, roysh, and the birds are, like, all giggly and stuff. But fifteen minutes of killer one-liners later, me and Oisinn have basically pulled them, me copping off with the one who looked like Andie McDowell, him ending up with the one who looked like focking Roddy McDowell. We tell the goys to steer clear of the Chuck Wagon for a couple of hours and we take the birds back. Lana, my one was called, roysh, didn't catch the other one's name, it being totally irrelevant to me. So there's me and Lana doing the bould thing on the airbed, roysh, her blabbing away in Argentinian, which I don't understand, although – not being big-headed or anything – I don't think any of us needs a translation for, 'SÍ! SÍ! SÍ!'

Halfway through, roysh, I hear my phone ringing and it's basically down the other end of the Vengabus so I decide to let it go to, like, the message minder. But then the next thing is, roysh, I hear Oisinn answering it and suddenly – the stupid focker – he's stood over me and Lana and he's going, 'Call for you, Ross,' and he hands me the thing, roysh, and of course I'm thinking, This SO better not be Sorcha. She hears this bird here panting with pleasure and it'll be a funeral not a wedding the goys'll be attending on the nineteenth of December. I'm there, 'Hello?' and all I hear is, 'Humphreys or O'Gara? You're standing in the shoes of the great Eddie O'Sullivan Esquire. Choose,' and I'm just there, 'Go and stick your finger in an electric socket and die, you penis,' and I hang up.

It's weird, roysh, but hearing your old man's voice while you're on the job is a bit of a passion-killer, roysh, and Lana seems to cop that the show is over. So we get up and head into the kitchen, where Oisinn is rooting through his dirty washing, looking for the portable DVD player he bought in Kuala Lumpur airport on the way over. Me and Lana and the dog Oisinn's with sit down on the couch, roysh, and he sets the thing up and he goes, 'Turns out our friend here,' – he's obviously forgotten her name as well – 'our friend here is actually from Uruguay,' and the bird goes, 'I from Montevideo,' which must be Uruguay for Pigsville or Bet-Down City if you're asking me. Oisinn's there, 'I told her I had this film she *had* to see.'

So he pops the disc in the machine, roysh, faffs around for a few more minutes, then switches off the lights and we all wait and it's all, 'Miramax Pictures presents. A Frank Martin Movie. Based on a true story. Starring Ethan Hawk. And Vincent Spano. And Josh Hamilton.' and then suddenly, across the screen in capital letters, it's like, 'ALIVE!' and – I don't believe this, roysh – it turns out it's that film about that rugby team from, where else, Uruguay, and their plane crashed in, I don't know, the Alps or some shit and they had to basically eat each other to survive.

We sit there watching it for, like, ten or twenty minutes, roysh, when all of a sudden I hear all this, like, sniffling and out of the corner of my eye I notice that Oisinn's bird is, like, bawling her eyes out. Of course I'm there putting two and two together, thinking that if she's from this Uruguay shithole and she's into, like, rugby and shit, then maybe she knows someone who was, like, involved. Maybe her old pair. Yeah, maybe her old dear ate her old man. But of course Oisinn's, like, totally oblivious to the fact that she's crying, roysh, and he's pointing out all the passengers as they're, like, strapping themselves into their seats, roysh, telling us who he'd eat and in what order. He's going, 'Him. Then him. I'd stick that big prop forward in the freezer. He'd keep. Oh my God, I'd eat her before the focking food ran out ...'

So the next thing, roysh – this is focking hilarious – his bird stops crying, dives on top of him and storts, like, beating the crap out of him with her fists, going, 'NOT SO FUNNY NOW. NOT SO FUNNY NOW,' and of course I'm cracking my hole laughing too much to help the goy. Then she pulls off one of her rhythms and storts, like, whacking him across the head with it and it's, like, five minutes before me and Lana can actually drag her off the goy. The two birds focked off, telling us we were very nasty boys, which was hordly, like, news to us. Oisinn could see the funny side of it the next morning, even though that's some black eye the dude's got. When the rest of the goys are in the back dozing, he turns to me and he goes, 'Thanks for not telling them, you know, what happened and shit?' and I'm there, 'Hey, it's Kool plus his significant other, my man.' He goes, 'JP asked me. I just said pure passion and tapped the side of my nose. He seemed happy enough with that.' I'm there, 'He believed that?' and he nods and goes, 'It turns out the goys came back about four o'clock in the morning, saw the Chuck Wagon bouncing up and down on its wheels and thought we were having the time of our lives. And we both crack our shites laughing and in the back JP shouts, 'Will you two faggots keep it down over there. Some of us are trying to catch some zeds.'

✳ ✳ ✳

We're about an hour from Melbourne when I get a text message and I don't know how, roysh, but I know before I even check that it's Erika with more of her games. I open it when Oisinn nods off and it's like, **Wnt out wth Clre lst nite. Cant hld her pis wen shes drnk. Tld me evrytng n I recrded al d intimat d tails. Congrats - ur getting quickr at it! Cant wait 4 u 2 hear d tape.** I'm focking toast.

✳ ✳ ✳

'The thing you have to understand about All You Can Eat restaurants,' Oisinn goes while we're sitting in this All You Can Eat restaurant, 'is that the house always wins. And the house always wins because the deck is loaded.' JP goes, 'Explain,' and Oisinn's like, 'Well, to start with, the food is never hot, just warm. So after one plate of it, you basically can't face anymore.' We all just, like, nod. The dude has a point. He goes, 'That's why I couldn't eat that focker out of business in Playa del Ingles a couple of years ago. But I'm going to smash the All You Can Eat cartel with *this*,' and he whips out this, like, miniature gas heater, roysh, and he puts his plate on top of it and Pip, this Aussie bird I've been throwing one into for the last couple of nights, she's in, like, total shock.

Christian is telling Alanah, her best mate – plain as a Rich Tea biscuit – that he has three words for anyone who thinks that the threat to the new Republic died with the Emperor in the new Death Stor and those words are Grand Admiral Thrawn, while Fionn's reading a book called *The Nexus and Olive Tree – A Bird's Eye View of Globalisation*, like the wanker that he is. I can see Pip looking at me, roysh, wondering what is this absolute stud doing hanging around with a bunch of focking muppets like this lot. And it is hord to explain, roysh, but I was watching that 'Happy Days' on the telly the other morning, roysh, and I suppose I'm a bit like that Fonzie in my own way. I mean the dude didn't hang around with geeks like Ralph and Richie for the good of his health, it was more to, like, make himself look cooler and shit? It's not the Crown Lager talking, roysh, but that's the way it is with me.

JP's pretty quiet today. I presume he's just wrecked like the rest of us after the Ireland v Australia game, the Melbourne Cup, blah blah blah, we're talking five nights straight on the total lash and we're talking totally. We ended up going to the Melbourne Cup in our Castlerock jerseys and shades, giving it loads, roysh, knocking back the old champers by the neck, chatting up birds, should have seen the scenario, we're talking wall-to-wall Blankers-Koen here, and there's us giving it, 'I like your hat,' worming our way in with the old Irish chorm.

Everyone was looking at us, roysh, all the birds' eyes were out on stalks, and it was only a matter of time before a TV crew rolled up and asked to, like, interview us? The goy tells us he's from, like, Channel 7 News, roysh, and we're all there, 'Get the camera rolling then! Make-up! Action!' basically giving it loads.

So the goy looks into the camera and he goes, 'Yes, it's a beautiful day down here, Julie. Now at the Melbourne Cup, race-goers come in all shapes and sizes. Now this crowd with me at the moment are from Ireland and they've come dressed up as a bunch of rugby jocks. Guys, are you enjoying your time at the Melbourne Cup?' and we're all there, 'Yyyeeeaaahhh!!!' high-fiving each other, the whole lot.

He goes, 'Any message for our viewers watching at home?' and of course we've been put on the spot here, none of us knows what to say, it's like stage-fright or some shit, and there's this, like, silence for, like, twenty seconds or something until Ross here saves the day as usual by going, 'My old man's a knob-end … and if he sees this, I need more dosh, man.'

It was a cracker of a day, roysh, even if Sorcha did do her best to ruin it, ringing me up in the middle of the night with her whole insecurity act, giving it, 'You're doing the dirt on me over there. I SO know you are,' and I'm there, 'How many times do I have to tell you, stop listening to Erika. She's just trying to stir shit.' She goes, 'She keeps saying she knows you better than I do, Ross.'

CHAPTER EIGHT
All the Days of Our Lives

Ended up forgetting to bring Sorcha back a present from Australia, roysh, but of course Slick Mick here saves the day by picking her up a *You've Got Mail* box-set in Kuala Lumpur on the stopover, the old team of Ryan and Hanks getting back together for the rom-com that took the genre into cyberspace, thirty Aussie dollars, with a T-shirt, a mouse-mat and six stills from the movie thrown in, happy days. I'll tell her that all the toy koalas and, like, didgeridoos were all, I don't know, tested on animals or some shit. No, this limited edition – only fourteen million were made – collector's gift-pack is gonna be the difference between getting my Billy Joel tonight or sitting in my room playing the old Japanese JCB operator.

We arrive in Dublin at, like, ten o'clock in the morning. Me and the goys come through the arrivals gate and Sorcha's standing there with Lauren, as in Christian's bird. Sorcha comes straight over, roysh, air-kisses me, then the rest of the goys, then goes, 'Come on, we've stuff to do,' and suddenly I'm following her over to the short-term cor pork, no chance to high-five the rest of the goys to say, 'Great trip,' and whatever. We're in the cor, roysh, and she goes, 'Did you sleep on the flight?' and I'm there, 'Yeah, the few beers helped,' and she's like, 'Good. We've a

busy day ahead of us. You've got your final ring fitting this afternoon. We've got a dance class tonight, just to refresh your
memory on some of the steps. And this traffic SO better stort
moving because we're seeing the priest at, like, half-eleven.'

I'm there, 'Sorry, my ears popped somewhere over Thailand
and they haven't gone back to normal yet. I thought for a second
there you said we were going to see a priest.' She's there, 'Ross,
do NOT stort your shit today. You can't get married in a church
without getting the approval of the priest first. We should have
seen him, like, months ago. You're SO lucky he's a friend of
Dad's,' and blahdy blahdy blah. We pull up outside the priest's
gaff, roysh, and Sorcha smokes two Marlboro Lights while giving
me various warnings and threats about how to answer and how
not to answer the priest's questions. We knock on the door,
roysh, and this old biddy shows us into this, like, study where
Father Whatever-His-Face is already waiting for us. Straight away
he storts going, 'How's your father, Sorcha?' – small talk, small
talk, small talk – then, after ignoring me for, like, five minutes, he
suddenly turns around to me and he goes, 'You must be Ross,'
and I shake the dude's hand and I go, 'Hey, what's the craic,
dude?' actually going out of my way to make the effort. He
doesn't appreciate it, though. He looks at me like he's walked in
and caught me giving his housekeeper a length while drinking his,
I don't know, whatever priests drink, crème de menthe. He goes,
'Don't think we've ever had the pleasure. Where do you usually
attend church?' and I'm not going to lie to the dude. I'm there,
'Church? Whoa, horsey. Sunday mornings I'm generally hanging
after the night before,' trying to lighten the old atmos, roysh, but
I have to be honest, it's not going well.

He goes, 'Listen to me. This is an informal meeting, but it's also an important one. I want to find out whether you are emotionally and spiritually mature enough to enter into the Holy Sacrament of marriage in the presence of the Lord, do you understand?' and it's obviously heavy shit here. I'm there, 'Hey, I'm Kool and the Gang,' and he goes, 'Hmmm! At this moment, Sorcha, I might ask you to leave the room while I have a little chat with your ... intended,' and I don't like the, I don't know, tone of the way he said that. *Intended.* Sorcha goes, 'I'd just like to apologise in advance for anything he says,' the crawler, and the priest goes, 'Am I my brother's keeper? Genesis 4:9.' When Sorcha focks off, the dude tells me to take a seat, roysh, and I sit on this, like, leather sofa he's got going on and he sits down beside me. He's just, like, staring at the door, roysh, and he goes, 'A great girl, Sorcha. I married her parents. Friends of mine. Do you love her, Ross?' and I'm like, 'Ah yeah, you know yourself, dude,' playing my cords pretty close to my chest. He just looks at me over the top of his glasses and he's there, 'Her father has told me you're quite the Jack the Lad. If you ever hurt her, Ross, I'm going to be ministering to you the Final Sacrament. Do you know what that is?' and I'm there, 'Em, I can guess,' and he goes, 'Good. I'll say a few words of prayer before Edmund puts you in the ground. I'll plead provocation before the Lord on the Last Day and face my judgement then. Do I make myself clear ... *dude*?' I'm there, 'Loud and clear, Father,' kacking myself because I know he's actually serious. He goes, 'Just want to make sure you understand the craic ... horsey.'

I go, 'Honestly. There's no way I'd ever do the dirt on the girl,' and he stares back at me and goes, 'What do you know about the Bible?' Straight out of left field, that one. I'm there, 'The Bible?' He goes, 'You've heard of this book, I take it? The bedrock of our faith? Basic Instructions Before Leaving Earth, I like to call it,' and I'm there, 'Oh, the Bible, yeah.' The dude's looking bored now, I'm losing him. He goes, 'What would you say would be your favourite story from the Bible, Ross?' What kind of a focking question is that? I'm about to say the one with Jesus in a manger, the wise men, blah blah blah, but I'm not even sure if that's in it. Then it hits me, roysh, we're talking inspiration here, we're talking maximum respect to the Rossmeister General. I'm thinking of that Elvis CD that JP drove us up the focking walls with while we were driving around Oz. How did that song go? He goes, 'You must know at least ... *one* ... story from the Bible?' like the teachers used to talk to me at school. I'm pretty sure condescending is the word. Then, quick as a flash, roysh, Ross is there, 'I like the story of Joshua,' and at that he perks up, roysh, suddenly all, like, interested. He goes, 'What do *you* know about Joshua?' and I'm there, 'Well, I know he fought the Battle of Jericho. And the walls came tumbling down.'

His face sort of, like, lightens. Smiles, almost. He goes, 'This is *extraordinary*. Joshua is *my* favourite book of the Old Testament too,' and I'm there, 'You can talk about men of Giddeon. You can brag about your King of Saul. But there's no one like Joshua. At the Battle of Jericho,' and the next thing I know, roysh, he's telling me he's, like, misjudged me and he's sorry, roysh, and he's got the drinks cabinet open and he's pouring me a glass of scotch – I was actually roysh, there was a bottle of crème de menthe in there – and he's going, 'I have to confess I have a deep spiritual attachment to the ancient city. My father fought in the First World War, you see. Helped capture it. February twenty-first, nineteen hundred and eighteen. Three-and-a-half thousand years after the great Hebrew leader himself.'

I go, 'He was supposed to have had a spear that was, like, nigh on twelve feet long,' and he's there, 'I don't doubt it. Of course there's a lot of archaeological evidence out there now that would contradict the Old Testament account of Joshua's, shall we say, military prowess. We *are* talking about theology here rather than history, but I love the battle scenes nonetheless, the sun standing still to extend the day for Israel – Iz-rie-ill – to defeat her enemies. Joshua 10:12 to 13. Old school!' and I'm about to mention that the bone in his hip was a double-edged sword and his mouth was a gospel horn, but the dude has probably forgotten more about Joshua than I'll ever know, so I don't push it. Anyway, he might have the CD. But suffice to say, roysh, that the last thing Sorcha expected to see when the door opened twenty minutes later was Father whatever-the-fock-he-calls-himself with his orm around my shoulder, telling me how sorry he is for, like, misjudging me and promising to dig out some book he's got on the valley of the lower Jordan. He turns to Sorcha and he's like, 'Young Ross here is quite the Biblical scholar.'

We get into the cor, roysh, and Sorcha goes, 'Ross, you are SO amazing,' and I'm just there, 'I know, I know. And you haven't even seen your present yet.'

✱ ✱ ✱

I walk into kitchen and the old dear's crapping away on the phone while shoving cake into her trap. Turns out she's talking to Sorcha. She's going, 'When Charles and *I* got married, my bridesmaids had bouquets of freesias and sweetpeas and I had a cloud of pink peonies.' I'm just there, 'Borf!' Sorcha obviously says something, roysh, then the old dear goes, 'I know cranberries are your theme, dorling. That's the beauty of white flowers. They go with anything. What about a nice shower of

Phalaenopsis orchids ... Yes? Oh *good*. I just want to feel like I'm doing *something*, Sorcha ... I'll talk to Hen, one of the girls from tennis. She owns a florists.' Then Sorcha says something else, roysh, and all of a sudden the old dear's going, 'Yes, he's here in front of me. Bold as brass,' while I'm, like, mouthing the words I'm not here, the stupid bitch. She goes, 'I'll hand you over to him, dorling. And don't forget, if you need any ideas for the cake ... *Su-per*!' I grab the phone off her, roysh, before she makes an even bigger tit of herself and I go, 'Alroysh, Sorcha. What's the Jackanory?' and Sorcha goes, 'Your mum is being SUCH a pet about the wedding. She's doing SO much for us,' and I'm there, '*What*-ever!' Sorcha's like, 'I want to talk to you about getting favours for people,' and I'm there, 'Favours?' obviously thinking *sexual* favours. As you do. She goes, 'Yes, Ross, favours. Especially for Christian. I met Lauren in Nine West yesterday. She said the poor goy's been SO stressed out about the whole best man thing. And then JP, Oisinn and Fionn. They're your groomsmen, Ross, you want to give them something they'll remember.'

So I'm there, 'I actually didn't think you'd be so cool about that kind of thing. Now that you mention it, we were thinking of hitting a lappy or two the night of the stag. If no one scores, obviously,' and there's, like, silence on the other end of the line, which is when I realise we've got our wires seriously crossed. She goes, 'I don't think I want to *know* what you're talking about, Ross. *I'm* talking about favours as in the little presents you leave on the table for guests. Now, I know we agreed it'd be John Rocha champagne flutes for the girls and Cuban cigars for the guys,' and I'm thinking, Don't remember that. It's like that trigonometry shit they pulled on me in the Leaving – must have been out that day. She goes, 'I just think we should get our friends a little something extra. I was thinking maybe gold lockets for my friends and maybe cufflinks for yours. Or maybe hip-flasks,' and I'm there, 'Yeah, with You Can't Knock The Rock on them,' and she goes, 'I HOPE for your sake, Ross, that that was a joke,' and I'm there, 'Er, yeah. A good one, huh?'

But she doesn't answer, roysh. She goes, 'I haven't got time for jokes. I've got to ring about the fireworks.' I'm there, 'Fireworks?' and she's like, 'Yes, Ross, FIREWORKS! At the end of the night, when the music's over, we're going to get everyone out onto the balcony for a toast and then, unknown to everyone, there's going to be a big fireworks display.' I'm there, 'Don't forget your granny's ticker isn't the Mae West. Probably should turn down her hearing aid for her at some stage in the evening,' but she doesn't respond, roysh, she just goes, 'Oh and I've decided to get diamonds on my wedding band. It's an extra four grand, but *everyone's* doing it these days.'

✳ ✳ ✳

We forgot to put a Typhoon baby blue kitchen scales on the wedding list – panic stations! – and also a Blossom and Browne's sycamore duvet with matching pillowcases. So Sorcha drags me into BTs, roysh, all the way up to the top level where the, like, wedding shit is and she walks up to the bird and tells her, whatever, a few essentials to add to the O'Carroll-Kelly/Lalor wedding list. All of a sudden, roysh, I'm suddenly, like, aware of someone standing behind me, roysh, and I look over my left shoulder and who is it, roysh, only – I actually don't believe it myself – we're talking Bianca Luykx. She probably forgot to put a baby blue scales on her list as well. I can feel my face get all, like, hot and I have to move away and sit down on one of the sofas in, like, the furniture deportment. The next thing, roysh, I see

Sorcha looking around for me and she spots me and goes, 'Ross, are you okay? Your face is all red,' and I'm there, 'I'm just a bit, I don't know, hot.' She goes, 'You're probably just stressed like me. I think I'm getting a cold sore.' Then she goes, 'Hey, you will NEVER guess who I just saw adding a John Rocha signature soup tureen to her wedding list?'

✳ ✳ ✳

Five o'clock in the morning, roysh, my phone rings and it's some bogger who turns out to be a cop, from Donnybrook of all places. He goes, 'Is this Mister Ross O'Carroll-Kelly?' and even though I'm still half-asleep, roysh, I go, 'The one and only. What can I *do you for*, officer?' He goes, 'We're releasing Oisinn Wallace. A friend of yours, I believe. Said you'd come and pick him up?' and I go, 'I'll be there in ten,' and it's only when I hang up, roysh, that I get my shit together and think 1) what the fock has Oisinn done to get himself nicked and 2) I've no focking driving licence. So I ring a Jo, roysh, which takes, like, half-a-focking-hour to arrive and when it does, roysh, I hop into the back and we're, like, not even out of the driveway when the tosser storts going, 'Interested in politics, are you?' I'm there, 'I'm interested in silence,' but he goes, 'Ever notice how you never see Bertie Ahern and Mary Harney together?' I'm too tired even to tell him to shut the fock up. He goes, 'That's cos there *is* no Mary Harney. It's Bertie dressed up. Everyone in the Dáil's known about it for years, but it's all hushed up. One day he's the Taoiseach, the next day he puts on the wig, and the dress, and he's the – what-do-call-it – Tánaiste. Live and let live, that's my motto. It's a big scam to claim two Dáil salaries. But don't be surprised now if you see Mary Harney stepping down before the next election. They're scared it's going to get out. I know a lot of shit, me. She's going to retire from public life. Like that Máire Geoghegan what's-her-face. You know that was Padraig Flynn, don't you? No? Jaysus, what planet have you been living on?'

I hand him twenty bills and I go, 'There's another score in it for you if you don't say another thing between now and Donnybrook, *capisce*?' and he goes, 'Game ball, son,' and fifteen minutes later, roysh, we're pulling up outside the cop shop and I'm peeling a couple of notes off the wad of bills that I, like, liberated from the old man's safe. I tell him to keep the engine ticking over, I'll be back out in a minute. So I peg it into the cop shop and there's Oisinn waiting for me in reception, roysh, and I'm about to ask the dude what the Jackanory is but he just goes, 'Let's skidaddle. I'll tell you everything in the cor.' So we hop into the back of the Jo, roysh, and we hit the Stillorgan dualler and Oisinn goes, 'Got busted, Ross. Busted big-time,' and I'm there, 'Busted for what?' He goes, 'Remember that last secret ingredient I told you I needed for the old *Eau d'Affluence*?' and I'm there, 'What was it, Oisinn?' and he goes, 'Hash.' I'm there, 'Hash?' and he's like, 'Yeah. As in dope. Cannibis. Doobey. Ganja. Weed.' I'm there, 'I *know* what hash *is*, Oisinn. But how *could* you? It's, like, SO working class.' The driver turns around and goes, 'The only actual woman in the Dáil is that Liz what-do-you-call-her, goodlooking bird. And even she spends half her time going round as Micheál Martin. All the PDs ever were was an expenses scam. Stands for Paid Double. I know a lot of shit, me.' I'm there, 'There's another twenty in it for you if you keep it closed,' and he goes, 'Game ball.' Oisinn's like, 'I wasn't *smoking* it, Ross. Hash comes from, like, hemp. We're talking the most versatile plant in the world here. You can make paper out of it. Rope. Wood. It also smells very nice, Ross. Skobies the world over will tell you that.' I'm there, 'So how'd you get busted?' and he goes, 'The Feds arrived last night. Raided the old lab. It's a good job the old pair were in St Moritz. The old man would have had a Sean Connery on the spot.' He goes, 'I'd been burning the shit for a few days. Just experimenting with it really. You could smell it all over the road. The poor old goy next door. Eighty-two-years-old and he storted wearing his hair in dreads. Well, someone must have tipped off the cops that there was working-class drugs being used in the area.' I'm there, 'Are you gonna get sent down?' and he laughs and goes, 'Shit the bed, I hope not. Luckily, I'd already burned most of the stuff. There was only enough left to charge me with possession. We're talking a fine and a slap on the wrist. Good job they didn't arrive two weeks ago or I'd be doing a ten-stretch for trafficking.' I go, 'That's what I'm wondering – where did you basically get the shit?' and he's like, 'Em, Australia,' and he suddenly seems a bit, I don't know, shifty.

I'm there, 'Hang on a sec. That big wooden elephant you asked me to carry through customs in Kuala Lumpur?' and he doesn't answer, roysh, just looks out the window. I go, 'Oisinn, they chop your focking head off in those countries for that shit. I've seen enough of those Amnesty magazines Sorcha gets,' and he's like, 'That's alroysh then. She'd have got you off with the Probation Act.' Which isn't focking funny.

✳ ✳ ✳

'I'll never forget the day Ross's father and I got married,' the old dear's going. She's there, 'We left the reception in a 1961 Imperial LeBaron. It was fab-a-lous,' and Sorcha goes, 'We chose the Bentley,' – correction, *she* chose the Bentley – 'because it's what Mum and Dad had when they got married.' The old dear goes,

'Fab-a-lous,' and tells her she'll make two fresh cappuccinos. Then she goes, 'Have you chosen a bag, dorling? To go with the dress,' and Sorcha's there, 'Just a small one. Fit a few bits and pieces in. My Christian Dior Sheer Skin-Lightening Make-up in Light Beige and my Sweet Cheeks Liquid Blush. My Volume Waterproof Mascara. My Crysanthemum Eye Shadow. My Sue Devitt Lip Gloss and my Penny Lane Cream Blusher. Oh and my Golden Goddess Shimmer Eye Cream Shadow, but that's it really. Oh and one or two things for the evening. My Givenchy Prisme Again. My Red Earth Mousse Shadow and my Sisley Glossy Gloss in Sparkle. My Argent Silver Automatic Liquid Eyeliner, my Jane Iredale Gold Dust and my Rimmel Natural Bronzer in Terra Compatta.' I'm there, 'You'll give yourself a focking hernia lugging that shit around,' and Sorcha looks at me and goes, 'Oh, it speaks.' I'm there, 'I'm not *used* to being up this early,' and Sorcha goes, 'Be grateful it's the weekend course we're doing and not the one my cousin did, one night a week for six weeks. Fionnuala, I'll pass on that second cappuccino. Better hit the road while Ross is still with us,' and the old dear laughs – the wagon – and I follow Sorcha out to the Rav 4 and we drive to some shithole down the sticks. I'd heard of these pre-wedding courses before, roysh, but I could never understand what you could spend an entire weekend talking about. Then I found out: How do you keep the romance alive? How has your fiancé been helping with organising the wedding? How do you arrange your joint finances? How do you resolve your arguments?

This is the shit they stort hitting us with, roysh, no sooner have we thrown our bags in the room. I thought they might give you an hour or two to get settled – maybe have a bit of the other – but no, roysh, straight away we're called down to our first meeting, roysh, or *group discussion* as they call it. There's, like, three other couples doing the course, roysh, we're talking Chris and Alison, Steve and Susan, Tom and Linda, drippy fockers every last one of them, a lot of side-portings and cardigan action going down among the blokes, who've all got that pussy-whipped look about them. The birds are obviously all, like, career girls and they're approaching this course, roysh, like it's some seminar they're doing for work. They've all got, like, A4 pads and pens and highlighter morkers, for fock's sake. Of course, I nearly fall off the chair when I notice Sorcha's got the same.

The man in charge – 'your host for the weekend' – is a dude called Tony and all you really need to know about him is that he's a tool. I'd say he studied to be a priest and changed his mind at the last minute, but is still devoted to doing good works. Stands out a mile. The sap. He sits us all around in a circle, roysh, and makes us all introduce ourselves. It's like a focking AA meeting or something. Then the questions stort. How do you arrange your joint finances? He goes, 'Chris and Alison,' and the two of them go to answer together, roysh, but Alison goes, 'No, you go first, honey,' and you can tell from the way the dude looks at her that it's, like, way out of character for her. He goes, 'Well, because we both work in the bank, I think we're both inclined to be sensible with our money. Our wages are paid into a joint account from which we pay the mortgage, but we keep some money by to treat ourselves occasionally,' and it's like, yawn focking yawn.

Tony has his hands, like, clasped together, roysh, like he's praying – I'm telling you, I'm roysh about him – and he's nodding really, like, thoughtfully. He goes, 'How do you keep the romance alive? Tom and Linda.' I'd throw Linda a length actually. She goes, 'Just by being attentive to each other. We're in the bank as well, the same branch actually,' – surprise, sur-focking-prise – 'so we see quite a bit of each other. We're probably more aware than most couples of the need to keep things fresh. That's why we like to surprise each other with little treats, don't we, sweetheart?' and Tom just nods like the nodding dog that he is. Tony goes, 'Sorcha and Ross,' and I'm there thinking, Please give us an easy one, but he's like, 'To what extent have you discussed one another's exes?' and I'm there, This goy's taking the piss, isn't he? He goes, 'Ross, you first,' and I'm like, 'Em, well ... Sorcha's only ever had one boyfriend aport from me and he was a tool. Cillian was his name. Some numbers hotshot. No offence to the rest of you. She went to Australia with him and he focked off with some other bird. So I don't worry about him. The goy's focking toast,' and there's, like, total silence in the room, then a few disapproving tut-tuts from the women about my language and I think I also hear the word, 'disrespect'. Tony goes, 'Thank you, Ross. That was very, em, *frank*. Sorcha?' and Sorcha goes, 'Ross has hundreds of exes,' and I'm just there nodding with a big shit-eating grin on my face. She goes, 'And sometimes I wonder whether some of them are ex at all. I overheard him telling one of his friends recently that he'd slept with more women than Julio Iglesias and he's still only half the man's age. Ross is what you would call a male slut,' and again there's total silence, roysh, and I'm thinking, Well, she's called it as she sees it. Like Hooky.

Tony tells us he thinks exes are an area we need to work on. He earns his money, this dude. Everyone in the room storts shaking their heads like he's just said something, I don't know, profound, if that's not too bent a word. So this is the basic vibe for the first day, roysh. Steve and Susan – who both work in mortgages – saying how they never let the sun go down on an argument, it's their one basic rule, and Alison saying how Chris proposed to her on safari as they watched a herd of wildebeest sweep across the Serengeti, and Tom saying how he and Linda want LOADS of children and are planning to stort straight away, mortgage or no mortgage. We seem to be the only couple in the room with shit to work through. To cut a long story short, roysh, on the Sunday we're given this, like, exercise to do, the vibe of which is basically to see how well you know your other half. There's all these, like, questions, roysh, as in what's your other half's favourite this, that and the other. Then you have to, like, swap answers with your, I suppose portner, and read out what the other one's put down. So anyway, roysh, Sorcha's reading my answers out and this particular question is like, 'As a couple, what is your ideal form of relaxation?' and Tony tells her to read out my answer, roysh, but she's going, 'I can't.' He's like, 'What do you mean, you can't?' and she turns to me, roysh, and she goes, 'I cannot BELIEVE you wrote this,' and Tony goes, 'Whatever it is, Sorcha, I want you to read it out. No secrets within the group, remember?' and she just, like, looks at everyone and goes, 'There's nothing Sorcha and I like more than ... a good fock.' I'm there, 'Flick, Sorcha. It says flick. As in the movies,' and she looks at it again, roysh, and goes, 'OH! MY! GOD! I thought that was a u,' and I'm there, 'No, it's an l and an i joined up, I just forgot to dot the i, that's all,' and the two of us just break our holes laughing. We're the only ones in the room, of course, no one else sees the funny side of it and that's when I realise, roysh, that, okay, we might have more issues than anyone else in this room, but at least there's something more between us than a joint mortgage and a joint VHI plan and a joint bank account and a joint life insurance policy. We laugh together. Why does no one in this room think that's important? With us, there's a connection, better than anyone here's got, even if we do get on each other's top tens most of the time. The meeting goes on, roysh, and Sorcha and me keep shooting each other sly looks out of the corner of our eyes and smiling. *Nothing we enjoy more than a good fock.*

✳ ✳ ✳

Kiss me. Beneath the bearded barley. Nightly. Beneath the green, green grass. Swing, swing. Swing your spinning step. You wear those shoes and I will wear that dress ...

Trevor's as excited as a Frenchman with ten mickeys. When all the clapping dies down, he goes, 'I used to say that *everyone* can dance. Everyone has the music within them. It just needs to be drawn out. And when he first walked in here, I thought that Ross O'Carroll-Kelly was going to be the exception to the rule. I think you've all just seen how wrong I was. Ross, you move like Valentino,' who I think is a racehorse. Sorcha whispers in my ear that she's SO proud of me. I go, 'You the man, Trevor,' pointing at the dude. 'You the man.'

✳ ✳ ✳

The CD the *Tribune* gave away free was total crap, it was all holy this and Jesus that and a stor in the night focking sky. It was like being at Mass. I had to tell the old man in the cor, roysh, I was like, 'Turn that off now or I'm grabbing that steering wheel from you and driving us both into a tree,' and he goes, 'Nothing wrong with appreciating the finer things in life. I wouldn't say our friend from Middle Abbey Street has ever heard of Mario Lanza. Sunk to new depths this morning. Made Charlie McCreevy look like an idiot. I expect that's why you're a little tetchy yourself.' I just look at him but stop myself from saying what I'm, like, thinking because – I hate to admit this – the goy's actually doing me a favour right now, which is why I'm doing two things at the moment that I wouldn't usually do and they are 1) being seen out in public with the tosser and 2) going to the northside.

Here's the *scéal*, roysh. The old man tells me last night that he's giving me and Sorcha 150,000 sheets as a wedding present, and of course I'm there, 'Well yippee-yahoo,' cracking on not to be impressed, roysh, because I don't want him getting the idea that we're suddenly all, I don't know, great mates. He's there pacing the floor of his study, going, 'Your mother and I always knew that you'd move on and find a little nest of your own and so forth. So we've been squirreling money away for you over the years. That's our wedding gift to you and young Sorcha. Should make quite a deposit for your own ... *gaff*, as you young people like to say. Quote-unquote, of course.' I'm there, 'Can I have it now? Have you got it on you?' and he laughs and takes a puff on his cigar and he goes, 'I haven't got it ... on me, as you put it. No it's, em ... offshore,' which means presumably it's so hot it'll come with a tube of aloe vera and a roll of focking bandages. He goes, 'I entrusted it all to Hennessy. Poor Hennessy. Languishing in jail, an innocent man ...' I'm there, 'How do I, sorry, me and Sorcha, get our hands on it?' and he goes, 'We'll go to see the man himself tomorrow.'

So we take the old man's Volvo and head for the Joy and, of course, all the way there Dick Features is crapping on about how him and Hennessy are going to head to Quinta do Lago for a golfing holiday when this is all over, in other words when the orsehole gets out of the slammer, which could be, like, fifty years from now. We pull up outside the prison, roysh – it's on this focking dump of a road – and I'm there, 'I'll wait here. Hurry the fock up. This is one of those streets where the local skobies charge you to pork.' He's there, 'Not coming in then?' and I'm like, 'What the fock do you think?' and he pats me on the shoulder and goes, 'I understand. It's difficult for *all* of us, Ross, seeing Hennessy like that. I'll give him your best,' then he gets out of the cor, walks a few steps, turns back and goes, 'If only *he* could see me now, eh? G Kerrigan Esquire – investigative reporter. Captain of Industry Caught Outside Mountjoy Jail. Banner headlines. Exclusive, what?' I'm there, 'Just hurry up and get me the focking sponds before the fockers have the alloys off,' and he focks off. Half-an-hour later – *half-a-focking-hour,* roysh – he arrives back and he gets into the cor and says fock-all. I'm there, 'How's Phil Mitchell?' ripping the piss, roysh, but he doesn't answer. The first time he says anything is just as we're crossing the East Link Bridge. He goes, 'He refused to see me, Ross. Can you believe that?' and of course I'm there, 'I presume this means my 150,000 bills is more offshore than you thought?' He shakes his head and he goes, 'I knew he was a crook, but I never thought he'd steal from one of his own.' I'm there, 'Well, the bad news for you is the money's going to have to come out of your focking pocket then. Do you think Hennessy ...' but he interrupts me, roysh, and he goes, 'Ross, I don't ever want to hear that man's name again.'

✳ ✳ ✳

I'm awake for, like, an hour, roysh, before I chance opening my eyes. Afraid the focking things will fall out. A hangover doesn't really kick in until you've opened your eyes, roysh, because that's when you're telling your body, 'There's no more sleep. Get up and face it, dude.' The light hurts. My mouth is dry. Feels like someone's focking carpeted my tongue. The old Ned Kelly's doing the 'Macarena' and my head feels like the focking Osbournes have been living in it.

Hang on, where am I?

Where the fock ... I don't recognise this room. I'm not in Fionn's gaff – he put that Periodic Table of Elements poster on the wall of his spare room because he knows it makes me dizzy and I end up spewing my ring just looking at it. And it's not Christian's gaff because there isn't a Millennium Falcon in sight. And it's not Oisinn's because his old pair wouldn't have me in the gaff since we drank that home-made elderflower wine and I ended up getting Moby Dick all over his old dear's Oriental rug. Maybe I copped off and was, like, so hammered she ended up putting me in her spare room. Maybe. I'll have to get up and investigate. See will she fix me a fry. I roll out of the old Margaret and get my threads together. I rip the L sign from the crotch of my chinos – JP's idea of a joke, no doubt. There's vom on the sleeve of my Henri Lloyd sailing jacket and what smells like Pernod on the front of my Ralph. Not too much damage. I'm, like, piecing the night together as I get dressed. I remember Sorcha having an eppo when I told her I was having a stag. She was giving it, 'I thought Australia was your stag,' and I'm like, 'Get over it, girl.' She was just bulling because she wanted me to go out to dinner with some knobby relatives of hers, Uncle John and Auntie Christ, I call them, because the aunt is basically a weapon.

I lash the bedroom door open and go out onto the landing. There's, like, voices downstairs. Don't think I'm ready to meet the parents yet. Big-time *Trainspotting* vibe going down here. Decide to tiptoe down the stairs, roysh, peg it out the door, ring Dick Features and tell him to come and get me. But just as I hit the last stair, roysh, I hear this old dear's voice in the hall behind me, going, 'Aha! *Guten morgen*!' I'm there, 'Guten what?' and she's like, '*Guten morgen. Frühstuck?*' I'm there, 'Are you ill or something?' She sort of, like, gestures towards the kitchen, roysh, so I follow her down, you know me, I don't like to be rude. I've just boned her daughter, the least I can do is stick around for half-an-hour. Have to say, roysh, I'm also pretty curious about what happened last night, or more to the point, what this bird looks like – are we talking honey or horror-movie material? – and anyway, roysh, by the smell of things, there's a pretty good nosebag going down.

Of course, nothing could have prepared me for what I see when we hit the kitchen. It's not a kitchen at all, roysh, but a dining room with, like, ten or eleven tables in it and all these people, like, sitting around them and shit. That's when I cop that I'm in some kind of, like, hotel or guesthouse. When I walk in, roysh, everyone stops eating and looks up at me. I'm there, 'Alroysh?' and they're all giving it, '*Guten morgen*,' which is when I twig, roysh, that something's seriously wrong here. I sit down and this serving bird comes over and she goes, '*Kaffee?*' and I'm like, 'Couldn't hurt,' and the next thing, roysh, this old biddy, who's obviously the owner, comes in and puts a plate in front of me and it's got, like, sausages on it, roysh, but not ordinary sausages, they're those big focking hotdog jobbies. I'm there, 'What are these?' and she's like, 'Um, how to say... *wurste*,' and I'm suddenly listening to the people talking, roysh, and it's all, Hunken dunken shmunken and Heil Hitler and whatever you're having yourself, and the goy at the next table's reading a paper called *Bild* and it's then, roysh, that I cop that, wherever the fock I am, I'm not in focking Ireland. I totally lose it, of course. I stand up and I go, 'SOMEONE TELL ME WHAT THE FOCK IS GOING ON? WHERE AM I AND

SHIT?' and the goy at the next table puts down his newspaper and says in this real, like, 'Allo 'Allo voice, 'You don't know vare you har?' and I'm there, 'The last thing I remember is leaving Ron Black's with a traffic cone on my head and the goys pushing me down Dawson Street in a shopping trolley. After that ...' The goy goes, 'You are in Deutschland ... Germany.'

Germany! Holy fock, I don't even know what country that's in. I'm there, 'Okay, okay, no one panic,' and then I just go, in a loud, clear voice so, like, everyone understands, 'WHERE ... CAN ... I ... GET ... A ... TRAIN ... TO ... IRELAND ... NAMELY ... FOXROCK?' and they must misunderstand me, roysh, because they all just break their holes laughing. I'm beginning to know how Tom Hanks felt in that film, no not the one about the steamers, the one where he ends up stranded on a desert island. See, my credit cord's maxed out, roysh, and now I can feel my legs shaking and there's, like, tears in my eyes and I'm thinking I SO should have listened to Sorcha when she said ...

And then all of a sudden I hear all this laughter, roysh, and the door swings open and in morch all the goys, we're talking JP, Oisinn, Fionn and Christian and they're, like, high-fiving everyone in the room and cracking their shites laughing basically. I'm there, 'Goys, thank God you're here. I've been trying to make conversation with these people. It seems we've ended up in Germany. As far as I can gather, it's in a place called Doichland.' Fionn goes, 'Ross, we're in a B&B on Haddington Road. We've been ripping the piss out of you. Everyone's been in on it,' and they all crack up laughing again. I'm there, 'Actually, I knew. I was just playing along.'

Dickheads.

✳ ✳ ✳

I send Sorcha a text and it's like, **Howd d hens go?** and straight away she's like, **Meaning?** and I'm there, **Jst askin did u hav a gud time?** and she goes, **Oh. Was fine.**

✳ ✳ ✳

The doorbell rings, roysh, and the old man answers it and ten seconds later who walks in only Erika, dressed to focking kill, but she always is. Straight away, roysh, I know she's come here for a showdown, to deliver me an ultimatum if that's the roysh word, so from the stort I decide to play it like Steve Silvermint. I go, 'Coffee?' and she goes, 'A cappuccino, if that machine makes them. You heard about the hen's weekend I take it. Your fiancé?' and I'm just stop, roysh, with the cup under the nozzle and I go, 'She didn't do the dirt, did she?'

Erika sort of, like, snorts and goes, 'HELLO? We were in a luxury spa resort, Ross, not Ibiza. And besides, the silly girl's devoted to you. If I thought she was even *remotely* interested in anyone else, I'd have shoved her in their direction ages ago, ended this ridiculous wedding charade.'

I put the cappuccino in front of her and she looks at it like it's just been scooped out of the toilet bowl. Then she shakes her head, pushes it to one side and goes, 'I've never laughed so much in my life. Sorcha decided she was going to have a *Brazilian*. I take it you know what a Brazilian is, Ross?' I'm there, 'I've seen a few magazines in my time,' and she's there, 'You won't have seen *anything* like this, Ross. She got ingrown hairs. Ended up with a huge rash you-know-where. Came running into me. I was having a glass of wine, relaxing before my facial massage. The girl had lost the plot. Kept screaming, "What is Ross going to think?" I told her, "You marry someone like Ross and you're going to have to get used to rashes, dear".'

I'm there, 'The poor thing,' but she just goes, 'And little Claire. The *bridesmaid*. Went for one of those spray-on tans.' I'm there, 'A what?' and she throws her eyes up to heaven, like I'm supposed to know about these things, and she goes, 'They put you in a paper thong and airbrush you brown. I'm surprised at Claire. Knackers usually go on the sunbeds. Anyway, it's like they say, you can take the girl out of Bray, but you can't take Bray out of the girl. Claire didn't bother having a shower beforehand – no surprise there – but what she didn't know was the tan doesn't take properly if the body's oily. So it went on in streaks. Oh, it's hilarious. She looks like a dirty protest.' I'm there, 'Serves her roysh. You have had to put up with so much shit from that creamer,' and Erika goes, 'There's no point in sucking up to me, Ross. Your *fiancé* tried that. Asked if I wanted to join her for a pedicure the next morning. Obviously thinking of asking me to step in as a replacement.'

I'm there, 'Okay, Erika, cords on the table. I'm asking you – no, I'm begging you – please don't tell Sorcha. There's nothing to be gained from it,' and she goes, 'Except a lot of unhappiness for a lot of people,' and I'm there, 'Er, yeah,' and she's like, 'Well, that's *hordly* nothing now, is it?' I go, 'You won't go through with it. You wouldn't let yourself down in public,' and she's there, 'You think I'm bluffing? Ross, I've got Orpha's diary and I've got Claire's confession, which incidentally she doesn't even remember giving. That'll be that ... *cider* she drinks. This wedding goes ahead and I'm staging a little Press conference at the reception. Don't for a minute think I won't.' I go, 'Still think you're bluffing,' knowing damn well she's not.

* * *

All of Sorcha's friends from music are coming over to the gaff tonight, we're talking Sophie, Emma, Chloe and Amie – the Ming Quarter as I call them, roysh, but only as a joke because there isn't one of them I wouldn't do. They're doing the music for the church, roysh, and of course the old dear – who wouldn't know a note unless it had 100 euro stamped on it – has appointed herself the Louis Walsh of the outfit, roysh, and has invited them over to the gaff tonight for their final rehearsal and to discuss one or two concerns she has with their version of 'How Great Thou Art', the stupid bitch. She's making a meal out of the evening. Literally actually. Focking cleaned out Marks & Spencer this morning and she's invited all her knobby mates over from golf and tennis and her various Fock the Poor groups. So for the sake of my own sanity, roysh, I have to get out of the house, so I ring up the goys and ask them if they fancy going for a few scoops, which they do. As it happens, roysh, there's something I need to talk to them about. This Erika business is wrecking my head. Terrible thing to say, roysh, but I'm dreading the wedding, not looking forward to it, and as a last resort I've decided to turn to my four best friends in the world for help. They're already there when I arrive. The first thing Christian says to me is, 'I know you said no *Star Wars* references in my speech, Ross, but would you mind if I mentioned Oolah, Jabba's dancing girl, just for the purposes of an analogy?' and I go, 'Yeah, whatever.' JP goes, 'Looking good, my man,' which I am, I have to say, roysh, wearing my new black Hugo Boss jumper. He goes, 'If this is what the big L does to a man, then here's my booking deposit and we'll close in a fortnight,' and I'm there, 'Thanks, dude.' Fionn asks me how the arrangements are going and I'm there, 'You know Sorcha,' which is all I really have to say. Everyone nods and then Fionn goes, 'But there's something up,' and I go, 'Er,' and he's like, 'Ross, every time you got a text message while we were in Australia, you jumped. It's like you're scared of something.'

Then Oisinn goes, 'And I'd wager that something goes by the name of Erika.' I go, 'How did you know?' and he's like, 'Me and Fionn bumped into her in town the other day. She looked a bit too pleased with herself. The kind of pleased she only ever looks when she's making someone's life a misery.' Fionn goes, 'Then she said she was calling up to your gaff later on.' I'm there, 'She has something on me, goys. And she's going to use it to ruin the wedding.' Fionn goes, 'I was going to ask what. Probably be closer to the mork if I asked *who*.' I go, 'Claire,' and all the goys just, like, groan. Then I go, 'And the sister, Orpha, or Aifric, or whatever she's called.' At exactly the same time, roysh, Oisinn and JP go, '*Both* bridesmaids?' though not in a *you're a total legend* kind of a way.

I go, 'I know, I know. I'm just too damn good-looking, that's my problem,' and Christian nods and he goes, 'There's no doubt you've been given a gift, Ross. But you're still too young and too reckless to use it properly. That's why Uncle Owen and Aunt Boru didn't want Obi Wan giving Luke a light-sabre until he was at least eighteen,' which I presume makes sense to someone. I'm there, 'Goys, I know I've been stupid. I'm marrying the greatest girl in the world and I scored the bridesmaids! If I could turn back the clock, I'd tell whatever-her-name-is not to put it in her diary and I'd ask Claire not to get hammered and spill her guts out to Erika. But I can't.' They're all looking at me, like, sympathetically. I go, 'You're the best friends I have. I wouldn't ask for your help if I wasn't desperate. I'm always the one who ends up humiliated – that French exchange student who turned out to be a bloke, then the movie, which I still haven't got my seven grand for, by the way. Please, goys, don't let me be humiliated on my wedding day.' Fionn – we've had our differences but fair focks to him – he goes, 'Ross, you're our friend. Personally, I'm a little hurt that you couldn't have turned to us earlier. But I'm telling you now – don't spend another minute worrying about it,' and Oisinn nods and goes, 'We'll stop her. We'll watch her like a bunch of hawks, we're talking really, really good-looking ones. We'll be miked up to each other. If she moves, one of us will alert the others and it'll be like, "Target, three o'clock and on the move".' JP goes, 'We'll sit on her if we have to, Ross,' and what can I do but tell the goys that they're total legends and we're talking *totally* here.

✳ ✳ ✳

The sooner I get my driving licence back the better. If I have to listen to one more taxi driver telling me that he knows things that could bring the Govurdenmint down I'll go loop the focking loop. I've actually resorted to saying, 'No interest in anything you've got to say,' the second they try to, like, draw me into conversation, roysh, and when they go to say something else, I just go, 'You're getting five bills as a tip. Every time you open your trap, it goes down by fifty cents,' and that generally shuts them the fock up. I'm actually on the way home, roysh. Scored in the Club of Love last night – Aibreann, doing architecture – last time I'll ever do the dirt on Sorcha and we're talking definitely here. Stupid again, but I just had to prove to myself that I still had the old magic.

My mobile rings, roysh, and it's her – as in, like, Sorcha – and of course the first thing that goes through my mind is, 'Deny *everything.*' Turns out it's not about that at all. She says she has something a bit, well, embarrassing that she wants to bring up with me. Totally relieved, roysh, I go, 'It's fine, Erika already told me. It's only a rash,' and I pay the driver, throw him five skins on top and go, 'Don't forget your hush money.' Sorcha's going, 'What are you talking about, Ross? Erika told you *what?*' and I'm putting the key in the door, going, 'About you getting the old whatever-you-call-it and ending up with a rash on your ... you know,' and she's there, 'OH! MY! GOD! I cannot BELIEVE she told you. She is SUCH a bitch.' I'm there, 'It's better I know there's, like, an innocent explanation for it, instead of thinking ...' and she goes, 'I would NOT have a sexually transmitted disease, Ross. YOU'RE the one with the history, remember?' which she didn't have to say, roysh.

She goes, 'Anyway, I don't have time for this, Ross. The menus arrived today, in *ivory* instead of white. It's like, *Duuuhhh!*' and I'm about to say, 'What's the difference?' but I manage to stop myself, roysh, and I end up going, 'How could anyone be so stupid?' and she goes, 'I know, it's like, HE-LLO? So I've got to go the printers to get it sorted out. I have SO got a cold sore coming on ...' I'm just there, 'So what's this embarrassing thing you're talking about?' and she goes, 'Oh yes. I want you to handle it, Ross. But it needs to be handled delicately.' I'm there, 'Sounds out of my league, Sorcha, but I'll give it a shot.' And she comes straight out with it – get this, roysh – she goes, 'The suit your mum's wearing to the wedding. I don't like it.' I'm there, 'O ... kay. Any basic reason?' and she goes, 'The colour.' I'm there, 'Pink? You love pink. Half your clothes are pink,' and she goes, 'I like pink, Ross. But Mum's wearing lemon,' and I'm there, 'I thought she was wearing, like, black,' and she goes, 'HELLO? She *was*? Then she saw this suit she liked in Paris.' I'm there, 'Hang on. If your old dear's wearing lemon, why can't my old dear wear pink?' and she flies off the handle, roysh, goes, 'Because when I'm being photographed with them I'll look like a block of Neapolitan!' and I'm there, 'Okay, calm down.' She goes, 'I'll calm *down* when I've got white menus like I ordered and *you've* told your mum that she is NOT to turn up at my wedding in *pink*.' I'm there, 'Okay, okay, I'll fix it.' She goes, 'Diplomatically, Ross,' like *she's* one to talk. I'm there, 'Piece of piss.'

I head upstairs, roysh, go into the old pair's room and there it is, roysh, the old dear's pink suit, or cerise as she calls it. I just pick it up, roysh, and reef off one of the orms, well, not completely, roysh, I leave it hanging on by a few threads. Then I go downstairs and lash on the telly. Columbo's on. He's unbelievable, that dude. Always knows a lot more than he cracks on. Half-an-hour later, roysh, the old pair arrive in, fock knows where they've been, roysh, but there better be food on that table in ten minutes or they won't be *invited* to the wedding. The dickheads.

Next thing, roysh, I hear the old dear going up the stairs and the old man comes into the sitting room and storts, like, talking to me, the usual old pals act, and suddenly there's all this, like, shrieking coming from the old dear's room – totally over the top if you ask me – and the old man pegs it out takes the stairs pretty much like I take my women, in other words two at a time. I leave it a couple of minutes, roysh, and I go out into the hall and basically earwig what's being said. The old dear's going, 'I'm *sure* I would have noticed it in the shop, Charles. Look, it's hanging off,' and Penis Head is there, 'We'll get you another, darling,' and she's giving it, 'But it was the last one.' I shout up the stairs, roysh, going, 'Will you two keep your big foghorn voices down. I'm trying to focking watch 'Columbo'.'

✱ ✱ ✱

The big day is, like, five days away, roysh, so I pick up my phone and send a text to every bird in my address book and it's like, **Getin married n 4 days. Pleas dont do NE ting stupid**, then I scroll down through the names and send it to them one by one. Ali. Happy days. She was doing, like, morkeshing in Mountjoy Square. A little bit like Monica Bellucci. Met her in Lillie's. Morched straight up to her and I was like, 'I've lost my phone number – can I borrow yours?' Corny, I know, but she fell for it. There wasn't much going on upstairs. As Fionn said, she thinks Sugar Diabetes is a Welsh middleweight boxer.

DELETE NUMBER

Are you sure?

Oh yes.

DELETED

Amy. She's been repeating first year law in Portobello for the last, like, four years, roysh, and she'll go on repeating first year law in Portobello until she finds a good-looking goy with loads of dosh – preferably Ethan Hawke – to keep her in gym memberships. I've been with her, like, a few times. We're talking behind Sorcha's back? Bit of a Make-up Monster. Was with her one night and had to take a detour through, like, a car wash on the way home.

DELETE NUMBER

Are you sure? Considering I'm about to marry one of her best friends next week, I think yes.

DELETED

Bianca. Ahhh, the lovely Bianca. This is it, Ross. Deleting this number is, like, a massive step. I've only actually seen the bird on the telly. Never met her. Ended up getting the number off Oisinn, who's mates with a goy who's doing a line with her, like, cousin's best friend. Course I bottled it. Rang it once, one night after Annabel's, when I was totally mullered, and I was like, 'Well, here I am. What are your other two wishes?' but she just hung up. And she's married now, so ...

Here goes.

DELETE NUMBER

Are you sure?

Be strong, big guy.

DELETED

Beibhínn. Oh yeah. Get rid. She's loop the focking loop. So I broke her hort. That was, like, two years ago. I'm like, get OVER it, girl. Every time I see her out, roysh, she ends up, like, staring at me for the whole night. Then she'll walk over to me, burst into tears and go, 'I can't believe it's happening all over again,' then throw her drink over me, usually something that smells foul, like Pernod, or an orange Bacordi Breezer.

DELETE NUMBER

Are you sure?

HELLO? Could Meg Ryan get a second job as a sink plunger?

DELETED

Críosa. The only one of Sorcha's friends I've never been with. I tried, but she was one of those rare Mounties who was never impressed by the whole rugby thing. Probably could have been in there if I had put the spadework in, but to me, roysh, it was like studying for the Leaving. What's the focking point?

DELETE NUMBER

Are you sure?

Next!

DELETED

Daniella. The original Body Off Baywatch, Face Off Crime-watch. Great to be with, but she gets a bit too John B. She's a bit like Playa del Ingles. Been there once. No intention of going back.

DELETE NUMBER

Are you sure?

Think now I may have been too hasty in deleting Bianca's actually.

DELETED

Elmarie. I suppose I could ask Oisinn to try to get it again. No, Ross. Focus. Elmarie. Elmarie? Who the fock is… Oh, Elmarie. The driving instructor's daughter. Uttered those four unforgivable words, 'I believe in waiting. I would never give myself to someone I didn't truly love.' Threw her out of the cor. She should be thankful I pulled over first.

DELETE NUMBER

Are you sure? Come on, *I* don't believe in waiting.

DELETED

Erika. The lovely Erika. Need I say more? Bitch whore from hell, about to ruin my life, yet still the most desirable girl on the planet.

DELETE NUMBER

Are you sure?

Er …

RETURN TO ADDRESS BOOK

Frederika. Memories, memories. Knew her in UCD. She was

doing Russian and Byzantine Studies. I convinced myself she looked like Charlize Theron, but to be honest, I was only with her because she was JP's ex and it pissed him off.

DELETE NUMBER

Are you sure?

She served her purpose.

DELETED

Georgia. Used to do the weather in RTÉ. I broke her hort, roysh, but she'd take another shot at the title if I offered it to her. Too much emotional baggage.

DELETE NUMBER

Are you sure? Yeah, come on, you're getting married, Ross.

DELETED

Melanie. She's actually in my phone as Melanie Institute because the Institute is where she did French grinds, though it could also be because she belongs in one. Dumped her by text, roysh, using the old Homer Simpson line: Welcome to Dumpsville. Population, YOU.'

DELETE NUMBER

Are you sure?

Yeah, don't know why it's still in there.

DELETED

Oreanna. How could I forget her! Killed her cat. Killed her dog. If she had a hamster, he'd probably be dead, too. Most birds, when they don't want to see you again, threaten to go to the cops and get a barring order. She threatened to go to the ISPCA. But she still wants me. So I've heard.

DELETE NUMBER

Are you sure?

It's all in the past now, Ross.

DELETED

Portia. Shannon Elizabeth's twin. Better-looking twin. Must have liked her because I took her to Roly's. There was a stage when I thought she was the one. It was at some point between the blue cheese and oven-dried tomato bruschetta and the vanilla crème brulee. But she was too nice. A girl like that doesn't deserve the shit I'd put her through.

DELETE NUMBER

Are you sure?

Quickly.

DELETED

I just automatically delete the seven Zoeys, roysh, and when I quit out of my address book I see that I've got, like, eight messages. Replies already. The first one I open is from, like, Georgia and she's like, **Do somting silly? Get a life! I've movd on ross. Iv got a nu byfrend. Hes 28 n he plays rugby. And by the way, u hav a tiny** ... well, you know, I'll spare you the details. The rest of the messages were, like, pretty much the same. Suffice to say, there's a lot of broken-horted birds out there putting a brave face on things.

✳ ✳ ✳

The old pair come in from, like, late night Christmas shopping, having bought half of Pamela Scott if the bags are anything to go by. The old dear says she got a *bea-u-tiful* navy suit for the wedding that it is going to go SO well with her Philip Treacy. And the two of them stort banging on about the wedding, as if it's, like, *their* day or something. I turn around to the old man and go, 'How's Hennessy?' knowing that'll, like, shut him up. He just goes, 'Never heard of him.'

✱ ✱ ✱

I'm a bad man, I know, but I ended up spending most of the rehearsal scooping the Ming Quartet, who, it has to be said, roysh, looked amazing, we're talking long black dresses, violins and whatever. For a minute, roysh, I actually thought that was the reason Sorcha was crying afterwards – me getting snared giving the old mince pies to someone else – and I give her, like, a hug afterwards and try to explain that it was the *music* I liked, bullshit bullshit bullshit. She goes, 'I can't BELIEVE you didn't notice,' still bawling, roysh, and I go, 'Notice what?' and she's there, 'That white floral summer dress by Kate Cooper with the Japanese orchid motif and the cranberry straps that I bought for my going-away outfit,' and I'm there, 'What about it?' and she goes, 'OH! MY! GOD! Did you not SEE what Erika was wearing in the church tonight?' and I didn't, roysh, I was too busy looking at her, like, sneering face. I go, 'It couldn't have been, like, a coincidence?' and Sorcha's there, 'HELLO? She was with me when I bought it, Ross,' and then I end up saying possibly the worst thing a bloke can ever say to a bird. I'm like, 'Just because she wore it doesn't mean you can't,' and she looks at me like she's just caught me in bed with her sister – actually, bad example there – and she goes, '*Everybody* was admiring it. Telling her how amazing she looked. It's going to look like *I* copied *her*. OH MY GOD! she is SUCH a bitch. If I get a cold sore over this ...'

This collar's choking the focking neck off me, roysh, and I feel like Reggie Corrigan dressed up in Peter Stringer's threads. Or maybe it's just, like, tension and shit, because I am kacking it, roysh, and we're talking totally here. There's, like, no other word for it. I just feel like me and Sorcha's happiness is in someone else's hands, and I'm basically cursing myself for being so stupid and damn handsome that I ended up being with her sister and her friend. And Christian's copped it because he's gone, 'Don't centre on your anxieties, Obi Wan. Keep your thoughts on the here and now.' But it's actually hord, roysh, especially with Ass Wipe babbling away over my shoulder. I'm standing at the altar and I can hear him in Eduard's ear, that tosser of a mate of his, and he's going, 'Corruption is what kept this country in the Middle Ages for so long. It's why hospital wards had to close. It's why there are children in this country who may never ski.' The tosser's been on this, like, clean up corruption vibe since he found out his best mate creamed off all the moolah he thought he had in the Caymans. I turn around to Christian and I go, 'Wonder will Frankie say all that to the judge when he's up in front of the tribunal?' and Christian does his best to laugh, considering it's his bird's old man we're basically talking about here. The old dear's telling everyone within earshot – which is quite a lot given her voice – that Sorcha looks 'fab-a-lous,' just letting everyone know that she was there in the gaff when she put the dress on and I'm, like, thinking about my old dear out there this morning, her and Sorcha's old dear having a see-who-can-fuss-over-the-bride-the-most competition. A couple of birds from Pizzazz were going out to do everyone's hair and some make-up artist as well, and I can picture my old dear, roysh, telling her she looks 'fab-a-lous' while Sorcha's throwing back valies with the champagne to take the edge off her nerves. Speaking of which ...

I look over my shoulder and there's Erika clip-clopping up the aisle, late of course, has to be the centre of attention, and she looks amazing, it has to be said. The Maria Grachvogel thing turned out to be bullshit, roysh. The word is she actually ended up going to New York to, like, pick up some Donna Karan number and I presume that's what she has on her – a jacket, trousers and this sort of, like, bodice, I think it's called. White, of course, just to upstage the bride. I look at her, roysh, and I know I've got my pathetic face on, begging her basically not to say anything, but she just gives me a wave, roysh, then reaches into her bag and whips out a tape and a piece of paper, which I presume is Claire's confession and the page from what's-her-face's diary. I turn back to face the front, roysh, and all of a sudden the violins stort up. *Here comes the bride, blah blahdy blah.* Behind me, roysh, all I can hear are these, like, gasps and people going, '*Oh my God,*' and 'Oh MY God!' and 'OH my God?' and 'OH! MY! GOD!' as Sorcha passes up the aisle. And the old man's going, 'There's a whole hidden underclass of people out there who couldn't tell you the difference between a four iron and a sand wedge ...'

When she's, like, ten steps away from the altar, roysh, I turn around and – OH! MY! GOD! – she looks … the only word I can think of is beautiful, if that doesn't make me sound too much of a benny. Even through the veil, she's … It's weird, roysh, I love the girl and everything, but it's like I'd totally forgotten until this moment how completely and totally incredible she is. And it's not just the slap either. She pulls up beside me, roysh, and her old man, who was linking her, leans over to me and he goes, 'She's all yours now, Ross. Handle with care,' like the total wanker that he is. Sorcha pulls back her veil and she smiles at me and goes, 'Hey, we made it,' and I try to say something back, roysh, something cool or whatever, but no words come out and then I realise that I'm crying – we're talking ACTUAL tears running down my actual face? – and she's got this, like, permanent smile on hers – that'll be the botox – and she just, like, squeezes my hand to let me know it's Kool and the Gang. Now the goy had actually warned us beforehand, roysh, that the ceremony itself is gonna be pretty much like Mass. And he's basically roysh, it's all Holy Mary Mother of God and whatever you're having yourself, Mrs Wembley. The two of us are kneeling there, bit bored basically, and I turn around to her – finally got my voice back – and I'm there, 'I love your dress,' and quick as a flash she goes, 'It's a bridal gown. Yes, Vera Wang did me proud. Did you see the shoes? They're Manolo Blahniks. I told the cameraman to zoom in on Erika's face when she clapped eyes on them.' Then she looks at the cameraman and storts, like, mouthing to him, 'Did … you … get … her … reaction?' And suddenly – whoa – it's all happening now. Our bit comes around pretty quickly, we're talking, like, vows and shit? The priest goes, 'Do you, Ross Kyle Gibson McBride O'Carroll-Kelly, take …' and of course everyone in the audience storts, like, breaking their shites laughing, and over my shoulder I can hear Dick Features going, 'Ah the age-old chestnut. Who's the greatest? Couldn't separate them with a cigarette paper, in my humble view. Quote me if you like,' and the priest's there, '... take Sorcha Eidemar Françoise Lalor to be your lawful wedded wife?' And it's actually pretty cool after that, just a matter of him asking you questions and you going, 'Yeah, whatever.' At one stage I hear the old dear blubbering away in the front row, roysh, and I have to turn around and give her a filthy before she makes a total tit of me in front of everyone. Blah blah blah, yada yada yada, then it's like, 'I now pronounce you ... man and wife. You may kiss the bride,' and we kiss each other, a big long one, roysh, and there's this big roar from everyone, and it's like – *whoosh!* – flashbulbs going off all over the gaff, and then all the goys – we're talking Oisinn, we're talking Fionn, we're talking JP, we're talking Ryle Nugent, the whole crew – they're giving it, 'MORE! MORE! MORE!' so we do it again, an even longer one this time, and all the goys are taking pictures of us with their phones, and then we're walking down the aisle together. As we're passing by Erika's pew, she goes to me out of the corner of her mouth, she goes, 'Later, Ross.' We get to the door of the church, roysh, and Sorcha sort of, like, pulls me to one side and goes, 'In case I don't get a chance to say this later ... this is the happiest day of my life,' and even though I'm smiling, roysh – like *I* was the one who had the botox – I'm wondering will she still be saying that at, like, ten o'clock tonight.' I'm thinking of coming clean to her then, roysh, but Claire and Orpha are standing pretty much beside us all of a sudden and then everyone storts, like, spilling out of the church and our old dears are the first over to us and fair play to them, they manage to interrupt this riveting conversation they're having about their hats to air-kiss us both – it's like, 'Ooh, snap! Mine's a Philip Treacy too ... Good luck, darlings. Moi, moi. Moi, moi ... Oh, ab-sa-lutely, Fionnuala. His online catalogue is fab-a-lous.'

And then it's, like, Oisinn and JP and, of course, they think it's, like, hilarious to shake Sorcha by the hand and kiss me on the lips, the steamers that they are. And then it's some old bird – might be an aunt of Sorcha's – who just goes, 'We forgot to sign the cord. The John Rocha napkin rings are from Alistair and I,' and she focks off, and throughout this time I'm not even looking at these people, roysh, I'm just staring at Sorcha in total awe because it's only sinking in now that she's, like, my wife and that I love her more than anything else in the world and within a few hours this is going to be snatched away from me.

She asks me a couple of times what's wrong, but I tell her I'm fine. We get the photos done – half-an-hour it takes to get Sorcha her Brad and Jen, during which time she keeps screaming, 'Ado-ringly, Ross. Look at me adoringly' – and then it's, like, in to The Berkeley Court for the reception. Sorcha decided, roysh, to get the speeches out of the way before the meal and we receive everyone in the President's Suite with a glass of either hot Port or mulled wine and a mince pie, and we all, like, make our speeches in front of this big log fire. I close my eyes throughout Dickhead's speech and try to, like, block it out. It storts with the line, 'We live in a country in which corruption is endemic, which is why occasions of joy, such as this, are so important,' and he prattles on for, like, twenty minutes about my rugby career and how I'd be playing for Ireland today if only Eddie O'Sullivan would take his head out of his orse. Then he talks about how me and him are not so much father and son as best friends, and how we have this bond, and I realise he must have had a couple of looseners in the Druid's Chair before he hit the church. Christian introduces Sorcha's old man – the focking muppet – and he storts giving it, 'The first time this beautiful daughter of ours brought Ross home, my wife and I weren't sure about him. The second time was different. We definitely, positively didn't like him,' and everyone cheers, especially the goys, my so-called mates. 'But the third time ... The third time, we absolutely hated him. In fact, we wanted her to go out with his friend, the chap with the glasses.' Focking Fionn. Dead man walking. Then he goes, 'But Sorcha wanted Ross. And what our little girl wants, she gets. She's singleminded, you see, which is why she's been successful at everything she's turned her hand to. College. Business. Travel. She's currently making a success of her mother's new boutique in the Powerscourt Townhouse Centre. And with a little bit of co-operation from this ... *fellow* here, she'll make a success of marriage as well.'

Yeah, yeah, sit down, you focking tosser. It's time for the big-hitters. Christian's speech is amazing. Not one focking *Star Wars* reference. He goes, 'This goy here is my best friend. And I've been through some ups and down with him.' Someone shouts, 'So has your old dear,' but he ignores it, roysh, and goes, 'There are a lot of people who don't like Ross O'Carroll-Kelly. He thinks he's *it*. If he was chocolate, he'd eat himself. But I speak from experience here. The goy has the best hort of anyone I've ever known. You just have to search hord to find it. I found it. So did Sorcha. I suppose one of us was going to end up marrying the loser, and thank God it's not me.' He gets a round of applause for that line, fair focks to him. Then someone – I think it's one of Sorcha's cousins, some Andrew's tosser – shouts, 'All you've got to do now, Ross, is get through the night without knobbing one of the bridesmaids,' and everyone laughs, roysh, and I catch Sorcha's sister staring at me with that big shork's smile she has and I look at Claire, who's, like, looking down in embarrassment. Then the man of the moment – yours truly – has to get up to make his speech and not blowing my own trumpet or anything, roysh, but it's shit-hot. Storts off with, 'Before today, I'd have said that winning the Leinster Schools Senior Cup with Castlerock in 1999 was the best day of my life. I said *before* today ...' and it just gets better.

Then Sorcha. She's amazing. She tells the story of how we first met, which I'd totally forgotten. It was, like, 1997. Me and Christian, roysh, we were the only fifth years on the Castlerock Senior Cup team and her and a few of her Mountie mates used to come and watch us play. Sorcha basically fancied me, but it took her until the semi-final – we lost to the Gick, I should have had a penalty try in the second half – to pluck up the courage to, like, speak to me. Me and Christian were drowning our sorrows in Eddie Rocket's in Donnybrook. We were the only two on the team who couldn't get served in pubs. She came over and she went, 'Congrats,' and I was there, 'We lost,' and she was like, 'Doesn't matter. Congrats anyway. You played amazing rugby. Why is that not something to be proud of?' and that, I remember now, made me feel amazing basically. She says I bought her a vanilla malt. She goes, 'I've still got the straw. When he paid the bill he said he'd ring – I'm sorry about this, Charles – Dick Features and get us a lift home,' and the whole place cracks up and I look over and see the old man clapping, fair play to him. The wanker. She goes, 'So Charles came into town and drove us out to Killiney. When I got home, I went into Mum – she was in bed, reading – and I went,

"Mum, tonight I met the boy I'm going to marry".'

What she says, roysh, just knocks me focking sideways. I couldn't tell you how long she talked for or a single thing she said after that. All I had was a feeling inside me of having been stupid all these years, that after all the time I'd spent mucking around – basically mucking *her* around – this was where I was meant to be all along, and it's all so obvious to me now.

Sorcha presents our old dears with the Birds of Paradise, which she got the florist to order in specially from, like, Mexico, and then I actually stort to relax and forget about the trouble that's brewing, roysh, and we take our seats for the banquet, roysh ... we take our seats ... we take our seats and everything ... suddenly ... becomes ... focked up. And we're talking *totally* focked up. I'm looking at the goys, roysh, who've placed themselves at, like, strategic points around the room so they can keep an eye on Erika and they've all got those little mikes and earpieces that Oisinn got from his brother, the one who does the security in the bor in Castlerock. I can see them all, roysh, discussing her movements, but when it all kicks off, roysh, there's nothing they can do.

The serving bird – waitress, I suppose you'd call her – is going around taking the orders for the main course, roysh, and she's going, 'Are you having the poached loin of Wicklow venison with roast root vegetables, the wild Irish mallard with Seville oranges and garlic and ginger Brussels sprouts, or the roast monkfish tail with Pernod butter sauce?' and she's a bit of a howiya, but there's no big deal. I order the venison, Sorcha asks for the vegetarian option – the gateaux of aubergine and Irish goat's cheese – and off she goes to the next table. So there we are, roysh, me and Sorcha, me and my wife, my wife and I, chatting away about how well everything's going, and how everyone seems to be enjoying themselves, when – all of a sudden – there's all this, like, commotion, if that's the roysh word, coming from the table in front of us, where Erika has plonked herself, roysh, totally ignoring the seating-plan. There's no mistaking the voice, roysh, it's her, and she's totally flipping the lid. Turns out the waitress may or may not have brushed off her wine glass, but one way or another Erika's ended up with, like, Châteauneuf-du-Pape all over her white suit and someone's going to pay. She's going, 'This suit cost more than you earn in a year!' There's, like, total silence in the room at this stage and I can see the goys, roysh, and they're, like, frozen to the spot. The best way I can describe it, roysh, is it's like they tell you that the best way to stop a pit bull terrier from savaging you is to, like, grab its two front legs and pull them aport, sending the bones into his hort. But then when there's an *actual* pit bull ripping your *actual* focking windpipe out, you don't think of it because you freeze. And that's like the goys at that, like, moment in time. Stopping Erika was all very well in theory, but now they've remembered how vicious she is and they're just, like, frozen to the spot.

Erika's going, 'I'm going to make sure you never work in this town again.' So, bearing in mind what Christian said about me having a big hort and everything, I stort to feel sorry for the waitress and try to, like, smooth things over, nice to be nice, blah blah blah. I walk over to them, roysh, and I'm telling Erika that everything's Kool and the Gang when, all of a sudden, the waitress is looking at me with her mouth wide open. After what seems like ages, she finally goes, 'Ross? Ross O'Carroll-whats-your-face?' I look at her and I'm there, 'Do I know you?' and all of a sudden she storts going, 'Oh, no. No. No. NO,' and shaking her head and, like, bawling her eyes out. Erika goes, 'You know this ... *slapper*?' and I realise that I know her alroysh. I look over at Sorcha, who's standing up, going, 'Who is she, Ross?' with a smile on her face that I'm pretty sure she wouldn't be wearing now were it not for the, like, botox. Who is she? Her name is Tina and who she is, well, it's a long and sordid story. Where to start ...

Don't know if I mentioned this before, roysh, but when we were in fourth year in Castlerock, the school organised this thing called The Urban Plunge. It was basically an exchange programme we did with this skobie school out in the middle of Pram Springs. Typical of the Brothers, that was. I remember Brother Augustus going, 'Your parents are loaded and most of you will never have to do a day's work in your lives. But it's important for your education as Christians to see how the fallen in our society live.' So we swapped homes with a bunch of focking creamers. They came to live in our houses and we went to live in theirs. I remember the goy I swapped with, the youngest person I'd ever seen with a moustache. He was a focking one-man crime epidemic. Went though Brighton Road like a dose of liver salts. If it wasn't nailed down, he robbed it. I think the old pair were sitting on focking orange crates by the time the month was over. Meanwhile, back at the ranch, not being big-headed or anything, but I ended up scoring his sister. His *older* sister. As in Tina. It was a kind of revenge basically. I'll spare you the gory details, roysh, but let's just say I chanced my orm one night and all her dreams came true and I ended up being a ledge when I got back to school.

But what I can't understand, roysh, is why she's crying now. It was, like, seven years ago, and it was only one night. Hordly meant that much. I know she rang the gaff, roysh, a few months later. I came home from rugby training one day and the old pair

said there'd been a call. Some *wan* called Tina, the old dear said. The old man went, 'She's not the type of girl we consider suitable for our son.' But I'm standing here now, wondering what the focking waterworks are all about. A one-night stand? Seven years ago? HELLO?

Then suddenly the old man stands up and he goes, 'WE TOLD YOU TO STAY AWAY,' and mouths drop everywhere. He goes, 'WE PAID YOU BLOODY GOOD MONEY TO STAY OUT OF OUR LIVES AND KEEP YOUR MOUTH SHUT ...'

The room is suddenly ... spinning.

Spinning.

Spinning.

Spinning ...

Sorcha shouts out, roysh, she goes, 'About what?'

Or maybe I say it, 'About what?'

I think we both say it. Tina looks at me. She's got this, like, locket around her neck – it's, like, a love hort – and she looks at my old man, roysh, and then back at me, and then she opens it and hands it to me and inside there's this, like, picture, of ...

A kid?

A boy.

And she doesn't need to say anything else.

Fock, he's even got my quiff.

And then I don't remember much. I have vague memories of Sorcha screaming – this crazy, high-pitched scream – made even crazier by the fact that the muscles in her face have been frozen into this, like, Joker's smile. Then I remember the room empty-ing out pretty quickly. And the last thing I know, I'm sitting at this bor – where, I haven't a focking clue – but I'm sitting there, just staring into space and Christian's with me – isn't he always? Doesn't matter how deep the shit is – and so are the other goys, we're talking Oisinn, JP, Fionn and Ryle Nugent, and there's a bottle of Jameson on the bor in front of us. Half a bottle. It feels like the early hours of the morning. In my horrendufied state, I go, 'I don't understand, Christian. Am I still married or what?' and he pours us both another shot and he's there, 'I think you should stay in my gaff for Christmas, Ross. Just till the smoke clears.' I'm like, 'Your old pair cool about that?' and he goes, 'They're cool with whatever I want, Ross.' My phone rings. I look at the screen. Thank fock. It's Sorcha. I answer it. It's not Sorcha. It's Erika, using Sorcha's phone. She goes, 'What a fascinating day, Ross. It was like something from 'EastEnders',' and I'm there, 'Is Sorcha with you? Put her on,' and she goes, 'I'm afraid she's been sedated, Ross. And on top of everything else, when she was getting into the back of the ambulance, she broke the heel off one of her Manolo Blahniks.'

We must be still in the Berkeley Court because outside I can hear fireworks going off. Our fireworks. Nobody thought to, like, cancel them. I'm there, 'Erika, I've got to talk to her. Look, that shit with Tina happened before I even met her,' but she's not listening. She goes, 'Oh and PS, Ross – the diary and the tape? You were right. I *was* bluffing. Claire never confessed anything to me and as far as I know Orpha doesn't even keep a diary,' and I tell her – sobbing down the phone basically – to tell Sorcha that I still love her, but she just goes, 'You're a loser, Ross,' and the line, like my life, suddenly just goes dead.

You want more of this goy?

I know you SO do ...

So there I was, roysh, putting the 'in' in 'in crowd', pick of the babes, bills from the old pair to fund the lifestyle I, like, totally deserve. But being a schools rugby legend has its downside, roysh, like all the total knobs wanting to chill in my, like, reflected glory, and the bunny-boilers who decide they want to be with me and won't take, like, no for an answer. And we're talking TOTALLY here. Basically, it may look like a champagne bath with Nell McAndrew with, like, no clothes and everything, but I can tell you, roysh, those focking bubbles can burst. And when they do ... OH MY GOD!

Book 2
The Teenage Dirtbag Years
(As told to Paul Howard)

So there I was, roysh, class legend, schools rugby legend, basically an all-round legend, when someone decides you can't, like, sit the Leaving Cert three times. Well that put a focking spanner in the works. But joining the goys at college wasn't the mare I thought it would be, basically for, like, three major reasons: beer, birds and more birds. And for once I agree with Fionn about the, like, education possibilities. I mean, where else can you learn about 'Judge Judy', fake IDs and how to order a Ken and snog a bird at the same time? I may be beautiful, roysh, but I'm not stupid and this much I totally know: college focking ROCKS!

Book 3
The Orange Mocha-Chip Frappuccino Years
(As told to Paul Howard)

So there I was, roysh, enjoying college life, college birds and, like, a major amount of socialising. Then, roysh, the old pair decide to mess everything up for me. And we're talking TOTALLY here. Don't ask me what they were thinking. I hadn't, like, changed or treated them any differently, but the next thing I know, roysh, I'm out on the streets. Another focking day in paradise for me. If it hadn't been for Fionn's aportment in Killiney, the old man paying for my Golf GTI, JP's old man's job offer and all the goys wanting to buy me drink, it would have been, like, a complete mare. TOTALLY. But naturally roysh, you can never be sure what life plans to do to you next. At least, it came as a complete focking surprise to me.